Please check out these other reads on Amazon
by Kate Anslinger:

Underwater Secrets
Saving Jason

The McKenna Mystery Series
The Gift
Buried Secrets
Never Tell

Family Photos

KATE ANSLINGER

To my Timmy, who has survived many near death experiences

Prologue

The child wore a dirtied white short-sleeve shirt affixed with a navy blue tie, knee-length shorts that exposed knees encrusted with mud, and blue and white saddle shoes over soiled white ankle socks. Looking every bit the proper schoolboy except for the tattered flannel blanket he clutched to his side. He moped while seated on a rocking tandem swing. His round face then contorted into wide-eyed horror with his mouth agape as he plummeted backward to the hard earth below. A rivulet of bright crimson seeped from a bullet-sized chest wound. His face turned ashen and his full lips turned bluish-purple, slackening as his chest no longer rose and fell with breath. His little body fell limp as his vacant hazel eyes released a trickling tear along the contours of his broad nose, blurring a cluster of freckles along the way.

CHAPTER ONE

Two Weeks Earlier

It was the third Saturday in May. Grace and Mark had been driving around Bridgeton with their real estate agent, Stephen, all morning, and between the limited affordable houses for sale and the nonstop rain, they were reaching the peak of frustration. Even Stephen, with his colorful and upbeat personality, was starting to lose patience.

Rain drummed the roof of the black VW Jetta and the dragging rubber of the windshield wipers worked overtime, providing a soundtrack to the awkward silence between agent and clients after a morning of disappointments. Grace sat alone in the backseat watching the raindrops race down her window when she suddenly perked up at the sight of a towering grey two-story Victorian with a charming, covered porch and a castle-like turret that accessorized the home.

"Okay, two more. Let's hope we score with one of these puppies," Stephen announced as he swung open the back door, shielding Grace with a large umbrella bearing the Rocky Shores Realty Group's logo of a home overlooking a grey, rocky coastline, with the agency's initials in a bold black font. Meanwhile, Mark jogged from the other side of the car and the three of them speed walked up the cobblestone path to seek shelter on the porch. The house sat on Court Street; a beautiful, tree-lined street in a family neighborhood known as the Highlands. On a whim Grace and Mark decided it was time to purchase a place together and it just made sense to live in the community where they both worked.

"Think about the gas money and time we'll save by being here," Mark said, as he flicked his hands and toned arms free of rainwater.

"I actually enjoy my thirty-minute commute. It gives me a chance to think about things and decompress," Grace responded while shaking out the umbrella Stephen had handed off to her so he could inspect something that caught his attention.

"Well, we can get rid of your Jeep or my van and I'll walk to work . . . saving on car insurance, oil changes, and everything else that goes along with owning a vehicle." Mark had been fighting his case hard. It wasn't that Grace didn't want to simplify their lives by moving to Bridgeton, it was that she was set in her ways in a house she had grown comfortable in. Like a favorite sweater, Grace's home in Cabotville fit her well, she had gotten used to all the little pulls and tears in it. What would hurt the most was saying goodbye to all of the memories she and her mother had made in her home. All the dinners they'd shared, the squabbles they'd have over what to watch while they were tucked under a shared afghan on Grace's couch. As an introvert, Grace would miss the seclusion of her home in Cabotville. She'd be going from having a closest neighbor a distance of two houses away to practically sharing a back yard with a Bridgeton neighbor. But Mark had sacrificed so much for her and he'd given up bits of his own career to help her solve cryptic cases, all the while accepting her for who she was.

Even in the rain, Stephen had gotten sidetracked and took his time surveying the landscaping and upkeep of the yard. Grace and Mark had reached their limit for the day and hadn't even looked at the specs on this house. As far as they were concerned, they were walking into a box of spiderwebs.

"We could get money knocked off for this," Stephen said, using a toe to lift a section of loose pavers lining the path, as he pulled the hood of his yellow raincoat forward to prevent the heavy droplets from pelting his face. "Remember what I said . . . even if you love it don't show it, okay?" He gave Mark and Grace his best serious nod as he joined them on the porch at the front door.

By this point in the day, Grace had lost all hope of finding an affordable home that didn't require a ridiculous amount of work. Two houses prior the owner was trying to sell a 1,400-square-foot home with a little yard, chipped paint, and a 1970s kitchen for half a million dollars. Any hope she had, had deflated from her. She felt like the wilted flowers sitting in the boxes framing the windows of that home.

Just as Stephen was about to pull the brass knocker on the white door, with an accent window at the top, a thirty-something female, with black hair piled high on her head, pulled the door open. Curly tendrils escaped from her topknot and danced along her jawline as she opened the door, revealing a friendly smile highlighted by raspberry-colored lips.

"Hello, Stephen!" It was clear she was more excited to see him than previous selling agents had been.

"Mel! Oh my goodness, look at you!" He held her shoulders and twirled her around before planting a kiss on her cheek.

"I lost all that baby weight finally . . . Lord knows I get enough steps in just by chasing the twins around, when I'm not slinging houses."

"You are beautiful." A sincere look was caught in his pale blue eyes. "What are you doing here!?"

"Oh, well, let me tell you . . . we've had some crazy turnover lately, and I'm covering for André who had to help with some condo showings in Boston. So, you're stuck with me!" Mel raised her arms with bent elbows and palms up, offering a toothy smile.

"Well, I was looking forward to gazing into Andre's smoldering brown eyes but I'm glad to see you too, honey." Stephen turned toward Mark and Grace, extending an introductory arm in their direction. "These are my amazing clients . . . Detective McKenna and Gym Guru Mark Connolly." Much to Grace's chagrin, Stephen insisted on introducing her as Detective. He claimed it put fear in the selling agents and made them less likely to lie about the property.

"I know you . . . you own Imperial Fitness!" Mel's small eyes expanded, transforming them into two green olives. "When I'm not busy with the twins, I get out and hit up Alyssa's kickboxing class on Tuesday nights. Best class I've ever taken and it helps me get my frustrations out."

"Awe Alyssa, she is one of our best instructors. She really loves what she does." Mark, in his comfort zone, reached into his pocket and pulled out one of the free class passes he carried with him.

"Is this the original hardwood?" Stephen interrupted.

"Yes, all original . . . that's what I love about this home." Mel flipped a switch, producing a dome of warm light from the chandelier over the entryway. She turned back to Mark to thank him for the card.

Grace made her way over to Stephen as he was scrutinizing the well-lit foyer. He already slipped off his wet shoes and was sliding his argyle socks along the hardwood floor. He bent down and used a hand to glide across the wood's texture, assessing the quality. Fine grain light maple wood with dark streaks and a few subtle blemishes reflected the ceiling lighting; making the area feel larger, brighter, and more spacious. Grace had trouble telling if he was happy about what he saw or if he found a flaw. Even in front of a selling agent that he knew, he had on a determined game face. The man loved his job.

"Looks like they've already moved out?" Stephen made his way to an empty living room. Front and center was a stunning brick fireplace that took Grace's breath away. She couldn't help but picture Brody sprawled out in front of the fire as she and Mark snuggled up on the couch on a snowy night. The dog loved nothing more than being as close to his people as possible.

"Yeah, U-Haul trucks were here two days ago, it's been a busy couple of days for him."

"Upgrading homes?"

"Actually, quite the opposite. My client is looking to downsize. Sick of the upkeep with an old house—" Mel caught herself, stopped, and twirled around as she pulled open two cream-colored solid wood doors to a sunroom extending off the living room. Even in the pouring rain the room filled with natural light, brightened up even more by the white tiled floor.

"This is nice. I bet the owners spent a lot of time out here . . . especially in the summer." Mark stepped down and ran a hand along the oak windowsills. Grace was already thinking about how she would want to brighten up the room with lighter paint colors, transforming the natural oak tones to a cheerful white.

"*Owner.* Believe it or not, only one person lived in this massive house. I've got twins and a pretty decent-sized husband and my house is half this size . . . and I'm in the business." Mel laughed, throwing a wink in Stephen's direction.

"Amen, sister, same here." Stephen swatted a hand in her direction and skated across the room toward the windows. He tapped on the glass of a window overlooking the back yard. An old, peeling forest-green swing set was situated just off to the right, its vacant swing eerily swaying in the driving rain, causing a muffled screech of its rusty hinges.

Grace's eyes were glued to the lone swaying seat held by two thin oxidizing chains. The metal slide had dents and burrs along its scuffed path. Clusters of tall grass and unwieldy weeds grew up beneath and around the metal set, so tall they protruded through the slats of a face-to-face glider swing rocking gently on the opposite end of the slide. A broken tandem swing dragged the ground, partially obscured by the overgrowth. A shiver dispersed up Grace's spine.

On the other side of the yard, in front of an age-worn white picket fence, was a pale blue and white metal shed leaning slightly sideways. One side sunk deeper into the ground than the other. Rusty patches were peppered along the elevated vertical ridges making the blue look even more faded against the russet tones of the flaking oxidation. Instead of a door that swung open and closed, like the sheds of today, this one had sliding doors. Age, or poor design, made the bottoms of the doors fall off the hinges and billow out. Grace imagined how easy it would be for rodents to creep in through the exposed crack. A small latch, where a lock was once placed, joined the two sliding doors, holding the lock loop tight—partly due to the rusty corrosion all around it. A slight hill rose up in the center of the yard, making it less than perfect, but Grace wasn't much for perfection. It was one of the reasons she immediately shot down the cookie-cutter neighborhoods that had to follow strict guidelines for lawn maintenance.

"Why the swing set if the guy was solo?"

"I believe it was his from when he was a boy. The house has always been in his family. Perhaps he intended to one day have a family of his own or didn't have the heart to remove a piece of his past?" Mel skimmed across the room in a pair of fluffy pink slippers. "They don't make 'em like that anymore. That was even before my time. Now it's all plastic and wood. A kid isn't happy nowadays unless they have an attached treehouse."

The house was nearly 3,000 square feet and the thought of so much space started to make Grace second guess the visit.

"Do you think it's too big?" Grace asked Mark under her breath.

"Let's see the rest of it before we jump to any conclusions. I can think of a lot of things that would fit in this space nicely," Mark joked, clearly not the least bit embarrassed about his hoarding tendencies.

"New windows?" Stephen kept his game face on, but Grace knew exactly how new windows made him feel. A few houses prior he nearly did a happy dance when he opened a kitchen window that rose and shut with such ease it wouldn't wake a sleeping baby.

Mel came back with a quick and proud response. "Brand spankin' new." She skated across the room, her furry slippers adding a childish look to her polished real estate-agent attire. "These are some of the best I've seen."

"You're not lying. Pella Architect Series. These babies are the Cadillac of historical home windows." Stephen flashed a confident nod with raised eyebrows in Grace and Mark's direction. Grace caught the confirmation before she headed back into the living room. Walking with arms hugging her chest, in her habitual stance, she made her way across the creaky floor toward the hallway connecting the living room and kitchen.

Upon stepping into the kitchen Grace's first reaction was utter awe. A large kitchen was on her list of non-negotiables and based on the expansive, bright kitchen before her, this one passed the test. Both she and Mark agreed the kitchen needed to be spacious enough to hold a gathering, if necessary. While Grace wasn't super keen on hosting house parties, she knew Mark's popular gym owner status would require them to commit to a few gatherings a year, showing appreciation for the wealthy clients who continued to keep Mark's salary growing. It was just one of the things she'd have to deal with as his girlfriend.

"Oh, ohhhhh." Grace took several steps into the room, spinning around as she took in the gleaming white and grey cabinets, the pristine appliances, and the expansive island central to everything. The lower cabinets were a pale shade of grey that pulled the grey tones of the granite countertop together. As if plucked from her very own internal Pinterest board; the upper cabinets were a gleaming solid white with a column of open shelving centered on each wall. Grace was already deciding which framed photos would offset the kitchen supplies to add some flair to the space; a tip she learned in one of Ellen's old *Better Homes & Gardens* magazines.

"What happened here?" Stephen stood opposite Grace; his composed game face ripped from his expression as an obvious look of impressed surprise etched itself in his wide eyes.

Grace looked over at Mark, already front and center, running a palm over the cold, smooth granite.

"What happened here is the owner got sick of the dark wood and decided to lift up the aesthetics of the place," Mel said, flourishing her hands.

"Damn . . . he must've paid a pretty penny for this." Mark circled around the large eight-by-three-foot island, smoothing a hand over the granite countertop and taking it all in. Grace caught the look that Stephen passed to Mark. *Shut up about money.*

"Are these new cabinets or just painted?" Stephen pulled open a cabinet, letting it shut in a silent, soft close.

"Brand new. Everything you see in this one room is brand new. In fact, the guy who lived here before probably hasn't used this stove more than once. He just had it done three months ago and from what I hear he was a heterosexual bachelor so . . . figure that one out." Mel walked toward a closed door on the opposite side of the galley portion of the kitchen. "The house is over one hundred years old, so it's to be expected that some major renovations were due to take place. Maybe he hired a designer."

"Hey, just because I'm gay doesn't mean I like to cook," Stephen joked.

"My bad. False stereotype got the best of me." Mel winked at Stephen. "Now, I don't know if you two like to cook but . . . I'll save this little beauty for last." Mel pulled the door open, and Grace's jaw dropped for the second time in two minutes. In front of Mel stood a pantry nearly the size of Grace's current bedroom.

"Oh my . . . you don't have to like to cook to appreciate that. Look at the space, Gracie." Mark nearly leapt into the room, his frame now surrounded by rows of shelving and cutting edge cabinets with brushed nickel knobs. A matching granite countertop separated the upper shelving from the lower cabinets, a place to stash décor or small appliances.

"Mark don't get any ideas . . . this won't house your fitness equipment," Grace interjected with a sly smirk, trying to keep him in line.

"No, but it could very well house my supplements."

As if a magnet were pulling her into the colossal pantry, Grace walked toward Mark and stood beside him, feeling just as mesmerized as he looked.

"Do you have any supplements that will get rid of this?" Mel pointed to the deep eleven lines forming between her brows.

"Or this?" Stephen came into the room rubbing his bald head.

"Bald is beautiful, Stephen," Grace said, as she sidled up to Mark, completely giddy with the house. She looked around at the four of them standing in the center of the oversized pantry and suddenly felt like she was home, and she hadn't even seen the second floor yet.

As if Mel had read her mind, she asked, "How about we make our way upstairs?"

"After you." Stephen motioned for Mel to lead the way, letting Grace and Mark file in behind her, as he took the last place in line. Grace rested her hand on the smooth railing, the sound of her silver bracelet tapping gently on the wood in between the parade of footfalls moving up the creaky stairs.

When the four of them made it to the landing at the top of the staircase, Mel expanded on her role as realtor as she effortlessly described the layout of the second floor. "This hallway leads to two bedrooms at the front of the house," she said, as she extended her hand down a narrow hall running parallel to the banister. The end of the hallway spilled out into a stretch of added living space, accented with a stunning window seat. A faded peach cushion, that looked like it was designed specifically for the mahogany perch, ran the length of the bench. The cheery color a charming element against the dark wood tones.

"Look, Mark, a window seat," Grace said in awe, as she advanced toward it. She dropped onto the cushion, positioning herself so she was leaning against the side wall and able to look out the rain-spattered window. Droplets raced down the glass, blurring her vision of the street below, distorting the neighboring houses into smudges of yellow, red, white, and blue. The seat was exactly what she had envisioned when she dreamed about passing the hours reading a book, pressed up against a window while snuggled under a blanket. A cup of coffee was always a given in those daydreams as well, held with both hands in front of an open book on her bent knees. Angling her head upwards she observed the height of the windows, the base starting at the top of the seat and stretching all the way up to a strip of dark crown molding. The wood was accented with etchings that swirled and dipped into an intricate pattern centered above the window.

"Just what you've always wanted, Gracie." Mark sat beside her, twisting his head so he was looking directly into her eyes and taking her right hand in his left.

Grace couldn't help but think about the truth in his statement. This was everything she'd ever wanted. Her career, her boyfriend, and now this house. She stood up, eager to see what else the second floor had in store. She kept his hand in her grip and hefted him up along with her.

Three steps to the left and they were in a small bedroom in the shape of a near-perfect square. White walls greeted wood flooring identical to the first floor, with less wear and tear.

"If you plan on having kids, you may want to use this as a nursery." Mel suggested as she stepped toward the closet door on the back wall. She pulled and twisted the glass knob, the loose hardware let out a slight groan as it dropped back into place when it was fully open and she released her grip. "Enough closet space to store diapers and supplies." She added. "Back when this house was built, occupants typically relied on wardrobes and dresser space for storage and, from what I hear, they traveled a lot lighter."

"That's probably why my grandmother always gives me a hard time for the massive quantity of shoes I own," Stephen said, as he padded toward the front window. Grace could tell he was pleased by the brand of window by the way he raised an eyebrow and assessed the quality, similar to how he had reacted on the first floor.

As they made their way past the window seat once more and into the bedroom on the opposite side of the hall, Grace picked up on a familiar scent. Christmas came to mind; her suspicion confirmed when she spotted the plug-in air freshener, filled with green pine-scented liquid, in the room that was slightly bigger than the last one. In the previous houses they had a plate of freshly baked cookies on the counter, for the purpose of what Grace assumed was, to stir up the sensation of feeling at home. Nearly identical as the previous room, with one additional window that overlooked the front yard, the four of them spent little time assessing what this room had to offer.

Mel led them back to the window seat. "Would you like to see the attic?"

"Absolutely," Stephen answered for all of them.

"Is that where this leads to?" Grace rested her hand on the glass knob on the opposite side of the window seat, flush with the hallway. She wiggled it gently and pulled it open, feeling the ridges of carved glass in her palm as it settled back into place.

"They are hard to manage sometimes, but you could make a fortune on these vintage doorknobs if you tried to sell them on eBay," Mel said.

The three of them watched as Mel disappeared into the darkness until the sound of a subtle click created a flood of light illuminating another flawless hardwood floor. Grace expected to see a dusty old attic space, with cobwebs strung in all corners, but her mouth dropped when she saw how pristine the space was.

"Now, I'm sure you could use this space for storage but, personally, I think it's a great escape from the kids." Mel spun a full revolution, coming to face the others with a pleased grin. Grace wasn't sure if it was the sound of Mel's soft laughter or the room that made her feel a sense of comfort.

"I can think of a lot of things I could put in this room," Mark said, stooping as he entered, ascending to full height once the angled ceiling gave way to vast openness.

"I think the key word is what we would *do* with the space, honey, not what we would *put* up here. So if you're envisioning stashing away more unusable fitness equipment then I'm going to override that decision right now." Grace established herself with raised brows and a slight tilt of the head in a knowing stance. Mark diverted his eyes, whistling in mock innocence as he continued to survey the space. Grace couldn't help but smirk at his veiled attempt at cluelessness.

Stephen walked over to a small octagonal window framed in a seafoam green border. "Looks like you could get a bit of air circulation up here if need be," he said with a nod, as he shoved his hands into the pockets of his black skinny jeans, continuing to survey the space that could pass for a small bedroom.

"Yeah, as you can tell, it's not that stuffy up here and it's well-kept," Mel said.

Grace couldn't help but think of how perfect the private room would be for her mother, but she was too far down the dementia tunnel to even leave the assisted living home for a day visit, let alone move in with them. Thinking of the advice her therapist gave her, she allowed the thought to pass through her, acknowledging it made her feel the sad emotion, before she accepted it and let it go. Only because she was in the presence of others did she manage to fight off the tears threatening to escape.

She still felt heavy with emotion after she allowed the thought to pass by. The four of them stood in the center of the room. A matching octagonal window sat on the opposite wall making Grace feel as if she was on a ship, the porthole her only access to the outside world.

"What's the deal with all the octagons?" Grace asked, as she sauntered over to one of the windowed walls and ran her palm over the thick wallpaper. A black fan pattern sprouted upwards on a white backdrop. A few slight bumps in the material gave way to its age and there were a couple of raised, curled-up edges.

"That's another fabulous question." Mel rested her hands on her hips, adjusting her black pencil skirt. "For whatever reason, whenever I show one of these old houses, I notice there is always a pattern or a theme. Sometimes it's flowers, sometimes it's paisley."

"Back in the day they had a thing for themed patterns," Stephen interjected. "It's not like today's styles where we have an anything goes kind of mentality. Homeowners were very particular about their patterns back then."

"Apparently, whoever lived here loved octagons." Mark's words came out somber, as if he was retelling a story of a long lost relative.

"Although, I will say, wallpaper is coming back . . . and with wallpaper comes patterns." Mel took a step forward, naturally moving the three of them along.

"Guilty as charged." Stephen raised a hand while crouching behind Grace as she took the first step down. "I actually just chose a wallpaper pattern for my new place. Black-and-white old newspaper. And I love it."

When they got to the bottom of the attic stairs Mel led them back to the master bedroom, likely saving the best for last. Much bigger in length and having the added bonus of an additional double window overlooking the back yard, this master bedroom seemed to be triple the size of the others.

"And this is where the magic will happen," Mark said, with a boyish chuckle as he glided his way across the floor, toward the back window. Grace playfully rolled her eyes while shaking her head in an *I can't take you anywhere* embarrassment. Stephen shot Mark another one of his *don't act like you like this house that much* looks.

By the time Grace's foot hit the bottom stair her eyes were feeling heavy thanks to the overabundance of homeowner information she and Mark had been inundated with over the past few hours. She had to admit there was something about this particular house she felt compelled to. The price, while in one of the better neighborhoods in town, was doable for their combined salaries, and she couldn't help but think of all the extra space Brody would have to romp in. Her house in Cabotville was a decent size, but the wide-open living room here was guaranteed to provide countless peaceful slumbers for the oversized fur baby. She could picture Brody sprawled out in the sunroom during both the summer and winter months. He'd have a front row seat to the parading turkeys said to inhabit the area, and the tiled floor would keep him cool underneath his thick black coat.

* * *

At the bottom of Court Street, Stephen turned right at the corner onto Somerset Avenue, hardly pausing to see if anyone was coming from the left-hand side of the one-way street. The rain had miraculously cleared, replaced by rays of brilliant golden sunshine breaking through the dull grey clouds. Grace's right arm was hanging out the window of Stephen's Jetta, bracing herself whenever he hugged the corners too closely or failed to come to a complete stop. He had somehow forgotten he had a cop in the back seat of his car.

"I mean, seriously . . . that house is perfect." Mark craned his neck to face Grace in the back seat. She couldn't stop the giddy feeling tugging at the corner of her lips, making her break out into a megawatt smile. They were so in love with this house they opted to cancel their next appointment.

"Okay listen, I'm as happy as the next agent when my client wants to drop a good chunk on a home but don't get too excited yet. I want to make sure we've crossed all our t's and dotted all our i's." Stephen rested a heavy foot on the break as he pulled into the parking lot of Imperial Fitness. "And you better believe we're gonna get some cash off for that shoddy landscaping."

Grace laughed. She hadn't even noticed the landscaping; her thoughts so preoccupied by that breathtaking kitchen. She would have to start cooking now or maybe she would let Mark take the lead on that. She pictured herself sitting at the island, with both of them enjoying an elaborate feast, and Brody at her feet collecting the scraps that fell to the floor.

CHAPTER TWO

Grace took a deep breath as she pushed open the door to the real estate attorney's office. In only two weeks she managed to get an offer on her house in Cabotville while her and Mark's offer on the Court Street home was accepted. She shouldn't be surprised considering Stephen repeatedly mentioned how fast things happen once the ball starts rolling. The only thing rolling was her eyes when he first said that, and now she knew he was one hundred percent correct. Her life had shifted gears drastically in the past few weeks and her rapidly beating heart was evidence of the changes that lay ahead of her. Having always been independent, it was difficult for Grace to give up the reigns on her living situation and share the responsibility with another person.

As she walked down the traffic-worn carpeted hallway into the waiting room, she concentrated on keeping her balance in the wedge sandals she wore for the occasion. Today was the day she and Mark were signing the closing agreement on their new house. It seemed like ages ago when she last went through this process, and she certainly didn't remember being quite as stressed as she felt today. Maybe it's because there was so much more at stake this time around.

Her anxiety lifted slightly when she entered the waiting room and saw Mark's goofy grin. "Hey, gorgeous." He stood up from the maroon chair, tossing a real estate magazine onto the side table. It landed face up before it slid off the table and onto the floor, as if riding down a water slide.

"I'll get it." Grace's need to move and keep her mind from stressing had her crouching on the ground picking up the magazine, before giving Mark a chance to offer. She placed it delicately on the table and slumped into the chair beside it; with an elbow on the armrest she cradled her head onto splayed fingers.

"What, no hug?" Mark stood over her with arms open wide and ready to present her with one of his all-encompassing bear hugs. "You're allowed to smile today you know . . . this is a good thing we're doing." He kneeled down in front of her to meet the gaze of her downcast eyes.

"I know, I know. I'm sorry . . . you know how I get." She forced a smile from behind a set of lips that formed one, harsh straight line.

"I promise you it will go smoothly and we will be having pizza with Brody in less than two hours."

"There's just so much paperwork. And gosh, anything could go wrong. What if the previous owner decides not to sell at the last minute? Then I got my hopes up. And all I want to do is have dinner with you in that ridiculously oversized, beautiful kitchen . . . heck, we can even set up a mattress in that pantry and turn it into a guest room—"

"Grace. Look at me." Mark used an index finger to turn her chin to look at him. "It's all going to be okay."

"You always say that . . . how are you so carefree all the time?"

Just as Mark was about to answer, a man and a pregnant woman erupted from one of the office doors located just off the waiting room. Both were glowing and grinning wide. The man rested a soothing hand on the woman's lower back, while guiding her out of the building, with a folder thick with papers tucked under his free arm.

"See . . . look at them . . . they are happy and I bet they just closed on a house," Mark said, jutting his chin toward the exiting couple.

"Yeah, but look at all that paperwork," Grace said, a slow smile puckering her tight lips.

"Grace and Mark? Hi, how are you?" Nadine Jenner stood before them offering an extended hand.

"Nadine, so good to see you again." Mark rose from his crouched position to accept her greeting; the crease in his black slacks revealing itself as he stood. For the first time since Grace saw him today, she was able to admire how good he looked dressed up for the occasion. She rarely saw him in anything other than gym clothes and the occasional collared shirt.

"Well, I gotta be honest, Mark, it's better seeing you here than at the gym." She then proffered a hand toward Grace and shook with a firm grip. "This guy kicked my butt this morning." She turned around and led them into her office. It wasn't rare for Grace to hear from Bridgeton residents about how Mark tortured them during personal training sessions and boot camp classes at his gym. The guy had become the town's fitness celebrity.

Grace was surprised by the office. Based on Nadine's bubbly personality, she expected the office to be filled with color and tasteful décor but instead a bland oval conference table stood centered in the room, surrounded by plain black chairs. A lone laptop sat at one end of the table, flanked by packets of paperwork held together with binder clips. At the center of the table was a glass jar with black and blue pens sprouting out in all directions like a bouquet of flowers. The corner of the room held a basic white table with three neat piles of bulging manila folders, all neatly labeled. Behind the desk was a shelf that held books strictly on real estate. With no sign of Nadine's personal life, Grace wondered if she was single and childless or if she simply liked to keep her personal and work life separate. She thought her office at the station was barren, but this one made hers look like a personalized sanctuary.

"So, take a seat and we'll get started before the seller and his attorney arrive," Nadine said, keeping it far more casual than Grace thought it would be. Nadine used a rubber fingertip protector to flip through one of the piles of paperwork. "We can get started on some of the documents in the meantime." With her gaze held steadily on the papers, she slid them across the table and pointed to the perfectly placed fluorescent tabs directing them where to sign. Grace bright yellow and Mark lime green.

Grace took another deep breath, plucked the cap off a blue pen, and signed her name on the line before she pushed it over to Mark who tossed a wink in her direction.

"Hello." A heavyset man appeared in the doorway.

"Oh hi, Frank, just getting things started here." Nadine looked up briefly, acknowledging the man, before she led her gaze back to the documents and continued business as usual.

"Hello, Nadine ... great to see you again." Frank waddled to the opposite end of the small room. He set his briefcase down on the table and in one gesture clicked it open and lifted the lid up and over. "My client should be here shortly." He looked at his watch, the silver links pressing so tightly into the skin Grace could see pinched grey hairs protruding. When he sat in the chair the table jolted slightly, bracing for his weight and releasing a sharp crack. "You must be the lucky buyers?" He breathed heavily as he spoke—no doubt winded from carrying around his substantial girth.

"Yes, this is Mark and Grace." Nadine motioned to each with a palm-up hand.

"That house is a beauty. My client . . . John, has a lot of history in that house. He took good care of it and I imagine this will be a pretty bittersweet day for him, but—"

"Sorry, I'm here." Frank's words were cut off when John Walsh pushed through the door. Both his words and his presence were soft, as if he didn't want to take up too much space in the world. In two long strides John reached the chair beside Frank and sat down, resting his hands flat on the table. "I apologize for my tardiness." He sat erect, reaching for one of the pens from the centerpiece, they clinked falling into new positions within the arrangement.

"No worries, we were just getting started. Lord knows it's just a lot of signatures." Nadine kept her head down, focused on placing stickers in the appropriate signature blocks and sliding documents across the table to Grace and Mark in rapid succession.

"Grace. Mark. This is John. As I was saying, he has a lot of history in the house but—"

"But, it's time for a change." John shifted in his seat so he was facing Mark, who sat on the other side of him. As Mark leaned back in his chair Grace was able to get her first official look at John. Mousy brown hair with thick flecks of grey was parted in the middle and feathered on each side, like he had just walked off the set of a movie that took place in the seventies. His face was sagging with age, jowls pulled his cheeks downward into a permanent frown. A small scar cut across one side of his forehead, evidence of stitches. Sporadic white specks of hypopigmentation marked his chin and jawline.

His gaze landed on Grace, offering her an acknowledgment and presenting her with a vision of a sullen little boy with side-parted blonde hair, slicked neatly into place. He wore a dirtied white short-sleeve shirt affixed with a navy blue tie, knee-length shorts that exposed knees encrusted with mud, and blue and white saddle shoes over soiled white ankle socks. Looking every bit the proper schoolboy except for the tattered flannel blanket he clutched to his side. He moped while seated on a rocking tandem swing. His round face then contorted into wide-eyed horror with his mouth agape as he plummeted backward to the hard earth below. A rivulet of bright crimson seeped from a bullet-sized chest wound. His face turned ashen and his full lips turned bluish-purple, slackening as his chest no longer rose and fell with breath. His little body fell limp as his vacant hazel eyes released a trickling tear along the contours of his broad nose, blurring a cluster of freckles along the way.

"Grace?" Mark bumped Grace's elbow, interrupting the vision revealed in the mystery homeowner's beady brown eyes.

"Sorry . . . sorry . . . what's that?" Grace blinked rapidly and attempted to shake the image from her mind's eye.

"Do you have your license so Nadine can make a copy?"

"Oh, yes sorry . . . " Grace fumbled with her wallet and retrieved her license, trying to hide her noticeably trembling hands. She was suddenly filled with feelings of anger and fear. She hadn't had a vision in months, and now here she was receiving flashes of a crime from the person she was purchasing a home from. In the past, when she was infiltrated with a surprise like this, she naturally got upset seeing pictures of horrid crimes committed. This time she was downright aggravated. Why him? Why did she have to be purchasing a home from a killer?

She slid her license across the table, keeping her eyes focused on the brown surface with flecks of tan and beige against the mahogany backdrop. She could feel Mark's stare boring into the side of her head. He knew. He always knew. Much in the same way her mother had developed a priviness to her visions, Mark learned when to recognize the signs as well. It normally started when Grace displayed some form of unease in the presence of a new person. And it was always accompanied by sweaty palms, a racing heart, and an obvious hesitation between bouts of eye contact with the criminal.

"You okay?" he whispered under his breath.

"Yeah." Grace dug her sandal into Mark's foot, silently informing him everything was *not* okay. She looked at him out of the corner of her eye, and before she could get up from the table and put a stop to the exchange taking place, she stopped herself. She wasn't going to let another criminal get in the way of moving forward with her life. Yes, she had a gift, she was able to see pieces of crimes committed in the eye of criminals. And because she was a cop, she was able to put the puzzle pieces together with more ease than a civilian. She expected that. What she was not about to accept was it interfering with her life. This was her dream home; it was Mark's dream home. Who was to say the next person she tried to buy a house from wasn't a criminal too? *Focus Grace and suck it up.*

* * *

"I would say congratulations but I have a feeling you have other things on your mind right now." Mark pulled Grace into his side as they walked through the parking lot.

"Damn it . . . why today?" Grace shook her head in frustration. "On the day that was supposed to be our day. Our moment. Buying our dream home . . . and I have to deal with this crap—" Grace threw up her hands in surrender.

"Listen." Mark stopped walking and maneuvered Grace by the shoulders so she was facing him. A slight breeze blew a loosened strand of hair across her forehead and he pushed it behind her ear. "Don't be upset about this . . . it's just a house. And we'll make it ours, without the tainted memories he left behind."

"It's just that . . ." Grace tried her hardest to stop the tear threatening to escape. As it cascaded down her cheek Mark used a finger to swipe it away. "I really wanted this moment to be ours . . . you didn't ask for this. You don't deserve some crazy cop who has unpredictable visions that come with a hell of a lot of emotion."

"You're right honey. I didn't ask for this. But to be honest with you . . . I wouldn't have it any other way. I love you and part of you is your gift, so I love that too."

"You know I'm going to have to get to the bottom of this right?"

"And again, I wouldn't have it any other way." Mark pulled her into his side and led them back to her Jeep. Once they got rid of Mark's van, they would share her vehicle; since they'd live and work in the same town, and Grace would have the cruiser fifty percent of the time.

"Thank you . . . you know . . . for being you." Grace slid into the passenger seat and looked over at Mark buckling his seatbelt, putting an end to the incessant alarm that reminded him to do so. "Wait, don't move!"

"Ohhhkay." Mark remained focused on the buckle with his head angled down.

"He's over there." She jerked her chin, directing Mark where to look. "Let's get his make and plate number." Grace watched as John Walsh slipped into a dark blue Honda Civic.

"I'll pull up behind him before he backs out. Follow my lead."

Mark pulled behind the Civic, to block him in, just as John was shutting his door. While there was still a slight chill in the air, the May weather allowed for open windows. They looked on as John rested an arm out the window, his oversized plaid shirt billowing slightly in the breeze.

"John!" Mark's friendly voice came out in a natural clip.

John craned his neck back, a look of confusion on his face before he recognized the man who just purchased his home.

"Hey."

"Any chance we can get your contact info . . . just in case something comes up with the house?" Mark used his kindest, go-to schmoozing voice. "Since you've lived there for a while, and whatnot, I figured—"

"Of course." John rose from the car and walked toward the passenger side window so he was inches from Grace. "Why don't you give me your number and I'll call you so you have mine."

As Mark read off his phone number, Grace made a point of turning her head so she directly faced John, close enough they could share a secret. As she felt his beady brown eyes on her, she tilted her head until her gaze fixed onto his like a padlock clicking into place. And with that came a barrage of horrifying images of the unknown slain boy. He was so small. He couldn't have been more than seven. What a sobering thought that this poor child was so violently robbed of his chance at a future, of growing any older.

"Grace . . . do you want to give him yours too?" Mark's voiced lured Grace away from the little boy's deadly expression. She was torn between two worlds, the current moment infiltrated by the killer standing inches from her. While she wanted desperately to keep looking at him to obtain more clues of the mystery, she needed to step outside of that world to show a sense of normalcy in front of John. Like in past cases, she was caught between solving a case, hoping for immediate justice, and putting on a performance that everything was okay. Not wanting to tip her hand at this juncture, she would be patient and show she could have a normal conversation with a man who likely had a hand in murdering a young boy.

"Yeah, that's a great idea, why don't you take my number too."

CHAPTER THREE

Boxes sat piled high, like blocks in a Jenga game, on the verge of falling over. Grace slid another one across the lawn and set it flush with the others and, with a grating sound of the tape gun, sealed the box with pride.

"Time for a break, Detective." Mark sat on the front steps and patted the spot beside him, motioning for Grace to join him. He held an iced coffee out in front of him, bribing her with the much-needed vice.

"I'm coming, I'm coming." Grace stood in front of what was now somebody else's house, breathing in a million memories from the time she lived there. "I'm gonna miss this place," she said, with her hands supporting her lower back as she gazed longingly through the open door, flooded with mixed emotions, before taking a seat beside Mark.

"Well, as much as you enjoy the thirty-minute commute, think of what we'll save in gas and mileage on the Jeep," Mark said, after he took a gulp of some vibrant green drink Grace had no desire to taste. He used his left hand to make circular motions on Brody's burly chest. The dog sat upright, his tongue hanging out the side of his mouth and bouncing around as he panted aggressively. He knew something was going on and was growing more antsy by the second. Even though they never left the dog at home for more than a few hours at a time, he always got panicked when he saw bags being packed and furniture being rearranged.

"You're right about that."

"And insurance money when we get rid of my van." Mark took another sip.

"Aren't you gonna miss that chick magnet of a vehicle?" Grace laughed, poking fun at the old van Mark chose to drive for years. Mark responded by sticking out the tip of his green-stained tongue and Grace recoiled in jest.

"Nah, it's time." Mark's hand dropped to the side as Brody made his tenth lap around the piles of boxes, investigating each one with his beefy sniffing snout. Just as Grace was about to continue making fun of Mark's mom vehicle, Brody lifted a leg and started to mark his territory on a box.

"Brody, NO!" Grace hoisted herself off the steps and lunged at the dog, tackling him to the ground just as a rainbow of pee arched out and onto the box, turning the cardboard dark and soggy. "Damn it!"

"Did you really think you were going to stop a dog midstream?" Mark rose, helping Grace as she started taking the contents of the box out, inspecting them to make sure they were dry.

"No, but . . . I thought it was worth a try. Brody . . . you naughty, naughty boy. What's your deal buddy?" Grace got down on her knees, so she was eye level with the big dog, as she aggressively rubbed his shoulders. She pulled his face toward hers and planted a wet sloppy kiss on his greying snout. "You're gonna love our new home . . . I promise you." When Grace was done petting him, he walked his front paws out until his belly was flat on the grass, then he dropped his head between his paws, giving into the sleep tugging at him.

* * *

After all the boxes were packed and the movers collected them, the two of them sat with Brody on the living room floor with a box of pizza open between them. It was the last night they would sleep in the house. Brody was on high alert anytime one of them made the slightest of moves, eager to scoop up any crumb that missed their lips and rained to the floor.

"So, do you want to talk about it?" Mark stabbed at the chef salad balanced on his lap. Crunching on a mouth full of lettuce, he gave Grace the all-knowing look of concern. Whenever she saw a vision, he waited for her to share the details, until of course, he couldn't wait any longer.

Grace dove in, eager to get it off her chest; packing up boxes only did so much to divert her attention from her latest case. "Well, it's a boy. Young boy. Five or six . . . maybe seven. But, here's the thing, in the vision, he is wearing a Catholic school uniform that is in line with the styles popular back in the fifties." Grace shared about how her search of boys' Catholic school attire came up with a variety of different styles over the years, but the saddle shoes and ankle socks were spot on for the fifties. "And the boy's hair . . . he had one of those harsh side parts very obviously gelled in place . . . the way they wore it back in those days. He looks like he could be plucked from a nineteen-fifties newspaper—except for his sullen expression and of course that bullet hole in his chest."

"Geez." Mark set his plastic salad container on the floor beside him and took a long swig from his water bottle. "I mean, I know you've had to deal with cases involving kids in the past but this dates back far. The fifties . . . that would mean our friend John is well into his seventies and he himself was a kid when the crime occurred Why would a little boy kill another little boy?"

"Your guess is as good as mine."

"I don't envy you, honey. I can't imagine how hard it is to see the faces of these victims." Mark rubbed his chin as he gave her a look of empathy. "But, as always, I'm here for you one hundred percent and I'll do all the digging I can to help you figure out who John Walsh is." He leaned back and slumped against the wall. "What are the chances we are moving into the home of a killer?"

"Based on our past luck, I'd say pretty damn good."

* * *

Grace woke with a knot in her lower back. She was starting to feel her age and sleeping on hardwood floors wasn't as easy as it was in her twenties. She rolled onto her side and, instead of seeing Mark's handsome face, was nose to nose with a sleeping Brody. As he let out a rumbling snore, she was hit in the nostrils with his pungent dog breath. She winced. Bringing the back of a hand to her nose, she tore the covers off with her free hand. She teetered as she came to a stand, groaning like a zombie. Disoriented, with eyes half-closed, she reached for furniture that was no longer there.

"Good morning, sunshine." Mark appeared from the kitchen, sniggering at her disheveled state, presenting her with a freshly brewed cup of hot coffee.

"How did you make coffee?" She greedily snatched the mug and cupped it with both hands, inhaling the rich aromatic steam. She sipped as if offered the last drop of water in the desert; closing her eyes as she swallowed liquid life. Mark chuckled at her antics.

"You didn't think I'd pack the coffee maker, did you? I know how you are without caffeine first thing in the morning." Mark grimaced like the walking dead with arms outstretched, mocking Grace.

"Well, bless your heart," Grace said, before breaking out into a giggle. She and Mark had a private joke about the phrase and had committed to using it as much as possible. In most cases it came out tongue-in-cheek, but today it was sincere.

Holding the small of her back, like a little old lady, she rotated her torso to stretch out the kinks as she looked around the empty room. "So, this is it, huh?" The reality finally hitting her. "I'm gonna miss this place."

Mark pulled her into his side and the two of them looked around the empty house one final time. It was the end of one season of life and the beginning of another.

* * *

Before Grace slipped into the passenger seat of the Jeep, she took one final gander at the exterior of her first home; tattooing a million memories on her mind. The front steps where she always sat with Brody when the weather was just right. To the right of the house were two Adirondack chairs she and her mother, Ellen, had spent countless hours sipping tea and talking about the little things in life. The new owners made an offer on the chairs and, since it was over the amount Grace paid for them, she agreed to leave them behind. It would've been hard to see those chairs at the new house, she had thought to herself, since Ellen would likely never be visiting and they would never be able to carry on their conversations in the matching set. It was time to let someone else create memories there and, as much as she hated to do it, it was time to accept the fact that Alzheimer's had stolen the best parts of Ellen. Now, on the rare occasions when Grace had the strength to visit her, she always ended up leaving angrier and more hopeless, souring her memories of the woman she loved and admired so dearly. She wanted to remember her mother on good terms, she didn't want to remember the angry and unrecognizable person she had transformed into. It was best for both of them.

"You ready?" Mark looked across the passenger seat as Grace slipped in.

"Yeah . . . I'm ready." She reached for the seatbelt and looked back at the house as Mark pulled away, down the long dirt driveway, for the last time. From the sideview mirror she could see the For Sale sign, with the status of sold advertised, shrinking in the distance.

"It's hard to say goodbye but I promise you we made the right decision." Mark rested his hand on her thigh and gave it a gentle squeeze as a tear carved its way down her cheek, landing on the open palm in her lap.

"I know."

CHAPTER FOUR

Using all her bicep strength, Grace carried an overstuffed tote of random kitchen supplies up the path and to the front porch, nearly tripping on the loose paver Stephen had stopped to inspect on the day of the showing.

"Looks like we found our first project." She kicked the offending chunk and it tumbled before coming to a stop in the grass.

"Easy fix," Mark said, following closely behind her with a square Tupperware container hoisted on one shoulder like a boom box. Behind him, Brody followed the rolled stone and sniffed at the grass, before raising his leg to mark the flowerbed bordering the walkway.

Grace dropped her tote on the porch and reached back for the key Mark offered with an amused expression on his face.

"Wait a second . . ." He reached into his back pocket to retrieve his phone. "We need to get a picture of this!" Just as Grace was rolling her eyes and jiggling the key in the lock, she looked back with raised brows and an overly animated smile in mock wonder. Mark chuckled, capturing the moment. "One day we'll look back on this, you know," Mark said, nodding as he returned the phone to his pocket.

"I know, I know." Grace shot Mark a crooked, thoughtful smile as she nodded in understanding.

With Brody close behind, the two of them hobbled into the house with their arms loaded and made their way into the infamous kitchen that sealed the deal for deciding on the home, plunking their goods down in front of the large island and stopping to take a breather.

"How does it feel to be home?" Mark leaned against the island and pulled Grace into his chest, planting a delicate kiss on her head.

"Good." Grace looked up and locked eyes with Mark. "Great." Now that the legal aspect of buying and selling a home was over, she finally felt like she could enjoy the rest of the moving journey. The back of her mind, however, was laced with the visions she saw in John's eyes, taking away some of the enjoyment of the new home. Making her feel uneasy, unsure of what she might uncover in this house. *Could there be an actual skeleton in John Walsh's closet?* She shook the absurd thought from her mind.

"Before we get started, how about a fresh cup of coffee?" Grace looked down seeing the top of the coffee maker extending over the tote she deposited at her feet. She reached for the flattened black surface, clutching under the brew basket. "It's not officially home until the smell of coffee permeates the air, right?" Grace said, while carrying the appliance, with the cord dangling, to its new home on the counter.

"You're right about that." Mark stepped toward Grace, pressing his body against her backside and wrapping his arms around her waist as she was about to fill the carafe at the deep stainless steel sink with a matching pull-down faucet.

Interrupting their moment, a loud noise came from the second floor. The cracking of wood against wood echoed through Grace's ears, followed by a loud thump. Grace nearly dropped the glass carafe when she flinched and both their heads jerked, in unison, toward the direction of the commotion.

"What the hell?!" Grace set the empty pitcher beside the sink and pushed herself away from Mark. With Mark following at her heels, she bounded up the stairs two at a time. Instinctively, she brought her hand to her hip where her sidearm was normally holstered to her like an additional appendage, but she didn't tend to wear it around the house.

As if they were about to take down an intruder in a threatening situation, the two of them hugged tight to the walls once they reached the top of the stairs and walked deftly toward the mysterious source of the disturbance. It didn't take long for Grace to recognize the culprit. Brody was sprawled out on the floor in front of the window seat, his beefy snout resting between his paws, looking at them with defeat in his all-knowing brown eyes. His rump was pressed against the base of the bench and when he stood to greet them one of the storage doors swung open, revealing a hidden compartment.

"Whoa, I didn't realize there was storage beneath this beauty," Grace said, rubbernecking as she walked around Brody to get a closer look.

"I'm surprised we failed to notice with all your ogling and examining the intricate carvings and design." Mark followed behind her, crouching down on one knee to peer into the newly exposed hollow. Maintaining eye contact with Grace he thrust his right hand into the dark recess, feeling around. After a moment he began convulsing, as if he were being sucked in by some unknown force, while shouting in mock agony. Grace, bug-eyed, toppled to her backside while clutching at her chest and Brody began barking fiercely at Mark's back.

Mark pulled his arm back out in great hysterics, collapsing backward with one arm across his ribs to stop his uncontrollable laughter. "Ah-ha, you should see your face!" Mark gasped, while pointing at an openmouthed Grace. She composed herself and came back up to a kneeling position and punched Mark's shoulder. Hard.

"Ow-ahh," Mark cried out, still laughing from his prank, as he dabbed at his watery eyes. "What did you think I'd find?"

"I don't know . . . I thought maybe a skeleton hand had grabbed you. It's not that far-fetched considering we purchased a house from a possible child murderer. And this space could be just the right size to . . . you know . . . hide small remains." Grace shrugged in a half-joking, half-serious consideration.

"Well, in all seriousness, I think I did feel something tucked in there. Do you have a flashlight?" He sniffled the last of his amused tears away, while patiently awaiting her response.

"Yeah. If I didn't crush it," Grace said, in a playful scowl, still recovering from her scare. She retrieved the phone from her back pocket and handed it over illuminated. Mark tried to focus with crinkled brows and a mouth twisted in curiosity. Grace knew he had in fact discovered something inside the mysterious alcove. He slid a small box over the lip of the cabinet. With darting eyes, they both moved their focus from the box to one another, silently questioning who was going to open it.

"Do you want to do the honors?" Mark asked.

"Sure." Grace braced herself for what came next, afraid the box would reveal pieces of a human skull. She leaned forward and stretched her arm out long, sliding the old cigar box closer. Reading each other's minds they both sat cross-legged across from one another with the box centered between them. Its outer edges decorated in red lines swirling like ribbon candy.

She lifted the lid, its age showing when it easily opened, the flap's crease displaying gaps and tears where it connected. An advertisement on the inside lid showed a dark-haired woman wearing a lace mantilla veil with *La Palina, The Quality Cigar* written above and below. Grace could still smell hints of tobacco as the box sat open before her, revealing the contents. A collection of haphazard black-and-white photographs sent an involuntary chill up Grace's spine. Rifling through the loose stack, her fingers felt a piece of cloth flattened at the bottom.

"Looks like old photos and . . ." She pulled the fabric up, spilling photos all over the floor between them. The material was pressed into a perfect square. Grace slowly unfolded it as they both watched it unravel and expand. "An apron?" It was an aged blue gingham, covered in a charming tiny red flower pattern. She held the apron on her lap and reached into the two large rectangular front pockets. "Nothing in the pockets. Weird."

Grace gathered up the spilled photos consisting of a few sepia-toned images and mostly black-and-white photographs, some with yellowing borders. Mark moved behind her, hovering over her shoulder as she flipped through them. She stopped at a picture of their house, with a young couple standing in front of a For Sale sign.

"I feel like people looked so much older back in the day." Grace laid the pictures down in front of her, making a mock scrapbook on the hardwood floor.

"It's because they didn't exercise." Mark's tone was serious, but Grace pulled the laugh out of him when she released one loud guffaw.

"Oh, is that what it was?"

"It's true! Exercise is scientifically proven to reverse the aging process." Mark flexed a bicep as he pulled Grace back so she was leaning against his chest, nestled between his legs.

"They were so good looking at the same time though." Grace held up a photo of a woman with short, cropped hair, styled in finger sculpted waves, framing her made-up face. Even without color in the photos she could tell the woman had slightly overdrawn, deeply-shaded lips and severely arched, thin eyebrows framing a pair of intense cat eyes. She wore a dazzling choker and a black beaded, straight-silhouette dress with a hem hitting just below the knee.

"Ahhh, the flapper days," Mark said, as he studied the image.

"Is that your go-to era?"

"Totally. The dancing, the underground parties, and the women were so risqué."

"I'm more of a sixties gal."

"You like getting high and wearing oversized clothing and flowery headbands?"

"Pretty much. I mean if I had to choose. Better than the nineties."

"True story. So, why do you think these photos were left here? Maybe it's some sort of time capsule?"

"Possibly. I wonder if this has been home to multiple generations of a single family? I know Mel mentioned John Walsh grew up here . . ." Grace considered this while flipping through the disorganized pile quickly, as though on a mission.

"Any pictures of the boy in your vision?" Mark asked, knowing full well Grace's quest.

"Not yet, but we got a lot of looking to do." She chewed on her lower lip as she concentrated.

While they waited for the U-Haul to arrive, they sorted through the photos. Several were of parties held in the house. Clouds of smoke billowing out from the mouths of the guests, martini glasses a natural fixture in everyone's hands. Most of the subjects in the photos had giant grins in common, some caught mid-laugh, on the receiving end of a group joke. Men were dressed in suits, several donning fedora hats. The women all had short hair and gazes that portrayed a feminine toughness, giving them an edge.

"I bet they all danced at these parties too," Grace said, as she held one up. A couple dressed to the nines, looking at each other with wide grins.

"I'm sure they did." Mark picked up a photo and paused. "It's not like it is today, where people wear activewear to themed parties or trivia nights . . . wait a second. What did that boy look like in your vision?" Grace shifted her gaze from the photo she was looking at to the one in Mark's hand. A little boy wearing a pair of stained overalls looked back at her. He was licking an ice cream cone, completely immersed in the moment. He sat on the front steps of the house . . . their house.

"That's not him." Grace's memory resurfaced an image of the boy she saw in her vision, with his sullen round face and parted full lips. The boy eating the ice cream cone had a narrower face, with beady eyes.

"Is he the same age?"

"This kid looks a bit older." Grace snatched the picture from Mark's fingers, surveying it more closely. "Does this look like the fifties to you?" She pointed to the white shoes. "Wait a minute." Grace held the photo closer to her face, observing the background behind the boy. "Look at the mailbox . . . what does it say?"

"Walsh." Mark's answer was proof that he saw the name as clear as day.

"So, if John Walsh is about seventy today, he was likely born sometime in the late forties or early fifties, the same time period that the boy in the vision appears to be in."

"Maybe he's a brother?"

"Could be I suppose. Why would he shoot his brother, though?"

"Again . . . great question."

Grace looked at her watch just as she heard a loud rumbling outside, alerting Brody to the Bridgeton Movers truck. Grace and Mark got to their feet and started directing a cluster of movers to the designated locations of the labeled boxes and furniture. Hiring movers had been a small argument they faced off about. Mark was determined to move all of their possessions with the help of his personal trainers and fitness staff, but Grace stopped him, making it clear that it was not okay to exploit his employees like that.

"And by the way . . . who will be working at the gym when you have your minions working at·our house?" She had asked him.

"Fine." He had said, more upset over the fact he wouldn't be able to experiment with some new box-moving workout he wanted to try on his staff. "I could've given them the best workout ever, and I was planning on having them do pushups and sprints between loads." He pouted.

"Really, and how long do you think that would take?" Grace had asked, as if she was reprimanding a toddler. "Remember we have some place to be the night of the move."

Longtime Lieutenant Joe Sullivan was retiring after more than fifty years of service at the Bridgeton Police Department. As her role model, and a man whom she respected dearly, Grace had to be there.

As she watched six movers parade by her, carrying boxes with militant precision, she knew she was right in paying the extra money to hire a team of qualified professionals. They were fast too, stacking boxes in the appropriate rooms, graceful and flowing through the process like the experts they were.

* * *

The Bridgeton Arms hotel and restaurant was already lined up with guests for the retirement ceremony. Before Grace got out of the Jeep, she gave her face one last look in the mirror. In normal circumstances, she wouldn't have thought all that much about her makeup, but tonight she was giving a speech on behalf of the police department, and she knew photographs would be taken by both the local newspaper and possibly even the Boston Globe. Knowing Joe had friends all over the city and several cop cronies in Boston, there was a good chance this event would receive significant press.

"You look beautiful," Mark said, as he opened Grace's door, offering her a hand. She reached for his hand and steadied herself on a pair of heels that hadn't been worn in years. It was unseasonably warm for May, and she could already feel the sweat accumulating under her arms and onto the edge of her sleeveless dress.

"Thanks." Grace inhaled a deep breath. Public speaking always made her nervous, but this time she was feeling exceptionally shaky. Joe Sullivan was like a father to her and she was starting to feel her emotions emerge, the reality of him no longer being her go-to person for police advice at the station seemed to hit her heavily as soon as they pulled up in front of the venue. The outside of the Arms was white and navy blue; a fresh, beachy look compared to the interior. Grace saw several familiar faces as she and Mark made their way up the stairs. The smell of seafood hit her as the door was pushed open and they were thrown into the subdued atmosphere of the old hotel and restaurant. Worn, uneven hardwood floors greeted her click-clacking heels, making her have to clutch Mark's hand even tighter. Dark wood paneling made the space look smaller than it was and a staircase covered in a navy blue carpet runner spilled out into the lobby joining the restaurant and hotel. It didn't take long for Grace to see Barb's red head standing at a small bar in the lobby, a beer in one hand.

"There's your girl," Mark said, as he nodded in the woman's direction. As always, Barb was wearing khaki pants. She had on a short sleeved, navy blue button-down shirt that was speckled with little white sailboats; making her stand out from the classier dressed folks who were gathered at the bar beside her. As they approached, Barb turned her head and locked eyes as if she had been expecting their arrival that very second.

"Well if it isn't tonight's spokesmodel." Barb assessed the two of them from head to toe. "Dang you two clean up nice." She leaned an elbow on the bar and flagged the bartender down. "What can I get y'all? The usual?"

"That would be great." Mark rested a hand on the small of Grace's back.

"Hey, Cody, a pinot grigio and a vodka soda over here . . . and fill the wine glass up to the brim, this girl's gotta soothe her nerves."

The baby-faced bartender gave Barb a nod and dashed back to the row of liquor bottles displayed unevenly on the mirror backed glass shelving.

Grace rolled her eyes.

"She's not *that* nervous," Mark said, pulling her into his side in a protective embrace.

"Yeah, actually I am." Grace held out a shaking hand.

"Geez, honey, did you eat today?"

"A bag of those cauliflower chips that you think are to die for." She glowered at Mark.

"Grace, how many times have I told you that you have to eat throughout the day." Mark attempted his best scolding tone, while equally coming to his own defense.

"I know, I know. But we were so busy packing and unpacking and I . . . forgot." She shrugged in his embrace.

Barb leaned in, throwing up a pair of air quotes. "Oh, Marky, she's one of those girls who 'forgets to eat.'" Grace ignored their teasing and took her first sip of wine. Mark fetched her some oyster crackers sitting in a basket on the other end of the bar. She could feel the wine burning in her empty stomach, its effects taking toll a lot sooner than if she'd eaten a full meal and not burnt a thousand calories ushering boxes across the multi-level floors of the new house.

Just as Grace poured the bag of oyster crackers in her mouth, she heard commotion by the door and immediately knew the guest of honor had arrived. She hastily chewed the crackers, spritzing white speckles down the front of her dress and washing them down with another swig of wine as she brushed away the crumbs to make herself presentable.

Several officers greeted Joe at the door. Many hugs and handshakes were passed back and forth, and he was suddenly lost in a sea of greetings, the crowd ushering him through the lobby like a slow-moving cloud. Grace knew Joe wasn't a big fan of gatherings that put him at the center of attention, but he seemed to be shining in this moment, his dress blues fitted to perfection.

As the cluster moved closer, Grace realized Joe had a woman on his arm and she, too, was glowing and donning a navy blue floor-length gown. While Grace hadn't personally met the woman she had heard Joe mention her in passing, never fully acknowledging her as anyone other than a friend who had the same hobbies—bowling, sailing, and frequenting annual town events that highlighted each season. For Joe to take the woman to such a meaningful event, she must be special to him. Grace was glad to see him happy, slowly recovering from the loss of his wife, even if there would always be a hole in his heart. Grace watched as an outstretched arm in the crowd handed Joe a brown liquor drink in a short glass. The woman by his side appeared to be giving her drink order to another inquiring officer.

"Shall we try to infiltrate the crowd to say our hellos, or let him pass?" Barb asked, as she took a long pull on her beer.

"Eh . . . let's let him go by . . . he's probably overwhelmed enough as it is." Grace took the final sip of her wine, promising herself she'd stick to water until after the speech.

On the other side of the lobby, by the entrance of the ballroom, Grace noticed a table displaying photos of Joe over the years. Having only been on the department during Joe's later years, Grace was intrigued by the photos of his younger days and made a beeline for the exhibit, with Mark and Barb following closely behind. Just as she approached the table, Mark got pulled into a conversation about fitness and Barb was rubbing elbows with an older gentleman, leaving her standing alone in front of a lifetime of the well-known lieutenant's memories. Joe as a toddler proudly wearing his father's too large and heavy police cap, with a crooked grin and happy eyes peeking out from beneath the tilted brim. Another one of Joe and his four brothers, all standing erect in dress blues from different locales. To say the Sullivans were a cop family was an understatement. Nearly all of the photos of Joe had some form of police sentiment and the career choice seemed to go back as far as Joe's great-grandfather. The only photo absent of dress blues or award ceremonies was one of Joe as a student, wearing a tux and standing beside a girl in a pale blue tulle dress that matched his tie. She held a bouquet of pastel flowers bound together with a matching pale blue tulle ribbon that looked like it was torn from her dress. Giant strawberry blonde curls sat on her head pinned securely in a fancy updo and side swept bangs highlighted her eyes. Grace wondered if that was Joe's wife.

"He was a cute one, wasn't he?"

As if she were jumping out of the memory, Grace nearly leaped forward at the voice that came from behind. She whirled around to see an unfamiliar face.

"Yeah, he was," Grace said, confusion evident in her expression.

"Betts." The woman extended a hand, offering a firm grip for her age. Her brown and silver hair pulled back into one long braid that draped over her left breast. Grace pegged her to be in her seventies based on her frail-looking height and weight and the deeply carved wrinkles on her face looked like contour lines on a map. "I'm Joe's older sister."

Grace, responding too fast, said, "Oh, I didn't know that he had a sister."

"Well that's because I wasn't a cop." She wafted a hand around the room, bringing the turquoise and silver bracelets to life on her wrist. "Everything in the Sullivan family revolves around police work . . . as you can see." Even the non-officer guests of the party were wearing navy blue, making it hard to distinguish who was a cop and who was a civilian.

"It's nice to meet you, Betts. I'm Grace . . . I worked with—"

"I know who you are . . . I may not be a cop but I'm privy to the gossip in all the stations my brothers have frequented." She tossed a wink in Grace's direction; revealing teal eye shadow that matched her loose-fitting dress, with contrasting rust-colored trim at the neckline, sleeves, and the ruffled hem dropping past her knees. A clump of layered turquoise necklaces rested on her deeply tanned décolletage. She was beautiful, with a heart-shaped face and full lips. Her eyes, a deep shade of brown, were wide-set in the way that Jackie Kennedy was known for. Grace noticed she leaned on a cane decorated with small, fancy cursive script, but Grace couldn't make out the wording.

"Oh, well I hope you've only heard good things."

"Very good things indeed." She nodded, giving Grace an all-knowing smile. Grace found it nearly impossible to take her eyes off the woman, as she was trying to pick apart her features and scramble them into a younger version of herself. *What was Betts like when she was younger? What did she do for work?* "And if you're wondering where I am in the photos . . . I was the one taking them." She took a step forward, limping on one foot. "This one is one of my favorites." With a finger, ornamented with a chunky orange ring, Betts pointed to the photo of Joe in his school uniform. "I picked up a camera when I was three, and I still haven't put it down . . . that was one of my first favorites. I just love how innocent Joey looks there. A perfect little Boston schoolboy."

"You mean, he's not innocent?"

Betts leaned back slightly, releasing a gentle chuckle while keeping her eyes focused on Grace. "Oh, he was innocent alright. Probably the most innocent of all the boys. But you didn't hear that from me." Adjusting her footing, she winked at Grace again.

"So, are you still a photographer?"

"I couldn't stop taking photos if you severed my hands off. Mostly landscapes now though, the occasional family photo, a new baby every now and then. I used to do strictly portraits but I gave that up for the most part. There is something calming and peaceful about nature . . . it changes from season to season but at its core it's the same. Unwavering. People, well, they're unpredictable, not always loyal to both themselves and others, and that shows up on film."

Grace was mesmerized by the woman standing before her. She had a rolodex of questions flipping through her head, questions she wanted to ask her, knowing without a doubt that this woman, this stranger, would have the answers to.

"Hey, Princess, shall we go pay Sully a visit before you do your famous speech?" Barb marched up to the table, taking in all the photos and somehow failing to notice Betts.

"I'll let you get to it then. It was lovely meeting you, Grace. I do hope our paths cross again."

"I too." The words spilled out of Grace's mouth as if a character in a historical romance movie.

"*I too?* What the heck was that?" Barb asked, staring at Grace's profile while she watched Betts limp off to a table alone.

"I have no idea." Grace, trying to change the subject looked around the room. "Where's Mark?"

"He's over there . . ." Grace's eyes followed the direction Barb was pointing and saw Mark wildly gesturing, pointing out certain body parts and displaying perfect posture, as if he was about to give a personal training lesson. A young couple stared at him in awe, bobbing their heads up and down and absorbing everything he was saying.

"Alright, I'm going to pass by Sully's table for a quick congrats before I take the stage."

"I already brought him a whiskey, so I'll meet ya at the table." Barb swiped a glass of champagne from a passing tray before she shuffled her way to the reserved table at the front of the room.

As Grace made her way to Sully's table she was suddenly overcome with unease. She felt self-conscious in the dress she was wearing, afraid she was spilling out in the wrong places. With one hand clutching her purse, she used the other to lift the front of her dress. She was suddenly fearful the press would get a photo of her bosom spilling out and regretted not wearing a more supportive bra.

She was grateful when she caught Sully in a rare moment when he wasn't in the middle of a conversation. He was sitting there sipping his drink while taking it all in. As soon as she approached the table, he looked up at her with adoration. "Gracie, you look beautiful." Setting his drink down he started to get up.

"Don't get up, I'll come down to you." Grace crouched, feeling her dress cling tighter to her hips and thighs. "I just wanted to officially congratulate you."

"Oh, you've already done enough, Gracie . . . the party at the station, the scrapbook . . ."

"My pleasure." Grace sucked in her stomach as she pushed herself up to a standing position. Just as she was about to step away from the table, Sully's girlfriend approached, carrying a small plate filled with appetizers.

"Oh, wait. Gracie, I want you to meet Susan."

Grace turned toward the woman, watching her as she set the plate down in front of Sully."

"It's a pleasure meeting you, Grace, I've heard so much about you. I'm glad someone has been taking care of Joe at the station." She reached for Grace's hand and held it in her own as she said the words, a gesture her mom always used to do when meeting people. Accepting the woman's kind words, Grace locked eyes with her and she was hit with a wave of recognition. The woman, with her mousy brown hair and small brown eyes that sparkled like two earthy gems, looked exactly like someone she knew but she couldn't place it. And then, as Susan kept talking, Grace picked up on the monotone voice and the thin lips that formed one straight line, only slightly curving upward when she attempted to emphasize a word.

After Grace expressed her gratitude for meeting the woman, she walked away and suddenly clung to the recognition that sat like a heavy weight on her chest. The woman was a spitting image of John Walsh.

CHAPTER FIVE

As soon as Grace was done giving her speech, she followed Mark to the bar. She felt like it was a success since her inserted jokes received loud rumbles of laughter and she only stumbled on one word. She made sure to point out the elephant in the room . . . that Sully was far older than most cops when they retired and his addiction to working at the station was brought up often over the years. When he finally admitted to being too old to be out in the field and partake in detective work, he downsized his career and strictly worked shifts on the console, managing the newbies and making the schedule. Even in the middle of the local reporter snapping photos, with her bright flash, she managed to keep it together. She had walked off the stage free of tears and by the time they made it to the bar, connected to the next door restaurant, her nerves had eased greatly.

"So, why did you want to go to this bar? Don't you want to receive all your accolades for giving, what will be, the most memorable speech of the night?" Mark asked, as Grace climbed onto a barstool at the smaller, and more private, bar in the event space.

As Grace told Mark about the similarities between Susan and John Walsh, he nodded his head between sips of his cocktail.

"But, aren't you thinking that Walsh had a brother, AKA the little boy on the swing?"

"Yeah, but who's to say he didn't have a sister too?"

"True."

"The ages match up . . . although it's hard to say if she is older or younger than Walsh."

"So, what's your next step?" Mark asked the appropriate questions like he always had. Grace felt comfort knowing he was on her side, prepared to tackle a case undercover. She was even more grateful that he passed no harsh judgement on her gift. Most men would either run as fast as they could away from her, out of fear, or have her committed. Mark, like a lighthouse in a storm, held steady in his commitment to Grace.

"That's the magic question." Grace took a long swig of the wine Mark ordered for her, her eyes darting around the room behind the glass, searching for answers. She saw Betts on the other side of the room sneaking a few photos with a massive camera, that looked like it outweighed her. "Gosh, I don't know how she lugs that thing around being so petite."

Mark turned to see what Grace was consumed by.

"Oh, Betts . . . that woman is a photography genius."

"Wait . . . you know her?"

"Yeah, she's the one who took all of my staff headshots, group shots, and images for our website."

"Hmmm . . . I didn't think she did that sort of work."

"Well, it helps that her boyfriend's godson is one of my best trainers."

"Ohhh. That's the relationship." Grace paused, absorbing the connection. "She didn't strike me as someone who would have a boyfriend."

"Well, I don't think they are exactly live-in status and she definitely has her own schedule. Maybe they are just really good friends."

"Does she have any kids?"

"Not that I know of."

"You know that she's Sullivan's older sister, right?"

Mark tilted his head and opened his eyes wide, as if connecting the dots for the first time. "Not until you just said that, but it makes sense . . . why I never put that together before is beyond me."

"Sullivan is a popular name in this area." Grace leaned on an elbow. "What do you say we get outta here, Mr. Connolly?"

"Are you sure you don't need to stay?" Mark leaned in closer, with only his eyes darting left to right for confirmation of a clean getaway.

"I did my part," Grace said, with a smug tilt of her raised chin.

"And you did damn good at it. That speech will be remembered forever." Mark's head bobbed with serious conviction that made Grace break into a smile at her sweet guy.

Grace hopped down from her stool and with a steadying grip linked arms with Mark, pulling him into her side, guiding them toward the exit. The hotel lobby was deserted, except for a couple out-of-towners checking in at the desk. A few twenty-somethings sat in the area between the event space and lobby, deep in conversation and oblivious to any passerby. Today's youth was so different from her generation. They were all conversing while simultaneously looking down at their phones, likely having dual conversations.

"Kids today, huh?" As if Grace's thoughts were extracted from her head, she turned toward the familiar voice. Sully was approaching her from the bathrooms by the main entrance. "Are you two heading out already?"

"You caught us," Grace said, raising her free hand in mock surrender.

"Gracie, you are a shining star. This night wouldn't have been the same without you. Your speech, your presence, your dedication to the department . . . honestly—" Sully swiped a hand over his face from top to bottom. "I wouldn't have survived these past four years without you."

Grace knew what he was referring to. She had been there the days following his wife's death. She'd consoled him on many occasions and offered him hope when she, too, was struggling with finding hope with her mother at the same time. They were each other's rocks at the department.

"You're gonna be missed, Sully." Grace could see a slight tear forming in the corner of his eye, his internal teddy bear coming out from behind his hard shell.

Sully opened his arms, welcoming her in. His embrace was like home. Just as her head peeked over his shoulder, she could see Susan headed in their direction after exiting the bathroom. She stood behind Sully, clutching her purse in front of her waist with both hands, a crooked smile turning her straight lips into an uneven line. Grace gave one last squeeze before she stepped back, meeting Susan's gaze, and alerting Sully to her presence.

"These two are sneaking away, honey," Sully said, a slight slur in his cadence. It was rare for him to show affection in public so she knew he was feeling the multiple whiskeys that had been sent his way this evening. Grace never pegged him for someone who used terms of endearment, let alone on a new girlfriend.

Susan took a timid step forward, adjusting her purse slightly. "Grace, your speech was beautiful."

"Thank you. He's a pretty easy person to speak highly about." Grace winked.

"Oh, I was so caught up in my big night I forgot to ask you how the move was." Sully, genuinely interested in their new house, shifted the attention off of himself and onto Grace and Mark.

"Well, we are still surrounded by boxes since the movers just came today, but we are taking our time unpacking," Mark said, "really taking the time to find the best places for furniture and storage." The words sounded foreign coming out of Mark's mouth. It was unlike him to be concerned about perfect placement, and he was typically the one stacking items one on top of another. Grace couldn't help but think that maybe he would change his pack rat ways now that he had a house of his own.

"Sue, these two just purchased a house in the area of your old stompin' grounds, in the Highlands," Sully said, as if he had just threaded the details of the related parties.

"Oh, really . . . where did you buy?"

"Ummm . . . Thirteen Court Street." As soon as the number tumbled out of Grace's mouth, Susan's slight smile dropped, her eyes a blank stare. Grace could almost see the memories batting around inside the woman's head. She knew the resemblance was uncanny, and Susan had to be the sister of John. Was she picturing the young boy being shot in the chest, or her own brother holding a gun? And what role did she play in all of this? Grace could see visions in the eyes of criminals but sometimes she wished she could also see the memories of the innocent, the ones who were there witnessing it all, or the ones who may have aided in the aftermath.

"That's a nice area." Susan forced the words out, a disguised nicety. "I wish you well there."

As if sensing Susan's uneasiness, Sully grabbed her hand. "Well, we better get back to schmoozing," he said, as he gave them both one last smile, his dimples deep and his eyes creasing into two slits.

* * *

Grace woke to the sound of an airplane rumbling overhead, its engine tearing into her sleep like an uninvited guest. She knew that the airplane noise was one of the top complaints about living in Bridgeton but she never imagined it would wake her up from a deep sleep, stealing her away from a dream about her mother. In the dream she and Ellen had been celebrating Christmas together. Alone as usual for the holidays. They had been exchanging gifts and Ellen was her old self again, with her memory intact and happy as she always had been.

"You'll get used to it." Mark's voice startled her from the corner of the room. She sat up, her heart jumping in her chest. "Sorry, I was trying to let you sleep . . . damn airplane ruined that for me." Mark was sitting on the recliner that had somehow taken up residence in the corner of their bedroom, his eyes peeking over the top of a fitness magazine.

"So you decided to sit there and watch me sleep?" Grace rose from the bed, heavy with slumber. "Kinda creepy don't you think?"

"In my defense I was worried you wouldn't know where you were when you woke up, so I wanted to be here."

"I'm not sure what's scarier . . . waking up seeing you watching me or waking up in a strange bedroom." Grace knew the bedroom would feel strange to her for at least a month, until she settled into their new home and learned all the creaks and little intricacies that made a home a home. Until then, she knew it would feel like a strange house until she and Mark were able to make some memories and stake their claim on the abode, matching moments with various parts of the house.

"Coffee?" Mark stood up and reached for a cup of coffee perched on the table made of stacked upside down milk crates.

"Yes, please." Halfway across the room Grace met Mark, retrieving her favorite mug, the one her mother had given her for Christmas just two years ago; although in this moment it had felt like a lifetime ago. She held the cup with both hands, embracing the ceramic snowman with a bright red scarf around the neck and a jolly round face that gave her an all-knowing smile. She brought her lips to the mug's edge and took a sip of the lukewarm beverage. *Bluck!*

Detecting her lack of enjoyment, Mark said, "Sorry, I've kinda had it sitting up here a little while." His retracted lower lip exposed his bottom teeth as he offered an explanation, while simultaneously begging for forgiveness.

"Creeping on me while I sleep *and* serving me cold coffee?" Grace joked as she set the cup down and stripped off the pair of boxer shorts she had borrowed from Mark. She walked toward the pile of garbage bags filled with their clothes and labeled accordingly. Without being gentle, she tore at the material beneath the knotted red drawstring and rifled through the garments until she found what she was looking for. Workout pants and a well-worn T-shirt.

"Need help getting dressed?" Mark approached her from behind, readying himself for some action. Until she looked up at him and gave him a look that was all business.

"If you ever want this house to feel like home, then we've got to get some work done." She slid on a pair of pants that clung to her thighs and hips, as Mark watched. As she headed for the bedroom door, she looked back over one shoulder with seductive eyes and a devious smirk, saying in a sultry voice, "Maybe once we have the living room unpacked, Casanova." She playfully sashayed her chest and hips while standing in the doorway, like a sexy Jessica Rabbit, attempting to entice Mark into chores with a manipulative come-hither look.

"In that case . . . I'll get to work." Mark dropped the magazine he was still holding, it landed splayed open with the cover face up.

"Whatever motivates you, dear." Grace winked and jogged down the staircase, leaving Mark and the cold coffee in her wake. Just as she was about to tackle the first stack of boxes in the living room, she heard a loud thump at the front door. Even though it was a bright and sunny spring day, every little noise seemed to make her jump lately. The new visions and historical home weren't helping her with staying calm. With Brody by her side she opened the front door. Not seeing a mystery package she assumed was the source of the thud; she looked around and saw a mail truck pulling away, hearing its distinct vibrating buzz, and stopping at the next house with rear yellow hazards flashing.

"Already?" She looked at her watch. The face revealed it was only nine o'clock. Hearing Mark hopping down the stairs she turned toward him with the doors still open. "Mail's already here."

"Yeah?"

"That's not odd to you?"

"Why would that be odd to me?"

"I don't know . . . I guess because in Cabotville I never got my mail till at least one o'clock."

"Well you're in the big city now, honey." Mark winked.

Grace lifted the lid of the rusty black metal mailbox affixed to the right of the front door. Wrapped in a rubber band were several papers and envelopes, of varying sizes. "I guess they wrap your mail neatly in the big city too." She pulled the elastic off the bundle, feeling it shrink back to size, as several smaller envelopes fell out from between folded flyers and advertisements. As she bent over to pick them up she saw John Walsh's name on a bill and a letter addressed to him from a Boston address.

"Anything good?" Mark asked, as he passed by with a box that was meant for the kitchen.

"Yeah, looks like we've got a couple of pieces for Mr. Walsh."

"Oh?" Mark set the box down on their dining room table and turned, his interest piqued.

"How should we get these to him?"

"Sounds like a great opportunity for you to see him face to face, don't you think?"

Grace knew exactly what Mark was saying. It was the perfect opportunity to glean more information from the man who had a past that was less than perfect. "Why me?"

"I know, I know. But, remember what your mom always said? You were given this gift for a reason." Mark wrapped his arm around her waist, pulling her closer to him. "And let's be honest . . . life would be pretty boring without your crazy ability, don't you think?"

She leaned into his shoulder, taking in the woodsy scent of his deodorant. "Boring sounds nice right about now."

* * *

As Grace made her way down the hill leading to the center of town, she took in the sounds of spring. It was approaching Memorial Day weekend and the nonstop sound of children playing outdoors made her think of her own childhood. Late spring was one of her mother's favorite times of year. Maybe because that's when her garden started to bloom, sprouting a rainbow of tulips she watered faithfully. It was the memories of her mother in that garden Grace clung to, the moments she seemed her happiest and most content.

The new street Grace and Mark lived on was one of the steepest roads in town and it spilled out into the main strip that cut across the town center. As Grace walked onto the crosswalk, a young boy, wobbly on a bike with training wheels, headed in her direction from the opposite side. Unaware of anything else around him, he nearly crashed into Grace as his mother screamed his name while pushing a stroller of fussy twins. It was in these moments Grace felt like summer was fast approaching and the town was coming to life. If only she could spend a summer without having to solve a gruesome mystery.

She reached into her pocket and slid out her phone, opening her GPS walking app. Stephen had alerted John Walsh she would be delivering some mail to his new residence. Unfamiliar with the location of the newly built condos where he resided, Grace needed the help of Google maps to find her way.

The smell of cinnamon hit her nostrils as she passed Betty's Bakery, a town staple known for the best cinnamon donuts. The door was propped open by a giant painted rock and workers bustled behind the counter, serving the line that wound between café tables and chairs. Beyond Betty's Bakery were a few other storefronts that led to the section of beach locals called The Greenbelt. Looking down at her phone, Grace followed the directions that took her up another high hill where a new section of condos was built. The building, tall and dark grey, stood high and narrow like a tower. The condos had been put up fast, thanks to a wealthy developer who was on a mission to build up the town. Grace hadn't pictured this to be the type of place John Walsh would reside, but maybe that was because all she knew of him were the quick flashes of images pegging him as a murderer. Having lived in the same house his entire life, Grace wanted to know the real reason he wanted to downsize. *Why now? Why hadn't he done this years ago?* Surely the visions she saw were the same that have been haunting him his entire life. Why stay in the home all this time, where something so disturbing happened?

Approaching the front steps, Grace stopped navigation and dialed the phone number Stephen had given her. After three rings John picked up the phone. "Hi, Grace," he said, much to her surprise. It was as if he had been watching her through a camera, his voice steely with an eerie tone.

"Hi, John, it's Grace . . . I mean—"

"I know, come on in." The door lock made one loud click, granting her entrance. Just as she was about to look at her phone to confirm what number condo, a door along the inner hallway flung open and John flagged her down with a wave.

Grace walked down the hallway, trying her best to put on a brave face. She hadn't expected this. She thought he'd simply come to the main entrance, retrieve his mail, and gift her with a few visions before being on his merry way. Based on his quiet nature at the closing he didn't seem like the chatty type. As she approached his condo unit he backed into the door, opening it wider, in a gesture that said he was inviting her in. Standing on the outside of the doorway, Grace passed him a tentative gaze.

"Oh, sorry . . . I have something for you actually, if you want to come in for a second . . . I'll get it." His eyes darted everywhere but on her stare, which made her even more hesitant to accept his offer.

Grace grazed her right hip with her hand, a subtle confirmation her Glock was still where she placed it hidden beneath her oversized windbreaker. It wasn't the type of look she usually aimed for but safety came before fashion. "Sure." Grace stepped into the entryway, her eyes assessing the layout of the place in case she had to make a run for it. She silently acquainted herself with any obstacles that had the potential to get in her way, and there were a lot of them. Like Grace and Mark, John was still in the midst of unpacking. Towers of half-opened boxes staggered throughout the living room, and the kitchen countertops were concealed by strewn-about appliances that had yet to find their home.

As John dug through a stack of paperwork piled on an old rolltop desk, in the corner of the living room, Grace made her way into his home. "Do you cook a lot?" She asked, as she took in the impressive amount of cooking gadgets lining the granite countertops. Crockery of various sizes were lined up, filled to the brim with wooden spoons, spatulas, and utensils. A recently used garlic press sat open with discarded skins scattered beside it.

"I try." John's words were followed up by a slight snicker. "Ahhhh, here it is." He walked toward her holding an overly stuffed envelope, reminding Grace what she came here for in the first place. She unzipped the front pouch of her windbreaker and pulled out the two pieces of mail.

Grace eyed the envelope he was holding before lifting her gaze to his button-shaped eyes. A flash of the boy against a backdrop of green grass and twisted roots above the earth's surface. Blood trickling down his chest, transforming his shirt from white to red as the stain spread across the fabric. His hazel eyes offering a lifeless stare. Beside him lay the flannel blanket, he no longer clutched, bespattered with his own blood. Shattered green glass rained down and a flash of something round and red. Shimmering flecks of sharp-edged glass twinkled in the air, catching the sunlight, like a sunlit Christmas tree. Putting a stop to the flashes, like a red light on a highway, John's voice interrupted the visions catapulting through her mind.

"So, this is just some paperwork that might come in handy. Warrantees on the kitchen appliances, my go-to painter and handyman, and a few other things you may find helpful in maintaining the house." As if they were part of a secret exchange, they passed their envelopes to one another, sealing an unspoken deal.

Peeling her eyes away from him, Grace looked around the condo once more. "Thank you . . . you must be glad to be downsizing . . . looks like this will be a lot easier to maintain." Grace took in the open-concept space that housed a small kitchen overlooking a spacious living room and an intimate seating area, complete with modern lighting, fresh pale grey paint, and wide windows allowing for a decent amount of natural sunlight to spill into the main living area. A door leading to, what Grace assumed was, the only bedroom, was set off the living room and halfway open, revealing darkness even in the middle of the sunny day.

"Yeah, it's nice to not have to deal with such an old house and have everything taken care of here. Besides . . . I was fooling myself thinking I needed all that space all these years." He paused, dropping and lifting his gaze along Grace's body. "I'm sure the space will come in handy for you guys . . . if you plan to start a family and all that."

Grace fought off her urge to shudder at the thought of him scanning her body from head to toe. What was he trying to assess . . . a growing baby in her stomach?

"Yeah, it's nice to have all that space . . . with our massive dog it certainly helps. Although he usually just lies in one spot on the floor, so . . . " Grace was rambling, partly because she was at a loss for words and partly because she wanted to gain more information from the man.

"Well, I'm glad the house went to a good family . . . and I hear you're a cop so I'm sure you'll keep it safe."

Grace's eyebrows raised, giving away her confusion about his statement. She thought about turning on a heel and getting out of there as fast as she could, but she pressed ahead to the unknown.

"So, how long did you live in the house?"

He paused, as if assessing his own thoughts. "My entire life. Couldn't quite get myself to leave, but . . . it was time."

"Well, thank you, John . . . for this." Grace waggled the fat envelope, its contents nearly spilling out with paperwork.

"Thank you . . . for this." He held up the two envelopes with his left hand and made a chopping motion into his right hand. Grace turned and started walking down the hallway, before she spun around one last time to see John still standing there. Watching her.

"Oh and, John?"

"Yeah?" His face colored at being caught watching her walk away.

"Are you still willing to make yourself available to us...you know in case anything else may arise?"

His eyes darted left to right, as he swayed with the closing door. "Yeah, sure." He answered noncommittally, most likely hoping he'd never hear from her again.

CHAPTER SIX

Grace was glad to be back at work. After a five day hiatus for moving and unpacking, she welcomed the routine and, even more so, welcomed the opportunity to focus on John Walsh. Aside from her routine work as the school resource officer in town, she'd have more time to research Walsh and the sad boy in her visions.

"Welcome back, Princess." Barb looked up from flipping through a magazine as Grace pushed the door to the station open.

"Hi, Barb. What are you reading?"

"Catchin' up on my latest celeb gossip . . . did you know George Clooney shops at Target?" Barb said, clearly not the slightest bit embarrassed she was caught reading trashy magazines on the job. She tossed the magazine into the wastebasket beside her massive metal desk. "Wait, do you want me to save that for you?"

"No thanks, I'm all set." Grace rolled her eyes. The last thing she wanted to do was read about famous people shopping at Target. She had her own people to read about . . . John Walsh, who was evidently famous in other ways.

"I'm sure you have plenty to keep you busy anyways. I left a note on your door. Your dad called looking for you. I don't know why he doesn't try your cell."

Grace didn't feel like explaining it to Barb, but her newly blossomed relationship with her father had led to multiple missed calls on her phone. In the short time she had known him, she had to admit she liked the man, but she felt the need to set up some hardcore boundaries. Part of it was due to the fact she was afraid that getting too close to him could lead to heartache and she didn't want to suffer any more parental pain. It was hard enough dealing with her mother's diminishing health.

"He probably just wants to tell me about a visit with my mom." Grace had stopped going to visit her mother in the assisted living home, ever since a nurse hinted it was probably best to stay away. For whatever reason, Grace caused heightened anger in Ellen every time she saw her, and her blood pressure was taking a hit because of it. Making matters worse, the man who walked out on both her and her mother was somehow a calming presence to Ellen. She had decided to let it go and be grateful that someone could calm her mother these days, instead of being bitter over it. Her father, Bruce Michaels, was a wealthy building developer and had been paying Ellen's rent ever since they reconnected, so Grace really couldn't complain. Otherwise the burden would be completely on her, and she and Mark would never have been able to purchase their new home.

Grace made her way to her office; habit stopping her at the main console. Every day she arrived at work, when Sully was on shift, she would check in with him. She'd lean up against the console and have small talk, that on more than one occasion got much deeper than the average chat about the weather. Behind the desk were two officers. One was a short-timer who was in the middle of training the newbie that would be covering Sully's shifts.

"Hi, Detective McKenna." The older of the two looked up from his binder of emergency checklists.

"Hey, Matt." Grace looked over Matt's shoulder, awaiting the introduction to the newer officer. She met him once before but had forgotten his name. The one thing she could tell, by the innocent expression on his face and the crisply pressed uniform he was wearing, was that he was brand new and straight out of the police academy. Grace never liked dealing with the younger guys. They had a tendency to suck up to her and she never knew if she was getting a straight answer.

"This is Jay . . . Jay Hanagan."

The last name caused a wave of recognition in Grace. "Wait . . . are you related to Mickey Hanagan?"

"I sure am . . . he's my uncle." The young officer stood at attention. His baby face and tight curly hair made Grace feel old. She had met the legendary Mickey Hanagan a few months prior and the guy had made an impression on her.

"Well, if you're anything like your uncle, then I'm sure you're a good guy." Grace gave him a quick wave before she took two long strides to her office door. A bright pink Post-It note was stuck sideways on her door in Barb's messy scrawl. *Call dad.* She peeled it off the door, twisted the knob, and tossed it into the trash can beside her desk.

As she sank into her old, creaky chair she felt right at home. Today would be considered a catch-up day. In between scheduling talks and events at the local schools she'd get through her emails and hopefully have a chance to do a little recon on John Walsh. She leaned back in her chair, resting her head in her interlaced fingers and looked up at the yellow stain on the ceiling. The station was in need of a serious upgrade but it seemed to be the last agenda item for the town. Maybe she could recruit the help of her dad to get a new building.

Using one finger she brought her computer to life and decided her school calls could wait. She typed "John Walsh Bridgeton" into Google and watched as a long list of results surfaced on her screen. As she clicked through the links, she discovered there were at least five people by the name of John Walsh who lived in Bridgeton at one point. Not an easy name in a prominently Irish town, Grace was well aware this was going to be a tricky mystery to unravel. There was a John Walsh who was now in the school system, likely a relative to her suspect. A John Walsh who was residing in the Bridgeton Nursing Home, a thirty-something John Walsh with a Facebook page, and another who appeared to be a reporter for the Boston Globe and no longer living in Bridgeton. She pulled up images and came across a grainy photo of what looked like her John Walsh, dated September 13, 2013. As she clicked the image it became clearer, bringing to life a closeup of John's face and hands as he placed a part on an airplane. The caption read, *"Airplane mechanic places newly invented part, designed to keep engine running longer on a Boeing 737."* In the image John was all business and Grace could tell he wasn't there for the photo op.

"Airplane mechanic," Grace said aloud to herself. While she really couldn't picture him in any specific type of career, she definitely didn't picture him in one involving the safety of millions of passengers. She supposed it was more of an accurate depiction than his being a public speaker or schoolteacher. It also made sense that he still lived in Bridgeton, a stone's throw away from Boston's Logan Airport. "Interesting."

After attempting a few more unsuccessful searches for him online, the front desk number rang on her phone. "Hey, Barb."

"Hey, it's your dad again . . . what do you want me to say?"

"Ugh . . ." Grace pushed out her lower lip, blowing a lose strand of hair out of her face; one of her go-to frustration gestures. "Just put him through . . . wait, Barb, I have a question for you . . . when you are searching for someone whom you can't find on the internet but you want to learn about their family . . . what do you do . . . do I have to go to the library and pull up the old newspapers?"

"You could do that . . . but first I'd try a free trial of one of those genealogy sites that tracks down your ancestors, lost siblings . . . all that crap people are into these days . . . in fact I think I may have a few brothers out there that I never—"

"Thanks!" Grace cut Barb off, anxious about tracing John Walsh's history down.

"Put my dad through." Grace picked up as soon as Barb transferred the call. "Detective McKenna."

"Hey . . . Grace . . . it's me, Dad . . . er, Bruce, I mean."

"Hey . . . what's up?" Grace wasn't quite ready to call him Dad.

"I just wanted to let you know . . . well . . . your mom has really been losing a lot of weight. They can't seem to get her to eat anything . . . to be honest she's really dwindling down to nothing. I know she's never been particularly curvy, but . . ."

Grace thought about the last time she saw her mother, nearly a month ago. She had already lost nearly fifteen pounds on her already frail frame.

"And how is her mind?"

"No better but not drastically worse . . . maybe a little more quiet than usual, if that's possible. She kinda just sits there and daydreams."

Grace thought about the various stages of Alzheimer's that Dr. Wexford had warned her about. The early stage was when the person could still function independently. Ellen had surpassed this stage rapidly. It all began when she started to forget the right words and names for things. This went from being a rare occurrence to one that was more common than not. Grace remembered Ellen had read a book for one of the book clubs she was in, and when it was time for her to host the club, she completely forgot everything about the plot and the main characters. Then there was stage two, also known as the moderate stage. Grace remembered this one lasting the longest. Ellen had started getting moody and not interested in her normal social outings. She knew it was bad when her mother chose to wear a thick, puffy sweater in the middle of July because she forgot what season they were in. By this point, Ellen was incapable of planning anything on her own because she'd forget everything just seconds later. And now, according to her father, Ellen was approaching the severe stage of Alzheimer's. Like being at the end of a long, dark tunnel where you have no hope of escaping. Ellen didn't know where she was at any given moment of the day. Grace had been feeling premature grief for her mother, knowing that she would one day have to say a goodbye she'd never be prepared for.

"Have the nurses said anything?"

"Yeah . . . that's kind of why I'm calling. She needs around-the-clock care, Grace." Bruce sucked in a long inhale with its slow release coming out fuzzy into the phone, penetrating Grace's ear sharply.

"Shit."

"Yeah, I know . . . I'm sorry, honey . . . I mean, Grace. This is the last news I wanted to bring you."

Before Grace could stop herself, tears pooled at the surface of her eyes, causing a deep, dull throbbing in her head.

"I have the finances all taken care of, but . . . I wanted you to know that things are going downhill fast. I'm sorry, Gracie."

The fact that Bruce used a pet name on Grace didn't escape her notice. Given the circumstances that she would likely be down to one parent soon enough, she allowed the name to slide into her heart just slightly. The two of them agreed to meet for coffee over the next few weeks, something Bruce had been trying to get Grace to agree to for months now.

As Grace hung up her phone, she couldn't help but feel the tug of war in her heart. One side was slowly preparing for the loss of her mother and the other side was starting to open up to the possibility of a growing relationship with her father. Like always, she put a Band-Aid on her emotions and immersed herself in her work. She next typed "genealogy" into Google and an instant list of ancestry site options appeared. Her eyes landed on one promising to provide family history in the form of newspaper publications, as far back as 1690.

"Bingo!" Grace's excitement tingled within as she signed up for a free 14-day trial. She dove right in, typing in John's first and last name. As the search results loaded, in the form of a slowly increasing percentage bar, Grace was asked other questions in the meantime. Spouse's name, affiliated organizations, and his parents' names. She didn't know anything beyond his full name so skipped the additional questions, but she wondered if John had ever been married or been in a relationship. A big part of her doubted he had, considering he lived in a big family home his entire life before settling into a little condo. As far as Grace could tell his condo showed no signs of a female presence.

When the loading hit one hundred percent, several blocks appeared broken up into categories of names, relationships, and events; with John T. Walsh prominent at the top. Grace scrolled down to the box listing father, mother, and siblings.

Father: Charles Walsh
Mother: Margaret Walsh
Sister: Susan Walsh
Brother: Timmy Walsh

Alongside Timmy's name was an obituary. As Grace clicked on the link, she braced herself for what was to come. Instead of an obituary there was only the dates of life and death followed by a poem, making the mystery even more cryptic.

Bridgeton: Timothy John Walsh December 6, 1950–August 12, 1955)

God looked around His garden
And found an empty place
He then looked down upon the earth
And saw your tired face
He put his arms around you
And lifted you to rest
God's garden must be beautiful
He always takes the best
He saw the roads were getting rough
And the hills were hard to climb

So He closed your weary eyelids
And whispered "Peace be Thine"
It broke our hearts to lose you
But you didn't go alone
For part of us went with you
The day God called you home

Services will be held at St. John the Evangelist Church
on August 18, 1955, at 12:00 p.m.
Visiting hours will be held at Callahan Funeral Home
on August 17, 1955, 4:00 p.m.– 7:00 p.m.

Grace scrolled farther down until she saw a familiar face in grainy black-and-white print. Staring back at her was the boy in her visions, who now had a name. *Timmy Walsh.* The same slick side part molded to his head, but here he displayed a contented, crooked smile. Grace enlarged the photo to get a better look. Even from a young age she could tell Timmy would've grown up to be a good-looking man. He had a more angular jaw than his brother. His eyes set an aesthetically pleasing distance apart; unlike John's beady, close-set eyes that looked pushed into his head. Even in the poor-quality newspaper photo she could tell his eyes were a lighter shade, different than the caramel tones of John's.

Grace couldn't help but wonder if Timmy died because of jealousy. Maybe he was the star child. The one that could do no wrong. Maybe John had a mental breakdown and killed his brother in a heated moment. Grace wondered if the Walsh family served as a cautionary tale for gun safety, an after school special in the making.

Pressing print in the upper right-hand corner of the computer, Grace heard her tired printer creak to life, slowly rolling off a two-page printout of Timmy's photo, the poem, and the times of the services held sixty-five years ago. But she couldn't help but wonder why there was no obituary write-up, nothing shedding light on how or why Timmy Walsh died at such a young age. There were several clues she would need to string together to get an answer, which would require the work of a little networking and a lot of searching.

After making a few calls to schedule safety visits to the schools and catching up on emails, the clock had made a surprisingly quick jump to lunchtime and, as promised, Mark sent a text reminding her of their first lunch date in the new house. Less than half a mile away, the house was walking distance from the police station and even less from Mark's gym, Imperial Fitness. With Mark's urging, Grace agreed to eat lunch at home every day they could, to save money to put toward any necessary projects for the aging Victorian. He also assured Grace it would do wonders for their health if they veered away from the local sandwich shops that slathered mayo on bread like a mom applies sunblock on her tot in the middle of summer. Grace was less concerned about the mayo and more about the money, knowing they would need a new roof and a decent paint job before too long.

"I'll be back for one o' clock," Grace said, as she rushed past Barb.

"Going home for a little one on one time," Barb said, with a knowing look and a mouthful of Italian sub. A tomato hung from one side of her mouth, bobbing as she spoke. She caught it with a pudgy finger moments before it was about to fall to the wax wrapping spread across her desk. An Italian sub every day for lunch was Barb's go-to meal, and that hadn't changed since Grace started at the station years ago.

Without saying a word Grace rolled her eyes, conveying everything she needed to. She pushed through the door and carved her way along the sidewalks and one-way streets that led her home. Seven minutes later she walked into their kitchen. Mark was pushing down on an onion chopper, adding to the columns of veggies already sliced and ready to mix into a colorful salad.

"You beat me home."

"Well, technically I ran." Mark used the inside of his forearm to swipe away the sweat accumulating on his brow. "Damn it!" He used his lower lip to blow air into his burning eyes as he looked up to the ceiling.

"I thought the whole point of the onion chopper was to prevent your eyes from burning." Grace mused with a raised brow, while biting into a crunchy carrot with a snap.

"It is, but my eyes are so darn sensitive it doesn't take much to get them tearing up." With an expert hand, he dragged a chef's knife across the cutting board toward him and, in one fluid motion, scooped the veggies into a mixing bowl. He put a lid on it before tossing the salad like a pair of maracas and then poured half the ingredients into another bowl, sliding it across the counter toward Grace. She looked down at the vegetables, some that were unrecognizable due to her life of choosing meat, cheese, and carbs over anything remotely healthy. She plopped down on a bar stool at the island and gave in, stabbing her fork into a medley of veggies.

"No meat?" Grace flicked through the ingredients with the tines of her fork, hoping to unearth something more substantial.

"There's some seasoned tofu in there . . . that should fill your protein needs," Mark said, matter-of-factly, as if he was educating one of his clients and not talking to his girlfriend over a lunch date.

Grace shot him an eye roll, similar to the one she had given Barb upon leaving the station.

"So, any progress on John Walsh?" Mark asked, between eager forkfuls of healthy goodness.

"As a matter of fact . . . yes." She gulped down some dry lettuce.

"I take it you didn't get much work done at the station this morning."

"Real work you mean? I accomplished what was necessary, made a few calls to the schools, but I may have put the focus on diving deeper into John Walsh's life for an hour or two."

"Bad Cop," Mark shook his head as he scowled in her direction, before he took a loud crunch of a baby carrot.

"Hey, I'm tracking down a murderer, aren't I? Isn't that my job?"

"So what did you find out?" Mark continued.

"John's younger brother Timmy, AKA the boy in my visions, died in 1955 when he was just five years old." Grace frowned at this unfair concept.

"Makes sense." Mark paused, stabbing at the last of his salad. "But what about the colorful glass you saw when you made eye contact with John during the mail delivery?"

Grace had filled Mark in on the eerie visit she had with John, including the vision of green glass shards and the flash of something round and red that shot through the air in front of Timmy. "That is something I need to investigate, but imagine how many things are made of green glass?"

"Just remember to keep in mind what era you're dealing with. What would be those colors in the fifties? Was stained glass a big deal back then? Maybe it was a busted window?"

"Genius idea." Grace pushed herself up from the bar stool, remembering something. "And one way I can do that is to go through those photos we found."

"Wait, you didn't take the photos back to John when you returned his mail?"

"I may have forgotten?" Grace said with a Cheshire cat grin, her questioning tone asking for forgiveness. "It's not like he really wants them anyway, he obviously left them behind for a reason."

"Perhaps that reason was he didn't actually forget them. My guess is he didn't even know they were stashed in that window seat. I mean, it was only by sheer luck we even discovered them after all this time." Mark mulled it over for a moment before a realization hit and his face contorted into an awestruck expression. "It's like we were meant to find them . . . maybe Timmy's ghost led us to them?" Mark mimed a spooky ghost impression, wiggling long fingers over her back and through her hair, blowing veggie breath at the back of her neck, causing her skin to crawl. She swatted him away with a giggle, followed by a scowl—remembering the death of a small child really isn't a joking matter.

"It really isn't funny, Mark. This is serious. Though you do raise a good point about the coincidence of the photos . . . almost finding us." Grace chewed on her cheek, pausing to consider this.

"You're not taking those to the station, are you?" He asked as she was gathering her belongings to head back to work, including the box of photos.

"No, but I'm going to leave them in the cruiser in the event I get a little downtime."

"So, I take it you'll be in your car for the rest of the afternoon," Mark teased knowingly.

"Are you questioning my work ethic, Mr. Connolly?" Grace picked up the box, holding it with both hands as if it was a breakable antique.

Mark held the door open for Grace and followed her outside. "Want a lift?"

"You're driving back to the gym?"

"Yeah, I'm bringing in some old equipment . . . trying to make use of it."

Grace looked at the back of the Jeep and saw it was filled to the brim with a piece of fitness machinery, several bright colored bands hanging off of it. "Shouldn't you be encouraging me to walk?"

"I should, but the more time I get to spend with you the better I feel."

"That may have been the sappiest thing you've ever said," Grace said, as she made her way toward the passenger side door.

"Looks like it's working though." Mark winked as he slid into the driver's seat.

Grace had to force herself not to open the box of photos, afraid she'd get immersed in them and forget about the things she had to do at the station. Mark turned onto Main Street and pulled into the small lot across from Imperial Fitness. "You're not gonna drop me off at the station?" Grace threw a pair of puppy dog eyes in Mark's direction.

"Nope. I think you can manage the five hundred feet." Mark nudged his head in the direction of the station.

"I already have six thousand steps today." Grace twisted her wrist toward Mark, showing him the face of her Apple watch he had given her as a gift.

"Well, walk to the station and you'll get that much closer to your daily 10K." He pulled her in for a quick kiss before opening the back of the Jeep to retrieve the equipment.

"Fine." Grace turned on a heel, still holding the cigar box of photos in her two hands like a tray of food.

CHAPTER SEVEN

Being May, the town of Bridgeton was starting to come to life. Seasonal stores were opening their doors and blinds for the summer, ready to cater to both the residents and many beachgoers who visited during the warmer months. The year-round stores seemed to take their marketing up a notch during this time of year, using bright colored signs and markers to jazz up their windows and walkways to attract a steady flow of customers. As Grace turned the corner onto the street of the station, someone walking backward stumbled into her. Just as she was about to offer a snide remark about walking backward on a busy sidewalk, she was stopped in her tracks with recognition registering on her face. She noticed the camera before she saw anything else; a colossal gadget held in both hands with one wrapped firmly around a wide lens.

"Betts!" Grace's excitement more enthusiastic than she expected.

"Grace!" Betts reciprocated the same inflection, a mutual synergy passing between one another. "I'm so sorry . . . I got a little caught up capturing the church. I wanted to get it from all angles before they tear it down." Sadness revealed itself in the lines on Betts's forehead and between her eyes as she lowered the camera from her face.

"I didn't know they were tearing St. John's down." Grace used a hand to shield her eyes from the sun, following Betts's gaze. Even though Grace wasn't really in-the-know about church happenings in town, she was certain she would've heard news about this.

"Yep, more condos. They literally just made the decision. I kind of have the inside scoop on it because my cousin is on the board." Betts adjusted her stance, letting the camera dangle freely at her chest. "The good news is that they are only tearing down part of the building . . . they want to keep the *church* vibe for the condos . . . I think it's a hipster thing." She waved her two hands, denoting uncertainty.

Grace thought about how many events she had been to at the church. It seemed to be the mecca for town happenings and she couldn't imagine it being anything other than a church. "That's news to me." She dropped her hand down and focused her attention back on Betts.

"It's about to be news to everybody." Betts winked. Changing the subject, she eyed the box Grace was holding. "Is that one of those old cigar boxes? Gosh, I haven't seen those in years."

"To tell you the truth, I had never seen one of these cigar boxes before now."

"Well, they are well before your time, and if your daddy didn't smoke cigars . . . well, you'd likely never stumble across them. I remember my dad smoked a cigar every night after dinner, sitting on the front porch. By the time he retired from the police department we had stacks of those boxes. I used to use them to store my film rolls. I'll never forget the aroma when I opened the box . . . I can still smell it today."

Grace lifted the open box and angled it in front of Betts's face, wafting a dose of nostalgia in her direction. Betts closed her eyes and inhaled deeply, as if drifting off into her childhood for a brief moment in time. Just as Grace was about to snap the lid closed, Betts's eyes popped open and took in the contents, her eyes widening in amusement.

"Ooo, another one of my favorite things . . . old pictures." Betts rubbed her palms together gleefully. "You're just gifting me with all kinds of goodies today," she said, bringing her fingertips to its rim, tipping the box toward her to examine the topmost photos.

"Oh, these are just some old photos I found in our new house."

"Intriguing. Where did you buy?" Betts's question came out in the form of small talk.

"Up in the highlands, on Court Street."

"Ahhh, one of the steepest streets in town," Betts said, bobbing her head in recognition.

"That's what they say." Grace nodded in confirmation.

"I used to take all my equipment to the top of that street and set up shop in the front yards. I'd get the best photos of the Boston skyline all lit up at night, the crashing waves in the most treacherous of storms, and on the Fourth of July I'd capture so many breathtaking photos of the fireworks."

"And what made you stop?"

"To tell you the truth, all of my friends who lived up there moved away . . . the town is starting to fill up with young professional Boston transplants and I'm not sure they would feel the same way about someone tenting out in their front yard for the night." Betts winked, revealing deep teal eye shadow that accented her chocolate brown eyes.

"I tell ya what . . . I'll let you set up shop in my front yard on one condition . . ."

Betts's eyes lit up. "I knew I liked you, Grace. What's your condition?"

"You give me a copy of one of your amazing photos so I can frame it and put it up in my new house."

"Easy . . . deal." Betts reached a hand out. As Grace extended hers to accept the shake, Betts's hand hit the box, causing it to plummet to the ground, scattering several of the photos along the sidewalk. Grace crouched down to pick them up and Betts followed to help, their two heads just inches apart.

"It's okay, I got it," Grace said, but it was too late. She watched Betts's facial expression transform from calm to disturbed, her natural smile peeled down into a frown accompanied by a furrowed brow.

Betts picked up one of the photos, holding it by the edges and smoothing the image with both thumbs. "Where did you say you live, Grace?"

Bracing herself for Betts's response to her answer, Grace paused before she said, "Thirteen Court Street."

Without lifting her eyes off the photo, Betts brought it closer to her face.

"I found these beneath a window seat in the house . . . I figured I'd bring them back to the previous owner." Grace lied.

"John Walsh." Matter-of-factly, the words spouted from Betts's lips. "I'm not quite sure he would want these photos back." She turned her head back, as if assessing who was around them, then rose up from her crouched position. "Unfortunately, I don't think these are days that John wants to remember."

"Were you a friend of his?"

"I was . . . yes. I was very close with John and his sister."

"Sister?"

"Yes, Susan . . . my brother's new lady friend. I'm sure you met her at the party the other night. They've officially *come out* as an item." Betts threw up a pair of air quotes highlighting the term *come out*. She passed the photo back to Grace face down. "That wasn't my best work. But given the circumstances . . ."

Grace turned the photo over in her hand. Standing in front of hedges—that were no longer there—was John, Susan, and Timmy Walsh side by side next to a woman, who Grace could only imagine was their mother, wearing a polka-dot dress that fell just below the knees. It was cinched securely at the waist with a belt, revealing a slender silhouette. White heels made her tower over the children and coordinated well with the white gloves and polka-dots. One gloved hand held a black sunhat and the other rested on Timmy's shoulder. The mother's face was glowing, a real Mary Tyler Moore moment, and her smile lit up with happiness for the camera. But her eyes were shifted slightly to the left, as if she was distracted by something off camera. Perfectly coiffed brown hair was coiled around her head, barely meeting her shoulders, in one side-parted swoop. All three children had half smiles like most young children do in forced family photos. Peeking out from behind the hedges was a hand painted sign that showcased the address. *13 Court Street*. Contrary to today's pale shade of grey, the house appeared to be a dark brown in the old photo.

"Not your best work . . . what do you mean?"

"I took that photo." Betts stood closer to Grace's side, looking over her shoulder.

"Let's see . . . Susie and John were about eight in this photo, so I was about ten. By then I had already been shooting for several years. I wasn't lying when I said I was born with a camera in my hand."

"Who is the other boy?" Grace asked the question tumbling through her mind in a series of back flips.

Betts paused, sealed her lips into a straight line before she said, "That's Timmy."

"I'm assuming he's their little brother?"

"Was." Betts corrected Grace, the one word conveying so much understanding between the two of them. "Let's see, this was taken not long before—"

"Before what?"

"Before Timmy died." Betts looked down at her watch, an opportunity to escape. "I gotta run Grace . . . got a shoot over by the airport. I'll track you down when I want to set up shop in your yard." Betts turned away fast, nearly bumping into a cluster of teen girls who were all looking down at their phones. Grace could hear her scolding them about watching where they were going. She took one last long look at the photo before lifting the lid and replacing it back in the box, where there was a whole world of mystery she had to unravel.

Grace held the box of photos pinned to her side as she walked up the station steps. Hoping to make a beeline for her office, so Barb wouldn't ask any questions about the box, she kept her eyes focused in front of her but was quickly stopped in her tracks. "Hey, Princess, I've got a surprise for you." Barb stood by the control station with one beefy forearm resting on the counter.

As if she needed any more surprises. In a monotone voice, she asked, "A homicide?"

"Tsss . . . you wish. No. Look who is here." Barb nudged her head in the direction of the control booth. Grace turned the corner cautiously, not super eager to see what Barb was up to. And then, just like that, Grace's outlook had taken an about-face. In front of her, lounging in a control booth chair in civilian clothes, was Sully, the man who could always make her smile.

"Sully!" She nearly climbed over the low door that led into the booth. "What are you doing here?"

Sully stood reaching across the door for a solid bear hug; his arms already tan from spending days outside, instead of being cooped up inside the station. "I thought I'd come by for a visit . . . and I forgot something from the other night. Matty here brought it home for me after I had one too many whiskeys." Sully held up the plaque he had been presented at his retirement party; clear glass engraved with his name and years of service on a backdrop of polished cherry wood.

Remembering the box at her side Grace excused herself briefly. "I'll be right back." She sidestepped to her office, pushed the door open, and dropped the box into the deepest desk drawer. "Sorry, I needed my coffee." She came back with a cup of cold coffee she hadn't sipped in three hours.

Barb scanned her from head to toe in one of her all-knowing manners. "So, how is retired life treating you so far?"

"Well, I feel like I've been busier than ever." Sully leaned back in his chair, as one loud creak erupted from the old furniture.

"Everyone says that when they retire," Grace said, as she forced herself to take a sip of the cold coffee, trying to hide her disgust.

"Well it also helps that he has a new girlfriend booking up his calendar," Barb interjected, tossing a wink in Sully's direction. A sheepish grin formed across his face as he looked down at the ground.

"How is Susan anyway?"

"Sully and Susan sittin' in a tree—" Barb broke out in the childish rhyme.

"Barb, seriously ... I think your phone is ringing," Grace said. In a saved by the bell moment Barb's phone had rung, cutting her embarrassment-inducing chant short. Matty had sunk into the background tending to the console duties of checklists and radio monitoring, like a good newbie, and Grace was grateful for that. She wanted a chance to talk to Sully alone, to perhaps obtain more information from him about Susan.

"So ... Susan ... she seems nice." She drove them into the conversation, like a car speeding through a green light at an intersection. The opportunity was there, the light was green and ready for movement.

"She's a doll, Gracie."

"I'm glad you're happy, Sully."

As if he was reminded of something, Sully continued. "Still though ... not a day goes by that I don't think about—"

"You don't have to feel guilty for trying to find happiness, Sully ... that's what she would've wanted for you." Grace picked up on Sully's tone, she could tell he was emitting guilt for seeing someone else besides his beloved late wife.

"I know, I know ... it's just that I have this big knot inside ... like I feel like she is watching and it makes me feel so guilty, ya know."

"I can imagine how that feels." Grace consoled him, thinking about how it would be after Ellen. If her father met a woman, would it be like someone was replacing Ellen? No one could replace her mother, she knew that, but she imagined how laced with guilt she'd feel just spending time with another mother figure.

Guiding Sully off of the guilt trip, she pressed forward for the benefit of both of them. "So, how did you meet Susan anyway?"

"Oh gosh, I've known her for years. Since I was a kid actually." Sully's face flushed a pale pink. "She was my first crush."

"Really?" Grace gave him a jovial smile. "Sounds like you've come full circle then. Did you two date in high school?"

"Oh gosh no . . . she wouldn't have been caught dead dating me then."

Grace pictured Susan and she saw her ordinary face, absent of any stand-out features. In fact, she was a spitting image of John Walsh with mousy characteristics and an overall bland appearance. Grace remembered how handsome Sully was in the photos that were on display at his retirement. While they showed him aging over the years, he did so gracefully, with a strong jawline that was still evident and eyes that could hold a steady stare and a tender gaze. He had a noteworthy stature that even on his last shift, filled out his police uniform handsomely. "Why on earth wouldn't she want to be seen with you?"

"Well, you see, the Walsh family comes from big money . . . high society. The grandfather was a successful inventor of some big airplane part, and he passed the wealth and business down to his son, who was Susan's father." Sully glided his hands along the arms of the chair. "The Sullivans were on the opposite side of the tracks, so to speak. We were all cops, and while you and I think that this is a good career to be in . . . high society folks scoffed at us. And back then they viewed us as servants, in a way, I suppose. Let's put it this way . . . Mr. Walsh made more money in a day than my dad made in a year, back in the day."

Grace had trouble seeing Sully as viewed as anything but a hero. At the same time she was intrigued by how the Walsh children grew up. If John, Susan, and Timmy were all siblings and lived a prominent lifestyle, then how would Timmy wind up murdered?

"So, is John Walsh Susan's brother?"

"Yeah, why do you ask?"

"Well, because John Walsh was the previous owner of the house we just purchased and they look alike, so . . ."

"Twins. They are twins." Suddenly Sully catapulted from the chair. "Wait a minute . . . what house did you say you bought?"

Grace knew she had told both Sully and Susan the night of the retirement party, but maybe the multiple whiskeys diminished some of his memory from that night. "Thirteen Court Street."

Sully put a hand over his eyes, shaking his head. "That's why!"

"That's why, what?"

"Well, I'll be honest . . . I don't remember a ton from the end of my retirement party but I do remember Susan acting very strange. Kind of reserved." Sully leaned on the counter joining the rest of the station with the console. "She was so high energy and excited at the beginning of the night and then . . . she kind of just fizzled out and withdrew. Just bits and pieces of it are all I can remember, but the next day she mentioned something that struck me as odd."

"What?"

"Well, we were in the middle of eating breakfast at the Center Café and she all of a sudden had to leave. She got a text or maybe she saw someone walk by the café . . . but she just jumped up and said she'd call me later."

"What happened when you saw her again?"

"Well, I actually haven't seen her again. I . . . she said that she was going to visit her son in Rhode Island for a few days."

"Have you talked to her?"

"Just a text here and there. I don't like to bother her when she's with her kids and she gives me the same respect. Kind of a past life privacy thing." Sully paused, as his eyes darted left to right, searching for his initial point in the conversation. "Thirteen Court Street. You live on thirteen Court Street. That is why, Grace. That's the house that Susan grew up in. That's the house where her little brother died. Gosh, I should've known." Sully wiped a hand down his face. "I should've put two and two together."

"What happened to her brother?" Grace asked the question knowing and not knowing the answer at the same time, like a soldier walking through a field of land mines. Something was there, but there was no telling the extent of the aftermath.

Sully leaned on the doorframe. "It was so long ago . . . but I'll never forget the look on my father's face."

"Your father?"

"When Timmy had his accident, my dad was the first responding cop. Having several sons of his own, well . . . I think the tragedy was that much more difficult for him to see. And in some sense, it was my dad's biggest fear."

"What happened?

"Timmy was only five when it happened, but his dad should've known . . . he should've taken precaution and locked up his gun. Like all little boys back then, Timmy was curious about guns. It could've been any boy his age really . . . he somehow got a hold of his father's gun and . . ." Sully paused again, the words struggling to come out. "He accidentally pulled the trigger. Someone figured out how to unlock it, or maybe it was never actually locked. Back then we didn't have afterschool specials about guns and suicide and bullying. Maybe Timmy's tragic accident is why those PSAs exist today. Who knows."

"He shot himself?" Grace faked the question mark at the end of her sentence.

"Not intentionally. But geez, what a tragedy that was for his family. For Susan. I never even stopped to think about how that must've impacted her own life. And to think . . . she has two kids of her own, both boys. One she named Timmy after her little brother."

"Wait, but why did her father have a gun?"

"That would've never been a question back in the fifties . . . it wasn't rare for high society men to have guns. Mostly they used them as toys or something to stroke their ego. But her father's negligence caused Timmy's death. I imagine the mother never did forgive him. The kids too, I'm sure John and Susan weren't too keen on forgiving their father after his stupidity caused their little brother's death."

"What about your sister Betts?"

"What about her?"

"Well, she said she photographed the family and was friends with the kids. If they were high society and didn't associate with blue collar families like yours then how did Betts get in with them?"

"Oh, that's because Betts had a natural talent to capture people on film . . . still does today. She's been a photography genius since she was a young kid. Some say she's a savant. You know she has photos in National Geographic?"

While Grace was impressed with Betts's resume, she wanted to keep Sully on track and find out more about the Walsh family. It was well known to Grace that Timmy's death was not an accident and John was the one responsible for killing him. But why?

"Wow . . . that's impressive. Betts must've been close to the family then, right?"

"As close as she could get, I suppose. She saw them from the outside, capturing them in posed family photos, but Betts is . . . well she's an artist so she thinks differently than you and I. It's all about capturing the photo from the right angle and in the right lighting, and less about getting to know the subject. If that makes any sense."

To Grace it made complete sense, but she still questioned whether or not Betts had the inside scoop on the family. Grace was the first to admit she was not an artist and her mind worked differently, but she didn't want to discount what else Betts knew.

"Makes total sense." Grace lied. She had no idea what it took to be a photographer. The only thing she knew right now was that she had to slice through the Walsh family tree, until it was in a million little pieces, so it could be broken down easier.

"Well, I better head out. Guess I should try to get a hold of Susan by phone now since she hasn't answered my texts."

"Good luck. I hope you track her down. I'm sure she's just caught up in spending some quality time with her kids. Speaking of . . . how old are her boys?"

"Right around the same age as my kids."

"Have you met them yet?"

"Not yet. We're taking it slow." Sully passed a wink in her direction. He pushed through the door and wrapped Grace in one of his famous bear hugs.

"We miss you around here already, Sully." Grace said, as she squeezed him back. "Behave yourself and keep in touch."

"You couldn't get rid of me if you tried, Gracie." He turned on a heel and stopped at Barb's desk as Grace made her way into her office.

She sat down and immediately pulled the deep bottom drawer open. Her excitement built as she lifted the lid, as if opening a treasure chest. Now was the time to look at each photo with care, and really dissect them, assessing each and every subject from facial expression to body awareness. Maybe there was a scene in the photos that would give her clues. This time, instead of just looking at the top photo and closing the box, she pulled the pile out and spread them out on her desk face up.

Moments captured in the Walsh family life stared back at her, some candid shots and others posed and planned. The one common theme in all the photos was the mother's smile and the crooked grins of the three children, tugging upwards like they were puppets performing with the help of strings. Grace's eyes scanned the collage before her as her mind memorized the faces and scenes of the images.

One, in the far corner of her desk, stood out from the rest. An added character was on the stage of the Walsh's lives. And while there were a few other photos showcasing additional players, this one was different. It was a woman who was poised and presented properly beside the family in a posed picture. Unlike the others containing celebratory grins and cocktail-filled hands, this one was intentional and less candid. The woman in the photo stood behind Timmy, her hand rested gently on his shoulders as if claiming him as her own. Beside her was Mr. and Mrs. Walsh, who sandwiched Susan and John in a loving huddle. Unlike Mrs. Walsh's perfectly posh dress and coiffed hair, the woman wore an apron layered over a long-sleeved dress with a frilly collar protruding at the neckline.

Grace's jaw dropped as she recognized the tiny red flower pattern on the blue and white gingham of the woman's apron. *The apron from the cigar box.* Grace had stored the apron safely in a kitchen drawer for the time being. Trained in detecting a fraud, she also picked up on the uneasy smile plastered on the woman's face. It looked unnatural and forced. Her stance over Timmy was one that was protective in nature rather than cozy and organic. *Who are you? And why do you have such a strong hold over the little boy who died?*

Grace's immediate gut reaction was to believe that the woman played a role in Timmy's death. Possibly an ally to John's perfect aim in the boy's chest, in what could've been an act of jealousy or maybe a psychotic break. It may have been cheap makeup, but the woman looked older than Mrs. Walsh. Her face, free of the well-blended colorful tones costly cosmetics achieved, looked far less flashy than Mrs. Walsh's. A few flyaways escaped her loosely pinned hair, and her ample waist was accented by the flowery apron hugging her body.

Comparing her to Mrs. Walsh, Grace came to the conclusion she wasn't in the same social status. In the other photos, the woman who appeared to be Mrs. Walsh's friends were all wearing heavy lipstick, carving out their smiles like Cheshire cats and donning evil, mocking grins. *We are elite, no one can touch us.* As if they were all in on the same secret, the women in the other photos were all huddled together, martini glasses clinking, with heads thrown back mid-laugh. The men in the photos were always standing proudly in crisp shirts and slacks, leaning into one another as if they were sealing sleazy deals.

Shifting her eyes side to side, Grace searched for the outcast woman in the other photos, until she locked eyes with the mystery subject. In the photo she was once again beside Timmy, except this time she was wearing a hat and not restricted with the flowery apron. A flowy dress cascaded around her on the grass, as she crouched beside Timmy holding an Easter egg. Eye to eye with her, Timmy reached for the egg, his smile tipped up to the side in a sloppy, tempted grin. Far in the background, Grace could see distant silhouettes of Mrs. Walsh and the other two children, as if they were backup singers to the two on the main stage.

Grace pulled the photo closer to her face, feeling her eyes cross. While she couldn't quite make out the facial expressions on the other three in the background, she could tell they were wearing dressy clothing like people often did for the holidays back then. The mystery still swirled in her head and she was left with only one option. She picked up the landline on her desk and dialed Barb's extension.

"What's up, Princess?"

"Hey, Barb, can you come here for a minute? I have a question for you." Without completely knowing, Barb had assisted Grace in cracking clues in her mystery cases in the past and she knew she could trust her. While Barb knew that something odd was going on with Grace during those moments, she never questioned it and was simply happy to go along for the ride. The woman was drenched in sarcasm but she was a hard worker and had no qualms about helping Grace with just about anything. Part of it was because she had no immediate family of her own, so she had the time to commit, and the other part was that she simply wanted to feel included.

"Uh oh, I know how these conversation starters usually go," Barb joked, before hanging up the phone. Within seconds Barb was barging through Grace's door. "What you got, Princess? Another AWOL student you need me to track down?"

"I wish." As Grace said the words Barb's eyes discovered the photomontage displayed on the desk in front of her.

"What have we got here?" Barb beelined for the folding chair propped against the wall opposite Grace's desk. Opening it up, she straddled it as she picked up a photo. "These are oldies."

"So, I found these in the new house."

"Creepy. So, who are they?"

"Well, evidently it's the family that lived there before we did. The son sold it to us. Most of these photos are from when he was a kid, when the parents were in their prime."

"Looks like they were a fun time." Barb turned a photo toward Grace. Several women were seated on, what looked like, a velvet couch. All had martini glasses, on the verge of spilling, in their hands. One woman lay sprawled out across their laps, her head rested on an elbow with a confident grin on her face.

"Yeah, they knew how to party back then."

"So, besides learning about the ghosts that are likely walking the hallways of your house, what exactly are you looking for?"

"Well, see these two photos." Grace held up both photos that had the mystery woman in them. "I'm trying to figure out where this woman fits in with the family."

Barb looked at the photo for less than three seconds and responded. "She's a maid . . . or, I guess, nowadays it would be politically correct to call her a housekeeper. Or a *domestic employee*." She spit the words out with sarcasm. "That was a big deal back then for people like this. High society."

"Damn it! Why didn't I think of that?" Grace hit herself on the head with the heel of her hand.

"That's what I'm here for, Princess." Barb picked up another photo and let out a long whistle. "Dang, the men were good lookin' back then. Makes them look like slobs today . . . but in all seriousness, Princess, maids were common back in the day and I only know this because my family had one."

Grace nearly dropped the photos she was holding and locked her wide-eyed stare on Barb.

"What? Don't look at me like I'm not worthy of having a maid." She paused and glanced around the room like she was about to release a major secret. "Okay, so it may not have been my immediate family who had a maid, but my second cousin's family in Boston had one. We used to go there for an annual New Year's party when I was a kid. And let me tell you these photos could've been taken from those parties. They were all the same. All the high society women sipping their cocktails and exchanging recipes to meals that they didn't even make themselves. To be honest, I always felt more comfortable hanging out with the maid at those parties. In fact, I befriended this one named Lena. She was a sweetheart . . . used to sneak me those strawberry candies with the delicious gel inside. She had a heavy Polish accent . . . straight off the boat—"

"Do you remember if Lena participated in family activities like this maid did?" Grace cut her off and showed her the photo taken on Easter, with the woman and Timmy dressed in their Sunday best.

"Sure. If the family liked her." Barb leaned farther forward and picked up another photo. "I remember one New Year's Eve when Lena got drunk. The women at the party were coaxing her to drink with them, and then they kind of just made fun of her. I felt so bad for her. Those women were so ignorant and I remember thinking that even at such a young age. When Lena got drunk, her accent thickened and the women all started mocking her. To them, I'm sure they claimed it as innocent fun but . . . what wenches, right? Poor Lena. She was a plain Jane compared to those women, with their fancy dresses and painted on faces. Sweet Lena was hefty and not so easy on the eyes."

"See this little boy? . . ." Grace felt safe enough to take Barb a step further in the story. She held up a photo of Timmy by himself, holding a massive frog, while standing in front of a lake where water stretched behind him for miles.

"They were so cute and proper looking back then . . . not like today's kids . . . all bratty and wearing those baggy pants."

"Those are teenagers, Barb," Grace said, slumping with a tilted head and blinking slowly, revealing her annoyance at wanting to stay on topic, "anyway, his name is Timmy and he died not too long after this photo was taken." Grace angled her head, assessing his age in the photo. She turned it over in her hand. On the back the date read *July 1955*, beside it was a logo for *Mahoney's Photo Lab* stamped in red. A store no longer on the list of local businesses. He didn't look much younger than he was in her visions of him on the swing—with a bullet in his chest.

"What? How? I know measles were big back then and it wasn't rare for kids to die from it, but usually high society families had access to better healthcare, so I can't imagine—"

"No. He was shot."

"As in murdered?" Barbs head dropped and she kept her stare on Grace, looking at her through bushy brows.

"That, I don't know. According to Sully, the boy somehow got his hands on his father's unlocked gun and it accidentally went off."

"Jesus." Barb dropped the photo she was holding and placed her hands on the chair back. "That's terrible . . . but wait . . . are you doubting Sully's statement?"

"Not doubting Sully, but I just have a feeling that there is more to the story."

"Ahhh . . . Grace and her feelings," Barb said, as she inhaled a deep breath. "Come to think of it, though, your feelings are usually right. I have no idea how you do that but . . . you got a natural hunch for things. How do you do that, Grace?"

"I guess it's just part of being a detective." Grace wished she could tell Barb about her gift. She so badly wanted to share her secret with someone other than Mark and her mother, but she couldn't take the risk. She couldn't chance Barb having a bad reaction and telling the whole station she was crazy. It would be a career killer.

"Did you do any research on the family?"

"That's the problem, there is such limited stuff online from that time period."

"What's the last name?"

"Walsh."

"Like, as in, Susan Walsh, Sully's new *friend*?" Barb held up four meaty fingers displaying quotation marks around the word friend.

"Exactly."

"So, you moved into Sully's girlfriend's old house?"

"Well, her brother John was the only one still living there when we bought it."

"She has another non-dead brother?"

"Yeah, she and John are twins and the brother Timmy, who died, was a few years younger than them."

"I'll bet that was scarring." She leaned back as a wave of empathy passed across her face.

"So, why not ask the brother John about it?" Barb asked matter-of-factly.

"First of all, I can't just approach the guy sixty-five years later and question how his little brother died." Grace paused, trying to think of the words to ease into the next part of the puzzle she wanted to convey. "And there is something creepy about him . . . I can't quite figure it out."

"Is this guy about the same age as Sully?"

"Yeah, from what it sounds like."

"That would make sense since he's dating the twin sister . . . I don't peg Sully for someone who would aim too much younger."

"Yeah, he doesn't have many *womanizer* qualities," Grace joked as Barb rolled her eyes.

"So, let me get this straight . . . you got a hunch that something else happened the day this boy died and he didn't accidentally pull the trigger?"

"Pretty much."

Barb rocked front to back on the chair. "So what can I do to help?"

"That's a good question." Grace looked at the ceiling, searching the yellowing water spot for an answer. "Well, maybe we should start by searching for old news articles. I can't seem to find anything online, so maybe you can help me out at the library . . . I have no idea how to pull up articles on those old machines."

"They're called microfiche readers." Barb got up from the chair and headed toward the door. "You may not know this about me but I did a stint at the library before I scored this gig. I had dreams of becoming a librarian . . . then I realized how much schooling it actually took."

"I learn something knew about you every day, Barb."

"Well, let's be honest . . . this station would never be able to run without me, so y'all should be thankful my librarian dreams were crushed."

"Touché."

"Meet me in the research section of the library tomorrow at nine."

Surprised by Barb's demand to start the process so quickly, Grace moved the photos aside and checked tomorrow's date to see what she had going on. "Tomorrow is Saturday."

"Exactly. Bring me coffee from The Depot."

"I thought we aren't allowed to bring beverages in there."

Barb placed a steady gaze on Grace. "What are you gonna do? Call the cops on me?"

"Touché."

"Besides, I know all the staff there . . . they let me do what I want." With that Barb turned and pulled the door open and exited, letting it slam behind her.

CHAPTER EIGHT

Grace was still getting used to the fact she now lived walking distance to anywhere she needed to go. She had wasted a good ten minutes searching for her keys before she left for the library to meet Barb. Thankfully Mark had been home for a morning break between clients, so he reminded her that they could actually see the top of the library building from their house. Standing behind Grace, in front of their bedroom window, Mark pointed to the peak of the old building where a statue of a man sat atop the angled roof. "See . . . you just walk down our street and take a left on Center Street," he said, as he pulled her backward into him and rested a chin on her shoulder.

She should've known. According to Betts, her house was the prime spot to view town landscapes and the Boston skyline. As she thought about Betts on her walk down the steep hill, an idea sprung to mind. By Googling the savvy photographer she learned her business was called Lighthouse Photography. She pulled her phone out of the front pocket of her bag and selected the number she saved. After three rings, Grace was greeted by Betts's voice. "This is Betts."

As soon as she heard the friendly tone of the woman's voice, Grace felt better about what she was doing. "Betts! This is Grace. Grace McKenna, the cop that—"

"Grace, yes, good to hear from you. Is my brother okay? Did he beg for you to take him back as an officer at the station? That guy can't stay away from—"

"No, actually, this isn't about Sully. It's personal."

"Oh?" Betts's voice suddenly descended, a concerned tone shadowing her words.

"Yeah, well . . . my boyfriend and I don't have any good photos of us and since we just moved into our new house . . . we thought now was the time to get some professional photos together. And we would love if our dog could be in them too . . . he's—"

"I would be honored, Grace."

Grace couldn't believe how easy it was. She was certain the woman would catch on to her fake photo shoot. "Thank you so much, I really appreciate it. It was perfect timing when I met you because we had been looking for a photographer." Grace already felt guilty for the lie erupting from her with ease.

"No worries. How's tomorrow?"

"Tomorrow?" Grace swallowed, as a pit formed in her gut.

"Yeah, I typically keep Sundays open for portrait stuff, and the family appointment I had just called to inform me one of their kids split his chin wide open and needed twelve stitches. So, needless to say, they're gonna postpone their shoot. So, the spot is yours if you want it? They had scheduled it for three thirty, after the baby's nap, but to be honest I'm wide open tomorrow so I can do any time that works for you."

"Oh, um . . . okay . . ." Grace tried to come up with a reason why they couldn't do tomorrow, but her mind was like a blank chalkboard—free of any answers. "How is two o'clock?"

"Perfect. Where do you live again? Oh, wait . . . yeah, I know where you live. Talk about walking into the past. I'll see you a little before two. Dress in solid colors, wear heavy makeup—but don't look like a hooker—and have enough treats to keep your dog content for poses."

By the time Grace reached the front steps of the library her mind was bombarded with the photo shoot she had inadvertently set up for tomorrow. "That's what I deserve I suppose," she said under her breath as she pulled the door open with more force, creating a sucking whoosh, thanks to the adrenaline surging through her. With the rapid motion, a taped-on flyer fell from the glass door and floated to the ground, face up, at Grace's feet. She picked it up to replace it, when the photo and name caught her attention. *Susan Jacobi, LMFT, Marriage and Family Psychologist.* Like blocks clicking into place, Grace's question was answered. Jacobi was apparently Susan's married name and she must've kept it after the divorce. While it wasn't surprising that she was divorced, considering she was dating Sully, Grace found it somewhat shocking that the woman was a marriage and family psychologist. *Although, losing a brother at such a young age may drive someone into a field that would help sort out some personal issues.* Grace read the rest of the flyer, smoothing her hands over it as she reattached it to the door.

Join Susan Jacobi, LMFT on June 1ˢᵗ for a discussion on
excelling in family relationships
and sorting through difficult conversations

Seating is limited
Please RSVP to Gretchen Calthrope, Library Assistant, by May 23ʳᵈ
Refreshments will be provided

Someone must be a big deal. Grace thought to herself as she looked at her Apple watch and saw it was May twentieth. Opening the door, for the second time, she marched straight to the front desk. As she was about to ring the silver bell on the counter, alongside a stack of books, a head popped up from the other side.

"Well, hello!" A woman with frizzy hair dispensed a friendly greeting more boisterous than Grace expected for a library setting. "What can I help you with?" Her eyes, massive behind a pair of glasses, bugged out as if high on caffeine. A blend of brown and grey coils sprung from her head and bounced as she spoke, like her voice was so overpowering it took over her entire body. This was not the disposition Grace imagined for a librarian. She read the nametag crookedly affixed to the woman's flowy navy blue shirt. Just the person she was looking for. Gretchen Calthrope.

"Hi, I'd like to sign up for the Susan Jacobi talk if there is still availability." Mirroring the woman's enthusiasm, Grace's words came out louder than she had intended.

"Let me seeeee . . ." Gretchen pulled a clipboard from a metal file holder affixed to the wall at her right. As she walked back she continued projecting her voice loudly. "Dr. Jacobi is one of our most popular speakers. She did wonders for my son that's for sure." She used an index finger like a typewriter, guiding it left to right making her way down the paper on the clipboard "You lucked out . . . there was a cancellation and no one has claimed the spot yet . . . looks like it's all yours . . . shall I put you down?"

"Yes. Wonderful! Thank you." Grace scanned the area behind the desk with towering stacks of books and DVDs covering all surfaces.

"Have you had the pleasure of hearing Dr. Jacobi before?" Gretchen searched high and low for a pen and burst out laughing when she realized one was behind her ear.

"No, I haven't, but I've heard wonderful things. If you don't mind my asking, what types of things does she specialize in?" Grace wanted to kick herself for not being able to find the right word. *Things* most certainly was not a scientific or professional term.

"Well, I only know from what she's helped me with in my own personal experience. But, from what I gather, it's anything from counseling kids while their parents go through a divorce to marriage issues. She handles clients that are simply having troubles in the home . . . which let's be honest . . . aren't we all? Susan is a pro at dealing with both kids and adults. She's so calm and patient and she makes it really easy to feel comfortable around her." Gretchen winked. "Can I get your name and contact info?" She readied herself with the pen on the clipboard.

"Of course. It's Grace McKenna."

"Ahhh, I thought you looked familiar. The female cop." Grace was used to the comment, but everyone followed it up differently and she was prepared for anything by this point in her career. "Thank you for your work in town. Not everyone might agree with me, when I say this, but I think it's crucial to have a female presence in law enforcement . . . women are much more likely to talk to and trust other women than they are men, especially in uniform."

"Thank you for acknowledging that, I appreciate it." Grace paused upon noticing a historical DVD on the top of a stack. "Now that I think of it . . . where can I find info on the town history, like the houses, noteworthy families, and such? I just moved here from Cabotville and, now that I'm both working and living here, I'd like to brush up on my town history."

"Well, you certainly came to the right place." Gretchen struck both hands onto the counter before turning and exiting her booth. "Follow me," she said, leading Grace into the main portion of the library.

"I have to admit I've never actually been here for pleasure. A few police calls, but that's about it."

"It's never too late to start." Gretchen led Grace through aisles of books with her long skirt swaying side to side, revealing a pair of worn Birkenstocks.

Just as Grace was inhaling the scent of books she felt her phone vibrate. Gretchen continued to feed her tidbits of the library's history as Grace read a text from Barb: *Did you stand me up?* It was only 9:04, Barb could wait a minute or two. The woman was a stickler for being on time and didn't hold back from calling out anyone who wasn't.

Grace nearly plowed into Gretchen's back when she came to a sudden stop rounding a corner. She was hit with the scent of patchouli and she couldn't tell if it was from Gretchen's shampoo or a perfume.

"Ahhh . . . here we go." Gretchen planted herself before a DVD display. "This is our town history collection. Now, you must be warned that the cinematography is shaky at best. Town collections are typically filmed by the town television station and, as I'm sure you know, we don't have a whole lot of money in this town to upgrade things. What timeframe are you looking for?" She leaned into Grace, stepping further into her personal space than she preferred.

"Do you have the 1950s?"

"I certainly do." Gretchen stood on her tiptoes as she flipped through several DVDs on the top row. "Ahhh, here we go; one of my favorite decades." She selected one with a picture of Bridgeton's Town Hall in black-and-white on the cover. From what Grace could tell it didn't look much different than today, with its manicured lawn and rusty black railings flanking the steps of the entryway. In the photo the flag was at half-staff, making Grace naturally question what day it was taken on. "I'll check it out for you at the front desk." Grace followed Gretchen back to the desk, where Grace opened a library card before the DVD was scanned and passed to her. "Don't forget, it was filmed a long time ago. In fact, if you go to the local TV station you'll see the actual video camera used to film this. We've, of course, transferred it to DVD since then. They have it on display in the main lobby. We may be behind, but we've certainly come a long way since the fifties."

"Thank you so much." Grace tucked the DVD into her bag. "One more question, where can I find the microfiche readers?"

"Wow, you really are digging deep into the history of the town . . . a gal after my own heart." Gretchen winked. "That would be in our reading room in the basement. Follow this aisle all the way down, take a right, and you'll see a staircase that leads to the basement. Go past the discounted books section and you'll bump right into the microfiche readers. I gotta say we don't have a lot of people coming into use those anymore. Have fun."

"Thanks," Grace said, making her way down the aisle.

"Oh and, Grace?"

"Yeah?"

"Don't hesitate to reach out to me if you have any other historical questions. I'm kind of a town history buff and this place is my home away from home, so I'm not hard to find."

"Thanks, Gretchen, I really appreciate that." Grace made a mental note to add Gretchen to her list of sources while trying to decipher the Timmy Walsh case.

Just as Grace made her way into the research section of the library, Barb's voice perked up from behind a massive machine. "I don't see a coffee in your hand, Princess."

"Darn!" Grace scolded herself. She had gotten so caught up talking to Betts on the way over that she forgot to stop by The Depot to pick up Barb's requested coffee.

"It's okay, I've got backup." Barb held up a small white cup before throwing her head back and taking, what was evidently, the last remaining sip. "Did you have trouble finding me in the dungeon?"

"Yeah, I had to ask the woman at the front desk."

"Ahhh, Gretchen . . . she's a treat, right? A bit of a close talker but she means well. The chick lives and breathes this library. Always been single but miraculously has a son. She doesn't seem like the type to get around but . . ." Barb shrugged her shoulders and threw her hands up. "Who knows."

"Is this the beast that is going to help us look at old newspaper articles?" Grace stood beside Barb in front of what looked similar to the first computer she and her mom owned, when she was in high school. A large opaque screen was framed in a bulky beige encasement. Beneath the screen was the film roll loader, magnifying lens, light source, and control knobs.

"Take a seat. This beauty right here should get us all the answers *we* . . . *you* . . . are looking for." Barb caressed the side of the box before giving it a little pat.

"This looks ancient. Reminds me of the computer I used to try and sneak into Matt Damon chat rooms in the nineties."

"She's an oldie but a goodie."

"So how do we get this baby moving?" Grace looked around, waiting for the machine to spring to life, anxious for a Google search bar to greet her on the screen like she was used to.

Barb wheeled herself over to a metal file cabinet beside the desk the machine was placed on. "Well, that's all up to you. This cabinet holds all of the microfiche for newspapers. Are you looking for a particular year?"

Grace had calculated the math in her head several times. She knew Susan and John were the same age as Sully, which meant they were born around 1947. She also knew, based on his obituary, that Timmy died in 1955 when he was five years old and the twins were eight years old. She'd need to research the years prior to gain more insight on the family, but she would start with the year of Timmy's death and backtrack if need be. "Fifty-five."

"Okey dokey." Barb used her weight to pull the drawer of the cabinet open. Her fingers danced along the tops of several small files. "Do you have a specific time of year?"

"Well, he died in August so maybe we can start with that month and go back? Maybe there's a news story on the shooting."

"August 1955," Barb said, as she plucked a small envelope out of the folder. She emptied the microfiche film in her hand, as if pouring herself a handful of M&Ms. As if on autopilot, Barb went to work loading the film and maneuvering the dials. "Let's just move this guy around a bit and see if anything stands out." As Barb turned the knobs, black-and-white articles scrolled along the screen. Grace kept her eyes peeled for two words. *Shooting. Walsh.* Regardless of what happened, if it made the news the family name would be in the story. "Eureka!" Barb leaned in toward the screen as she blinked one eye and emitted her classic discovery exclamation.

"Walsh!" Grace nearly tipped back in her chair as she saw the name in a headline: "Walsh Family Grapples Over Death."

"Geez, Princess . . . good thing we are the only ones down here. The knitting club would've had a fit if you screeched like that while they were midstitch," Barb said, half-serious, half-joking.

"Sorry." Grace leaned in so she was shoulder to shoulder with Barb, taking in the article dated August 19, 1955. The front page showed a grieving Mrs. Walsh in the center of her family. Clad in a simple black dress with a hem hitting below the knee and a high collar up at her throat. A pillbox hat sat on her head with the mesh veil doing little to obscure her downcast eyes; equally dark eye makeup made her point clear. She was desperately grieving. *Who wouldn't be.* Grace thought to herself. She lost her son. In the photo Mr. Walsh gripped her elbow, as if his main purpose was to be her crutch. The look on his face was empty, with a mouth that formed a straight line, free of emotion or maybe so entrenched in pain his face was unable to form any expression. His gaze was set ahead, propelling his family forward after a tragedy. Susan and John were on opposite sides of the parents. The short distance appearing more noticeable because in most photos Grace had seen of the twins, they were always side by side; still sharing the same space long after birth. In the background a black blur formed two lines with funeral guests parting for the well-known family.

"You'd think this family were the Kennedys of Bridgeton." Barb leaned back in her seat.

"Well, they very well could've been the Kennedys of Bridgeton." Grace leaned forward, squinting her eyes so she could read the blurb below the photo. "They certainly dressed like it anyway." Grace said under her breath.

The Walsh family grieves over the loss of their son, Timothy, as they leave the funeral at St. John the Evangelist Church.

"Hey, is it possible to print this stuff?"

"Of course . . . you want this entire article?"

"I want every article I can find on the family."

Barb turned the dial until the image and article filled the printer paper dimensions. "That could take a while, but I got nowhere to be."

Grace was suddenly overcome with gratitude for Barb. She may have been over the top sarcastic at times and sometimes a little too rough around the edges, but she was always there when Grace needed her and she never questioned her too much about the hunches she had. Whether Barb admitted it or not, she was a loyal friend and had a natural tendency to help.

"What would I do without you?" Grace asked.

"Well, for one, you probably wouldn't be with Marky . . . I take full responsibility for that relationship if I do say so myself." She hit a button on the machine and a nearby printer sprang to life.

"I do owe you that one . . . even though you were far too pushy about us dating at the beginning and nonstop embarrassed me."

"Look where it got you two though . . . living in a house . . . that is potentially haunted." Barb laughed. "Okay, let's see if we can find more articles on this unfortunate family."

The two of them sat on the edge of their seats as Barb turned the knob on the machine. Her hand stopped turning when she found an article titled: "Town Laments Fatal Accidental Shooting."

"Bingo," Grace said, this time under her breath. Words, black-and-white and blurred together flashed across the screen in a jumble until Barb had it centered in the frame.

August 14, 1955

In what is considered one of the town's greatest tragedies, the death of five-year-old Timothy John Walsh has residents filled with sorrow. At 4:13 p.m. on August 12, 1955, Walsh was reported dead after he accidentally discharged a popular .38 caliber Walther PPK pistol. Timmy was a well-loved member of the community and adored by his parents, Margaret and Charles Walsh, and his siblings, Susan and John. The Walsh family housekeeper, Karina Balik, who was present at the time of the incident, has refused to comment at this time. Further information to be reported at a later date.

Grace looked at the date again. "How did they have this printed so soon after?"

"Well, you have to remember that back then the Bridgeton Press was a daily paper."

"Damn. It's hard to believe they had enough news to send to print every single day."

"Trust me . . . they managed to fill up entire papers . . . and they used to have a socialite section."

Grace remembered the photos she saw of Mrs. Walsh and her friends, dressed to the nines and tipping back cocktails. "Wait . . . can I see that socialite section?"

"That only came out on Fridays so let's backtrack a little here . . . that will take us to August seventh." Barb turned the dials backward until she landed on the previous Friday. As she scrolled through the articles of that day, she laughed. "If you really want some entertainment you should read the police blotter from back in those days. They are hilarious."

"How do you know so much about the newspaper, Barb?"

"When I was a kid my dad worked for one of the Boston papers . . . one of the many that disappeared over the years. He used to do the formatting, he wasn't a reporter or anything like that, but I used to go to work with him a lot and I'd watch as he did the layout for the paper . . . that's when I became fascinated with the news. From a very young age, I read the paper every day. I've been a news junkie since. Pair that with my library background and I guess you could call me a "historical news junkie." Barb laughed. She used the dial to center another section of the paper, filling the screen with a picture of women poised perfectly on a plush lawn. All wearing summer dresses and smiles fixed on their faces, the women looked at the camera with shoulders back and heads tilted in practiced poses. "Now that you live in Bridgeton maybe you'll become one of the town's elite and have garden parties like these lovely ladies," Barb joked.

"Yeah right. Does this town even have elite ladies' groups anymore?"

"Not really, unless you consider the yoga-pant wearing mommy's groups, elite."

Grace grunted. She could never picture herself traveling with a mom tribe, sharing recipes and workouts and planning playdates like it was their job. And it wasn't because she looked down on these moms. Instead, it was the opposite and she actually felt a tinge of envy every time she encountered a gaggle of moms with strollers walking down the street or huddled together watching their children play sports. To Grace it was like a cult she'd never be worthy enough to join, a way of life she'd never be invited to take part in.

"So, what exactly were all these women so happy about here?" she asked, as she looked at the flawless faces smiling back at her.

"They were probably all taking mother's little helpers."

"What?" Grace turned her head toward Barb, her eyebrows rippled together in confusion.

"Benzodiazepines," Barb said, matter-of-factly, "you know . . . the housewife drug back in the day."

"Women took drugs back then?"

"Geez, Princess, do I have to teach you everything? Do yourself a favor and take out the DVD *Valley of the Dolls* on your way outta here today. You'll learn all about women and pills in the fifties and sixties."

Grace rolled her eyes. "Okay, what else do we have for the socialite section?"

"Let me see. . ." Barb turned the dial until she reached a page that included a collage of photos, square snippets of adults socializing. The women on the front page were all divvied up in different groups on this page, some with their husbands and some in action shots speaking publicly, all with that spotlight sparkle in their eyes. The section was titled: "Bridgeton Ladies Host Garden Party, Annual Fundraiser a Success."

"Can you print that one out too?"

"Sure." Barb pressed a button and the printer once again sprang to life, delivering the page. Grace stood up and took two steps to the printer. She pulled the paper off the machine and scanned all of the photos before settling on the one in the top left corner. Margaret Walsh was standing beside another woman with cropped blonde hair, long cigarettes extending from their fingers in a way that could only be seductive on women from that era. As Grace's eyes zeroed in on the picture, she saw something familiar.

"Wait a minute." In the background of the photo, she could see the familiar back yard except, instead of looking like the setting for a scary movie, the landscaping was plush and full of life. She recognized the tree line separating her yard from the neighbor's, except the trees today were massive and extending in every direction. In the photo they were lined up the proper distance apart and each tree was equal height. "This is my yard," Grace said, as she sunk back in her chair.

"For real?" Barb leaned closer, her hair touching Grace's shoulder.

"Yep, that's our back yard. And if you look really closely, you can see the edge of that creepy shed that's still there today. Trust me . . . they definitely don't make sheds like that anymore, so it stands out."

"Those Pinterest ladies would have a field day with that shed."

Grace turned her head and gave Barb a look of confusion. "You're into Pinterest?"

"I dabble. But I know some of those mom groups in town who are big into fixing up stuff like that. You could sell that puppy for a small fortune, I bet."

"I'll keep that in mind." Grace shifted her eyes back to the photo. Even though the image was in black-and-white, she could tell that the blue on the shed was more vibrant. Seeing the photos from the past and today was like watching a movie in black-and-white and then seeing it in color for the first time. As opposed to the back yard she knew today, the one in the images was bright and colorful and full of life, an oxymoron considering the visions that she had. Grace thought about little Timmy on the swing and tried to insert it into this image next to the glowing happy face of his mother, the social buzz of the gatherings hosted in their yard. She pulled her eyes away from that photo and scanned the others. Grace could tell that it was a women-only event; female figures filling the photos, capturing their goodness and showing the rest of the town how they were dedicated volunteers. In another photo several women gathered around a table, a selection of ornate appetizers placed before them. Some held bite-sized snacks elegantly, with their polished nails adding to the decorative finger food like artwork. Grace's eyes anchored on the figure standing behind the table. *Karina.*

"That's the maid," Grace said, pointing out the woman to Barb. She held an elaborate tray filled with glasses holding colorful seafood. Pieces of hearty shrimp were blended with cut red bell peppers and cilantro.

"Dang, they must've been loaded if they hosted a party that had seafood."

Grace looked at the perfection in both the food and the display. "Why's that?"

"Only the rich could afford to treat their guests with seafood back in the day . . . even in a town that has a plethora of fishermen."

"Not surprising," Grace said, as she thought about the perfectly fitted dresses the women were wearing, the flawless makeup, and the lush landscape. "Look at her face . . . she looks so serious." Grace pointed to Karina; her lips formed into a straight line, absent of a smile, her eyes locked on the tray, as if she was afraid to look at the guests directly.

"Our little Lena wasn't like that . . . that woman was always jolly." Barb laughed. "Could've been because the family was always trying to get her drunk."

"Where do you think the children were during this party?"

"Likely inside being tended to by Karina when she wasn't presenting the snobby guests with food. Maids had multiple jobs back then. And I'm guessing that being attached to a family like this, our little friend Karina made a decent living and had some major perks."

"It looks like Mrs. . . . Margaret Walsh liked her." Grace didn't miss the glowing smile spread across the woman's lips as she looked up at Karina, proud of her work, happy to show her off to the other guests. She imagined all these women had maids and they probably regularly conversed about them, comparing and contrasting their work ethics.

"Yes, but keep in mind there was a reporter snapping photos at this event . . . that whole *putting a good face on* probably came into play a lot at events like this."

"True." At the bottom of the page, Grace read the blurb.

The Walsh family hosted another successful garden party, raising $1,000 for the Town Beautification Committee. "We are honored to open up our home and host this event every year," said Margaret Walsh, Treasurer of the Bridgeton Ladies. This marks the fifth year the Walsh family has hosted the event.

Barb went through and printed all the articles that included the Walsh family while Grace gathered them into a neat pile. Images of little Timmy flittered through her head and frustration gathered around every thought. She found herself even more confused now than when she first arrived. She had been excited to learn more about John Walsh and the family dynamic, but all she really gleaned from the trip to the library was that Margaret Walsh was a socialite and her maid seemed less than happy.

CHAPTER NINE

"How's this look?" Mark ran his fingertips along the collar of the navy blue polo shirt he pulled over his head. His hair was rumpled, making him appear boyish and uncomplicated.

"Good . . . annoyingly good," Grace said, as she tossed the fourth failed shirt onto the bed. "I swear the last time I wore these shirts they fit just right and now they're hugging and falling in all the wrong places."

This time her hand landed on a thin cotton shirt she knew fit perfect but it was a different shade of blue, with more of a periwinkle inflection. She pulled it over her head and it fit just as she remembered. This was her style. Baggy but not sloppy, as comfortable as a T-shirt but classy enough for a photo shoot or a night out for dinner. "Think she'll approve of the different blues?" Grace asked, as she sat on the edge of the bed and pulled on a pair of nude ballet flats.

"Well, it kinda describes us doesn't it? We clash."

"True. I'm the periwinkle to your navy blue." Grace laughed just as three loud knocks sounded at the front door.

"We really gotta get that knocker replaced with a doorbell, don't you think?" Mark said, before he leaned down and kissed Grace on the forehead.

"Unless we want to hear that old fashioned door knocker pounding every time someone comes over. Then again, I'm not opposed to never having people over." Grace raised her eyebrows, delighted at the thought of not having visitors.

"Maybe you should stop booking photo shoots twenty-four hours in advance, then." Mark pulled her up off the bed and led her down the stairs.

Stepping over Brody, who had already forgotten that someone was knocking, Grace pulled the door open and was surprised to find no one there. She stepped onto the front step and looked left to right. Standing off to the right side of the house, Betts was as still as a statue with a bulky bag resting on her hip and one hand clutching a case dangling past her knees. Her other hand rested on the cane with the cursive writing. For a moment Grace watched her, wondering what she was looking at, curious about what memories were surfacing now that she was standing in front of the house she had visited as a child. She was wearing her hair braided the same way she wore the night of Sully's party, and the same turquoise jewelry stood out on her tan skin, the silver edges glinting in the sunlight.

"Betts?" It came out as a question, as if she were asking the woman to leave her memories and step into the present time.

A solid three seconds went by before Betts's face expanded into surprise, remembering why she was there. "I'm so sorry!" She spun toward Grace, leaning harder on the cane, to balance herself, as she adjusted her shoulder bag. "I haven't been here in years so it's like taking a trip down memory lane."

Mark peered out the doorway. "Betts, let me help you with that." He speed walked toward her. She released her grip on the case as he hefted it up in both arms. "Geez, how are you carrying this thing around?"

"It is for that reason my right bicep is so strong." She winked at Mark as she hobbled beside him, clutching the strap on the bag. "I figured you would be proud, gym guy."

"You're too funny."

"Thank you so much for coming on such short notice, Betts," Grace said, as she walked toward the two of them, her arms crossed below her chest, guarded with nerves.

"Well thank you for filling in the spot of my cancellation, dear." The three stood in a circle. In the sunlight Grace picked up on a few more wrinkles she hadn't noticed in the dim light at Sully's party. Crow's feet stretched deep from the edge of her eyes, fanned out like a waving hand. "And lucky for you guys some poor kid has a nice row of stitches on his face." She laughed.

Grace heard a thump by the front door and turned to see Brody, dropped into a sitting position, his full attention on the three of them. A string of viscous drool dangled from his lip, the result of his excitement from seeing someone new. Someone he hoped would pet him.

"Good Lord, is *that* your dog or did a bear wander onto your property this morning?" Betts's jaw dropped in awe, her wide-set eyes two giant saucers.

"Yeah . . . sorry is he too—"

"My God, he is gorgeous."

Grace's shoulders immediately relaxed as Betts made the declaration. There had been times when people had not been so welcoming of Brody's size, and it always made for an uncomfortable moment. "Do you want to pet him?"

"Do I want to pet him? I want to take him home and snuggle him for the rest of my life . . . yeah I want to pet that beautiful baby."

Grace didn't think she could like Betts any more than she already did right now. She jogged up the porch and opened the screen door, releasing Brody from the house while she gripped his collar. He could easily knock Betts over with the shake of his rump. She made sure to keep him tight to her side as she walked him over to where Betts was now kneeling on the ground, Mark standing behind as if he was ready to break her fall if Brody made one misstep.

"Bless your heart, sweet boy." She placed a hand on each of Brody's ears, as she nuzzled his snout. "Let me have a look at you, big boy." She stood up, with one hand petting his head, as he leaned into her side, delighted with the extra attention. His head came up well above her waist, but he sat on her foot like he was a lap dog. "I don't think we are gonna have any problems getting good photos of you," she said, as she fluffed up the hair on the top of his head, making him look like a rock star dog.

"Where do you think we should do the photos?" Grace asked, ready to take direction.

"Well, let's see . . . the sun is coming in from the left side of the house, so if we have you guys on the right side . . . that'll give us some good natural light. Luckily the sun isn't too overpowering today. I typically wait till a little later in the day to do outdoor shoots but we got lucky."

"Whatever you say." Mark stepped forward so he was standing beside Grace.

"Okay, just give me a minute to get my equipment set up."

"Do you need any help?" Mark asked.

"Nope, I'm all good." Betts knelt down beside her case. She flipped a switch on the side and pulled the lid open, revealing various lenses tucked neatly into their compartments.

"How are our outfits? Do we clash too much?" Grace asked, as she moved closer to Mark, comparing their shirt colors.

"Your outfits are fine but, Grace, you could use a little more lipstick. Just a dab darker if you have it."

The comment caused Mark's lips to tug into a smirk. He always told her how good she looked when she wore lipstick, but she never liked wearing it because she felt it made her look like she was trying too hard. "I'll see what I have." Grace purposely bumped into Mark's shoulder as she turned around and headed inside to assess her limited lipstick collection. Walking toward the house, she whipped her head around and saw Mark mocking her in an *I told you so* manner.

Upstairs, as Grace unzipped the small bag that held three different lipsticks and a lip gloss, the house was silent, but she couldn't help but think how differently this house was almost sixty-five years ago when the Walsh family lived here. What secrets had that family held onto so tightly all these years. And what really happened to Timmy Walsh? What drove John to shooting his baby brother and how did the family convince the police it was an accidental shooting? These were the questions endlessly circling around in Grace's head like a thought tornado.

After discerning the difference between Hot Shot Red, Berry Blaze, and Nude Night Out, Grace opted for the red. She stretched her lips against her teeth as she applied the, barely used, lipstick. She puckered them together, then opened wide releasing a popping sound. The red was a dramatic shade but she had to admit the color brightened her face. Gazing at her reflection, she tilted her head and imagined what it would be like to be Margaret Walsh getting ready for a night out with her wealthy friends. One of Bridgeton's debutantes mingling with her tribe and being envied by the masses.

With her freshly applied lipstick Grace made her way down the staircase, leaving behind a series of creaks with each footfall. She imagined wearing a long gown popular in the fifties, with the flowy hem gliding across the stairs. Surely, Margaret Walsh walked down these stairs on numerous occasions, enrobed in high-end gowns, ready to flit through social events only the elite were invited to. By the time Grace returned, Betts had her equipment in place and was guiding Mark and Brody in a private snapshot.

She snapped a quick photo of them before directing her line of vision toward Grace. "Ahhh, much better. You are a beauty."

"I tell her that all the time." Mark smiled.

"It's true, he does. And it's incredibly sappy."

"We were just testing out the lighting over here with a few shots of daddy and doggy." Betts pressed an index finger to her chin, contemplating the next pose. "Okay, let's have you two holding hands behind the big boy."

Grace got into position, embarrassed by her sweaty palm gripping Mark's. Being the center of attention was never her favorite place to be, and she was typically more on edge when she was in the presence of someone she was intrigued by, someone who may have answers to her latest mystery.

After an hour of arranging themselves into various positions in front of the house, Grace was officially done with fake smiles and unrealistic poses. She wanted to move forward and tackle the real reason she set up the shoot. Hopefully some memories would be triggered in Betts and get her to talk about her time at this house. "So, it must be weird being here after so many years." Grace pried, clutching Brody's collar, as Betts went to work removing the lens from her camera and securing it in its nook within the case. Still hanging from her neck, the camera swung side to side as she stood up. "You could say that."

"So, were you really close with the Walsh family?"

Her words came out more ambiguous the second time around. "You could say that."

Just when Grace thought she was going to get nowhere with the woman, she was gifted with her next words. "Would you mind if I looked around inside? Just to see if it's changed at all?"

"Of course!" Grace's words came out more excited than they should've. Mark took over the duty of holding onto Brody's collar and leading him into the house as Grace walked beside Betts, keeping her stride slow. Based on how agile Betts moved with a cane, Grace imagined she had a lot of practice with it and had perfected taking photos with one hand. She couldn't help but wonder what warranted the cane. Was it old age?

An accident? Grace added it to the long list of questions she already had scrambling around in her head.

Mark led them inside and released Brody. The dog flopped down on the floor by the door, happy to be back in his sleeping spot. "Can I get you ladies anything to drink? Tea, coffee, water, wine?"

"A man after my own heart. You have red?"

"That's all I have." Mark presented her with a glowing smile and his signature wink. The man was a natural flirt, but Grace knew it was simply an extension of his personality and not used in a harmful way. "Grace?"

"Sure." Grace had started getting more into wine over the past few months and even learned how to detect certain notes on her tongue. While she and Mark weren't big drinkers, they allowed themselves to enjoy a good bottle once in a while and had even joined an overpriced wine of the month club.

Mark went to work selecting a bottle from the pantry as Grace retrieved glasses from the rack alongside the island. A minute passed before she realized the room was silent aside from the clinking glasses and Mark's movement in the pantry. She looked over to see that Betts hadn't followed her into the kitchen, but instead she was still standing in the foyer, looking up the staircase as if watching a ghost approach. Grace watched her and held up a hand to stop Mark from saying anything when he emerged from the pantry. The two of them stood there observing the woman as she seemed to be watching past memories unfold. Grace imagined it was like pressing rewind on a VHS tape. Brody adjusted his position on the floor, the sound of his body dropping back down pulled Betts from her thoughts and brought her back to the present moment.

"Sorry . . . I . . . this is just so surreal . . . being in this house again." She looked around as if she had been transported into a different world, taking in her surroundings for the first time.

Grace leaned on the island and accepted the stemless glass of wine Mark slid in her direction. She cupped it with her palms as she watched Betts sort out the memories in her head. Grace had never seen Mark struggle with the right words to say, but in this instant all he could do was raise his eyebrows and stay silent.

"I'm sure it's strange being in here after all these years." Grace pushed ahead.

"Yep, it definitely is." Betts shook her head, jolting the memories around as if trying to unscramble them. She turned slowly and walked over to the island, her limp seeming more prevalent than it had earlier. After dropping her bag on the countertop she lifted the glass of wine Mark set in front of her and gave it one long sniff. "Burgundy?"

"You're good." Mark spun the bottle in her direction, revealing the label.

"One of my favorites."

"We aim to please at Chateau Connolly." Mark grinned as he wafted a hand in front of him.

"So, I'm guessing the kitchen looks quite different from when you were last here," Grace said, as she lifted the glass to her lips, allowing a tiny sip of wine to seep past. Always wanting to stay in control, she was a slow drinker and took her sips carefully, being sure to savor the taste.

"It certainly does." With wine glass in hand Betts walked toward the pantry. "Do you mind?" She rested a hand on the doorknob.

"Go for it." Mark was quick to respond.

She pulled the door open and walked in slowly. The shelves were still practically bare, with the exception of a few bottles of wine, a bulk box of rice, and a tub of oatmeal. Grace imagined this pantry would never be fully packed with just the two of them living here. "Before this pantry was here there was a dumbwaiter right here." She placed her hands in front of her showing the space it was in. Grace remembered seeing a dumbwaiter in one of the other old houses they toured during their house hunt. "In fact, one day, Karina caught the twins putting Timmy in the dumbwaiter." She shook her head. "I'll never forget that day . . . and standing here now makes it feel like it was just yesterday that it happened."

Grace played dumb, a skill she had mastered since trying to solve these crimes on her own. "Who is Karina?"

"Oh . . . she was the Walsh family's maid . . . poor little Timmy was stuffed in the dumbwaiter." Betts stepped out of the pantry, looking around the room as if she were reliving the moment. "Karina came barreling down the stairs. I'll never forget the look on her face." Betts turned her head toward the staircase then back to the island. She walked toward the countertop to the right of the pantry. "Right here was the fridge. I remember there was a smaller countertop beside it where Karina used to cut vegetables." She turned facing the other side of the current countertop. "And oddly enough, they had a stove facing outwards right here. There was an oval table right there." She pointed toward the other side of the kitchen and then the dining room. "But it looks like John must've tore down the wall separating the two rooms to create this one open space." She turned in a circle, comparing the home she remembered with the home of today, likely reassessing the space in her head. "Poor Timmy . . . the twins were always picking on him. It was like he was born into a world that had two bullies ready to knock him down. They even tried stuffing him in the dryer once." Betts walked to the other side of the kitchen facing away from Grace and Mark. "The laundry room was over here, off the dining room. I feel like Karina was doing laundry nonstop because Mrs. Walsh did not like when the kids' clothes were dirty." She turned and walked back to where Grace and Mark were sitting, taking it all in like they were watching a movie. After she rested her cane against the island, she slowly lifted herself onto a bar stool. "My mother on the other hand had been so used to dealing with my filthy brothers she didn't give a darn if I got dirty. Mrs. Walsh must've thought we were such slobs." She laughed.

Grace kept seeing the maid's somber facial expressions in the photos she found in the old newspapers. Something was urging her to find out more information on the woman. "How long did they have a maid?"

"Oh, they had Karina for as long as I can remember. I started coming around here to play with Susan when I was eight and she and John were six."

Grace couldn't help but wonder why she was welcome here when her brother Sully wasn't. She remembered Sully saying he ran in different circles because of the difference in their social classes, but why would Betts be accepted? She had to figure that out without coming out and blatantly asking. "Did Sully hang out with Susan back then?"

"No . . . and that's not because he didn't want to. In fact, he had a crush on Susan all those years ago, so it's kinda funny how they ended up together so much later in life."

Grace didn't tell Betts how Sully had mentioned that to her in their last conversation.

"So, did you take photos of the family a lot?"

"Yeah, that's kind of how I started spending time at this house. It all started when Susan got interested in photography. Being a rich kid, her parents got her top of the line equipment before the girl even knew which button to press to take a photo. They made Susan promise to learn how to use the equipment if they bought it for her. I had been two years older, around nine at that time, and everyone knew I had this weird obsession with photography. It's simply not normal to see a young kid toting around a big camera, snapping shots of everything in her path. But that was me . . . I was a freak. I still am. The thing about Susan was she was one of those wealthy kids who didn't really want to be seen as wealthy. She'd rather be like me . . . middle class with tunnel vision on one hobby. I never could figure it out. If I had all that money, I'd have used it to get ahead, and I'd have no problem letting my parents shower me with gifts. But like they say . . . the grass is always greener."

Susan hadn't come off uppity when Grace met her at Sully's party, so she wasn't particularly surprised by this news. "So, why was she suddenly into photography?"

"Beats me. My guess is that I was older and easily accessible . . . her family knew me because my dad was a cop, so I was accepted even though my parents raised me and my five brothers in a house a quarter the size of this house. So, like I said. I came over to give her a lesson in photography. I was thrilled to use all of her high-end equipment. It was really a dream gig for me. In fact, I still have her old photo gear today. One thing I never throw away is a camera." Betts winked. "And like I had expected, Susan lost interest by our third lesson. By then I had snapped so many photos of the family I kind of became a fixture in their . . . *this* house. I took some of my best photos here. And the family appreciated that I was capturing their happy moments. Some I even submitted to the newspaper for their socialite section."

"How long did that go on for?" Grace thought about how full circle this all was. Betts may have been the one who had taken the garden party photos she and Barb were studying yesterday at the library.

"Well, until they kind of wanted me to stop taking photos of them."

"Why would they want you to stop?"

"Hard to say. To be honest I still question it to this day. At first, Mrs. Walsh loved my photos and invited me over to capture every moment. She even bought my film for me and urged Susan to give me her equipment, knowing her daughter wasn't really into it like I was. And then one day I was walking up the hill toward the house, like I did every day after school, and Mrs. Walsh met me at the end of the driveway. It was the strangest thing because most of the time I never even saw her. She was kind enough when she asked me to stop taking photos, but it still baffled me and I thought that I had done something wrong."

"What exactly did she say when she asked you to stop?"

"She said something about how Mr. Walsh didn't want his family's life on film and it made him nervous because he wasn't home very often . . . you know he was a big time traveling salesman. I guess he was trying to protect his family."

"From what exactly, though?"

"All I could think of is that back then there were all of these gossip magazines that were emerging. They would basically feature wealthy, well-known families and people would just devour them word for word. They were mostly sold in the city . . . I know Boston had a few that had been flying off the shelves. Maybe he was just a private man?"

"Did you ever meet Mr. Walsh?"

"Only a handful of times. Some of my best family photos were taken with him . . . although, that says more about his good looks than my photography . . . the man was a looker."

Grace thought about the few photos she'd seen of Charles Walsh. She knew he had a slender build but she didn't memorize any of his other features. It wasn't that they didn't stand out but more because she had been so focused on Margaret Walsh. The woman was always front and center in the images, with clusters of other women circled around her, while Charles was always in the background.

"What was he like?"

"Quiet if I remember correctly." Betts took a hefty swig of her wine, swirled it around in her mouth and swallowed before she spoke again. "I'm kind of embarrassed to admit this but . . . I had a big crush on him when I was a kid. Weird right? A ten-year-old crushing on her friend's dad? Maybe it was because he was so mysterious, so soft spoken, and appeared calm all the time."

"If you're weird because of that, then I am too. I had a major crush on my junior high school gym teacher." Grace laughed, feeling the warmth of the wine rushing from her stomach to her head.

"Not weird at all, Gracie, that's why you chose me . . . your personal gym teacher." Mark laughed.

"You two complement each other well." Betts used her fingers to make the near-empty wine glass swivel on the counter. Before the conversation turned to them, Grace had to get it back on track, so she launched into the next question.

"So, what exactly happened the day Timmy died?" Grace pushed ahead.

Betts paused, took in a deep breath and let it all out in one long exhale. Mark took the next logical step and poured more wine into her glass. "You're a cop . . . but I sense you think beyond the black-and-white of the law. Am I right?" As she said the words, a chill ran up Grace's spine. Did this woman know about her secret? Her gift.

"I try to . . . but it doesn't always work out." Grace thought about all the times she had been empathetic when arresting someone, thinking about the criminal's *situation* and why they were committing crimes. Did they have a reason to? Were they raised to believe stealing, killing, and corruption was the only way to survive. Was it a way of life for them? Maybe it was female intuition, or maybe it was because she untangled crimes that were often the result of passion.

"Well, I'm about as opposite of *cop* as you can get," Betts said. "Having five brothers who were all cops it only made sense that I balanced them out by being the hippy artist." Betts lifted the glass of wine to her lips, this time she took a smaller, daintier sip. She set the glass down and with an unsettling stare, looked directly at Grace as she continued.

"I used to walk up this street every day after Mrs. Walsh told me not to photograph them anymore. I guess, in some sense, it made me more intrigued about their family. It's like they were hiding something now, and being the curious photographer I am, I guess part of me wanted to uncover what exactly they didn't want me to capture on film. If they were such a good role model family hosting happy events, then why would Mr. Walsh not want me to get snapshots of that?"

"It does sound strange." Grace leaned forward, ready to devour more of Betts's words.

"Did you stop hanging out with Susan at that point?" Mark interjected, his cop questioning coming back into play. He may have been a gym guy now, but his past as a police officer would always surge through his blood, surviving even when it was pushed down.

"No, not really. The Walsh kids went to a private school, so it's not like I saw them every day. To be honest, Susan and I didn't have a whole lot in common, so I was less concerned about the loss of friendship than I was about having the inside scoop on the family."

"What about John . . . were you friends with him when you spent time at the house?"

Without flinching Betts answered. "No. John has always been what some would call an 'odd duck.' Never talked much . . . still doesn't today. I guess he let Susan do all the talking for him when they were growing up. Sometimes that's the way with twins . . . one always speaks for the other. The day that Timmy got shot I walked up the street, going about my normal business, taking photos of everything that struck my fancy. I'd taken photos of houses, unique trees, gardens, all the way up the street. When I got to the top I had planned to take shots of the town. Right in front of the Walsh house . . . *this* house, is the highest point in town. The Walsh's knew that and I'm sure they saw me taking photos on several occasions. They didn't mind, as long as I didn't take photos of them, I suppose." Betts pulled her gaze away from Grace and Mark, angling it on the countertop as she used her thumb to make tiny circles on the granite. "As long as I wasn't taking photos of their family . . . they didn't mind."

Grace pictured Betts as a little girl walking around town, snapping photos of everything. "Did they let you take photos from their front yard?"

"Yeah, that was part of the deal when Mrs. Walsh told me to stop taking photos of their family . . . I think she felt a little bad, so she told me that I could always use their front yard to get photos of the town. She was well aware their house was in a dream location for photographers. I mentioned it, in awe, quite often. Us photographers are a bit weird when we find something that helps us capture our art."

Grace understood. It was similar to how she felt when she found clues in her cases. Nothing could get in the middle of her and those clues. Like a tornado, she would whirl her way through until she got to the bottom of it.

"Anyway, I heard the gunshot. It was in the afternoon, after summer day camp. I remember because I looked at my watch and it was four thirteen. I don't know if you guys ever hear that cannon that goes off at night? Well, it's been going off for years. Some Bridgeton tradition. But it usually goes off between six thirty and seven fifteen. On this day, I thought maybe it was going off earlier. But it actually wasn't the shot that stuck out in my head . . . it was what I heard before."

"What did you hear?" Grace, with eyes wide like she was watching a scary movie, leaned in closer.

"It was like a flurry of screaming . . . all coming from the back yard."

"Were the voices familiar? Could you tell who was screaming?" Mark asked, his curiosity appearing to be just as piqued as Grace's.

"That's the hard part. It was like a blend of Mrs. Walsh, the maid, Timmy crying, and John yelling." Betts paused, moisture making its way to her eyes. "Today, all these years later, I still hear that blend of voices, the shouting, the screeching. It's like it's haunting me."

"So, what do you think really happened?" Grace got to the point, she needed to pounce on the woman's memory while she had her sitting right in front of her, essentially at the scene of the crime when memories were their most clear, unblocked from everyday life and the many things that get in the way of past thoughts, past traumas.

"That's the question of the day? I still don't know, but there is something else that has stuck out in my mind all these years."

"What's that?" Grace urged her to continue.

"If someone in your house accidentally shot himself, how soon would you call the ambulance?"

"Immediately," Grace and Mark said at the same time, the syllables of the word blending between their two voices.

"Like I said, when I heard the shot, I looked at my watch . . . it was four thirteen. But what happened next stood out even more. I ran. With all of my equipment I ran down that hill. I ran so fast I nearly stumbled forward. Physics had my body weighted forward thanks to the hefty equipment and the steep decline of the hill. I still don't know why I ran so fast. Maybe I thought someone would come after me with a gun or maybe I thought that someone thought I was the one shooting the gun. I really don't know . . . the things that go through your mind when you're in that situation." Betts shook her head.

"Where did you go? Home?"

"That's what I was about to get to. You know that steep staircase that joins this street and Chestnut Street?" she asked. Grace knew the staircase. It was made from old, cracked cement.

"I know that staircase well," Mark said. He had taken his clients there often, making them walk up the stairs wearing weighted packs.

"Well, I turned toward the staircase and got halfway down where that landing is . . . you know . . . the section where someone added a little garden in the middle." Grace thought about the trees that hovered over that section of the stairs, the pansies that were planted by some kind, elderly gardener in town. "I plunked down right there with all my equipment. And I just sat there, I sat there until I heard an ambulance barreling up the street behind me. I knew in my heart of hearts something went wrong and someone was hurt. Badly. I knew without knowing, if that makes sense."

Grace pictured a young Betts racing down the steep street, sitting on the steps beneath the trees, like a fort in the middle of town.

"Did you happen to see what time it was then?" Mark beat her to the question.

"You're a natural cop, Mark . . . I was just about to get to that."

"It was four fifty-five when the ambulance came up the street. I remember thinking to myself, if that wasn't the cannon, if that was a real gun . . . why is it taking the ambulance so long to get here? I was only ten at the time but I knew a thing or two about the timeline for responding to accidents. My dad had started training my brothers and me on police work since we were old enough to walk. All those lessons came in handy that day. Well, maybe not handy . . . but I certainly put to use what my dad had taught me all those years."

"So, you're saying it took the ambulance forty-two minutes to arrive on the scene?" Grace inquired.

"In a town like Bridgeton, where the only ambulance calls are typically ones involving elderly falls." Betts pointed out.

"So, things haven't changed much over the years," Grace said, as she methodically brought the wine glass up to her lips, taking the last sip.

"Trust me, I researched the average ambulance response time and found out it's eight to fourteen minutes."

"So, much longer than average." Mark used his index finger to make small circles on his temple, his thinking habit.

"So, you are both cops with, what I've perceived as having, good gut instincts. You tell me why it would take so long for the ambulance to arrive when a five-year-old boy had a gunshot wound."

"My guess is that they called it in late, long after the shot was fired, but the better question is why? Why wouldn't a call to the ambulance be the first thing the parents did?" Grace added.

"My thoughts exactly," Betts said, as she pursed her lips together, displaying a matter-of-fact expression. Grace thought about her vision of Timmy falling off the swing set, the shattered green glass, and the look of sadness and betrayal set like stone in his features before his facial muscles relaxed and death's grip took him. Taking away all the hurt and pain. "And I presented this to my father . . . I researched the case for days after they deemed it an accidental shooting. Something didn't sit right in my gut."

"Maybe you should've been a cop," Mark said, as he locked eyes with Grace, the two of them thinking the exact same thing at the exact same moment.

Betts threw her head back, letting out an explosive guffaw. "You guys are funny. I'm about as opposite of cop as they come. Every time one of my brothers graduated from the academy, I would blatantly wear the most gothic attire to the ceremony. I was my own island in our family, standing strong to oppose the black-and-white characteristics of cop thinking."

"How did your parents feel about that?"

"My mother had an inner-hippy and I think she was happy to have me as her sidekick. And my dad and brothers learned to accept me." She smoothed her hand on the granite surface. "I think it helped that I was the only girl too."

Grace thought about her own mother, and how opposite she was from her. Ellen McKenna was a diehard hippy and looked at life through an artistic lens. A wave of sadness washed over Grace as she thought about how her mother would've probably loved to delve into an artistic career like photography, but was stuck spending all of her working years doing mindless work at the post office so she could sustain her life as a single mom. While Grace had trouble admitting it, she had found more similarities with her father's personality. She still hadn't completely opened up to the idea of a full-on father–daughter relationship with the man, but she had seen fragments of their personalities mesh together in the times they had spent getting to know each other.

"So, what did you do when you heard the ambulance?"

"I did what every good photographer would do." A sly expression moved across Betts's face, transforming her full lips into an impish grin.

Question marks grew evident on both Mark's and Grace's faces, urging Betts to continue.

"I snuck on the scene . . . and snapped photos."

"What!?" Grace was shocked by her admittance and secretly hoping she still had the photos to share.

"I honestly don't know how I managed to go unnoticed, but there was so much commotion going on and they had these trees lined up in their back yard, making for an easy angle to capture everything."

"The same trees that are now so overgrown and taking over half of our back yard." Grace walked to the back of the kitchen, where it sat flush with the sunroom and stood in front of the window that offered a perfect view of their back yard, creepy old swing set included. Taking her lead, Mark and Betts followed.

The three of them stood side by side looking out the window like they had just discovered an unconquered land.

"Things certainly don't change much," Betts said. Grace turned her head toward the woman and set her gaze on her profile, discerning a teardrop coming to the surface of her outer eye. The tear made her teal eye shadow shimmer even more, making her brown eyes shine on a backdrop of color.

"Except the fact that we desperately need a tree trimmer to come over and tackle those overly extended branches." A thought struck Grace as she continued to scan the tree line. "Was the fence there back then?"

"Yeah, that fence hasn't moved in years, except maybe to sink deeper into the ground." Betts laughed. "In fact, I used the fence for balance so I could take quick shots. Back before I needed the assistance of a cane, I could maneuver my body any way I wanted to capture a photo. Gosh, and being ten . . . it was so easy. Don't get old, whatever you do."

"So, where are those pictures today?"

Betts paused, turned back toward the counter, leaning on the cane for support. "They are put away." Grace wasn't sure if Betts's clipped response emerged from her need for privacy or from bitterness about the past. She looked toward Mark, as they followed her back to the center of the kitchen, hoping he had an appropriate response. Grace had always been able to count on Mark to shimmy his way into conversations and fix them when they went amok, since he was the one in the relationship who excelled at sweet talking.

"Betts, this had to have been incredibly hard for you to see at such a young age."

"It was. But what bothers me more is that there are some holes in the story and I was never able to convince my father to look deeper."

"Did your dad know you were at the scene that day?" Grace asked, as she slipped back on her bar stool.

"No, he didn't know then, but he did after when I showed him my pictures and told him about the lost time between when the shot was fired and when the ambulance raced up the street."

"And what did he say?" Mark asked, tilting his head as he crossed his arms across his chest, one of his classic stances from when he was a police officer and one he still used today when training clients.

"He wanted nothing to do with my 'theory.'" Betts displayed a set of finger quotes, sarcasm hugging the word *theory*. "You have to remember that I was a ten-year-old girl, it was in the fifties, and I was the black sheep of our family . . . the looked down upon artist. I didn't have a whole lot going for me."

"Your dad must've kicked himself in the butt when he saw you blossom into a well-known photographer, huh?" Mark laughed, but Grace was submerged in the type of stress that goes along with having a tight deadline. *Don't get her off topic, Mark.*

"He came around, but let's just say that the shooting at the Walsh house was never brought up again."

"What exactly was your theory, Betts?"

"Well, to be honest I really didn't have anything I was anchoring my story to, I just knew that Timmy didn't shoot himself, and if he did . . . it wasn't an accident."

Grace had a million questions surging through her mind. *What exactly does Betts think happened? What isn't she telling us?*

Before she was forced to ask any more uncomfortable questions, Betts continued. "There was the whole timing thing that was off, and the scene when I hid behind the trees . . . it was off."

"How so?" Mark adjusted his stance, maintaining eye contact with Betts.

"I can't say for sure. But, do you know when you feel like you are in the presence of wrongdoing? That's how it felt."

It was as if Betts was testing Grace. She, out of anyone, knew exactly what it was like to be in the presence of wrongdoing, of that helplessness you feel when you know there are demons but there is nothing that you can do about them. *Yet.*

"I just remember their maid Karina . . . being so distraught. But it was so over the top that I felt like she was putting on an act." Betts looked through the space between where Grace was sitting and Mark was standing, as if she was looking out the very window that led to the back yard. "You know how when someone is guilty of something and they try to make it look like they're not, by overcompensating?"

Grace had seen that many times since she'd been a detective. Criminals were often award-winning actors. "Yeah, I do know what you mean."

"Where was the mother when you were there?" Mark asked.

"Mrs. Walsh? Distraught as you can imagine, but rightfully so. I mean, sobbing this loud guttural cry that still haunts me today. The sound of a mother losing her child. I never had kids myself, but when I hear about incidents where parents lose their children, I think of that cry. It was like she was crying and growling at the same time, like the intensity of her emotions was causing her entire body to convulse. I wouldn't wish that feeling on my worst enemy."

"And Mr. Walsh?" The natural next question erupted from Grace's lips.

"He was on a plane home by then, I assume . . . unless the call to notify him was just as delayed as the ambulance." Betts scoffed at the idea, but Grace could tell she thought that scenario was entirely possible.

"What did Mr. Walsh do for work?" Mark asked. Whether Grace had told him or not, he was asking the right questions, keeping Betts talking.

"He was born into money . . . his grandfather invented a part on airplanes that evidently changed the way of air travel. Mr. Walsh was head of sales for that company."

Without needing more information, Grace could see dollar signs. She remembered her mother telling her about the golden age of travel. Ellen had always said that only the wealthy traveled back then. She told Grace about her friend who had obtained a sought-after job as a glamorous air hostess and all the wild things that happened in the sky back then. *"Gracie, it was like a nonstop party up there, glamorous meals, people smoking cigarettes, and an endless supply of drinks for all passengers. Not like it is today . . . they even had way more leg room back then."*

One thing Grace did know from air travel back then is that it was less safe than it is today, so if Mr. Walsh was selling a big-time airplane part, then that money was probably still coming in strong today. The Walsh siblings were likely still sitting pretty on loads of cash.

"That's big money," Mark said, exhaling a whistle between his lips.

"It is." Betts paused, slid her bag off the countertop and hoisted it onto her shoulder. She looked at the two of them thoughtfully. "But if I've learned anything in my lifetime . . . it's that money doesn't buy you happiness."

She started to turn toward the foyer, as Grace erupted one last question that she knew half of the answer to. "What about John and Susan? Were they at the scene that day?"

"John was. Susan . . . no."

"I imagine John was a mess seeing his little brother like that?"

"Quite the contrary, actually. The boy was always kind of odd, but that day he looked as if the emotion had been sucked out of him. He didn't speak, he didn't cry, and he looked like he was simply going through the emotions of everyday life." Betts shrugged her shoulders. "Maybe it was shock. And like I said, Susan usually did all the talking for him and she wasn't there, so who knows."

"Could've been," Mark said, as he followed Betts toward the door. Grace trailed behind, like a puppy dog being strung along with a tempting slab of meat. She wanted more info while she had Betts here, but there was a fine line between asking questions out of curiosity and sending red flags up for being too pushy.

"I'll send you the top ten photos I took and let you choose what you like, then from there I'll edit them and send you the files." Just as Betts was about to head toward the front door, Brody sat upright, blocking her in. *Good boy, buddy.* "You were so quiet I almost forgot about you, big boy." Betts leaned over her cane and roughed up the hair on his head. She turned toward Mark and Grace and said, "I don't think you two have to worry about a bad shot . . . this boy can make any photo look good."

Mark started to pick up her case but Grace silently intercepted. "I'll get that." She hefted the case up and followed Betts out the door, shifted to her side as they made their way across the front yard, toward her car. "Thank you again for coming over on such short notice."

"You're so welcome. Thanks for keeping me company this afternoon." A pleasant smile sprung across Betts's lips, erasing the harsh expression she had just moments before while they were in deep conversation about the Walsh family. She took the case from Grace, as she raised the trunk of her Subaru wagon, and gently set it down on a folded up brown and orange afghan. It reminded Grace of the many afghans her mother had lying around the house growing up. They had all been made by a great-aunt who was like a mother to Ellen. "Oh and, Grace?"

"Yeah?"

"Can you keep our Walsh family discussions between us . . . and Mark?"

"Of course."

"My brother would kill me if he knew I was talking about it. He kinda had the same views as my father on it. Either that or he was brainwashed by our dad. I'm sure all of my brothers were, come to think about it. And now that he is dating Susan . . . well he'd really be mad if I was talking about the case."

"They seem to make a good couple . . . how do you like Susan?"

"Susan is Susan . . . I can't say I have a feeling either way." Betts tossed her bag into the car beside the case and slammed the trunk closed. "That reminds me . . . I gotta see if he ever got in touch with her. Ever since his wife died, he worries about every little thing. I think he has a fear that everyone is going to leave him. Poor guy."

As Betts slipped into her car and drove off, Grace was pummeled with thoughts. *Where is Susan?* She had remembered Sully saying that she hadn't answered his texts, but that didn't stand out until Betts mentioned it again. After Grace waved to Betts on her way out, she slid her cell phone out of her back pocket, punching a quick text in to Sully.

Hey, just checking to see if you ever got in touch with Susan…
you know how I worry about you. ;)

As Grace made her way to the front door, she kept her eyes focused on the three grey dots flickering within a conversation bubble. Sully wasn't always the fastest text responder so the fact that he was already replying laced Grace's anticipation with worry.

His reply marked the screen with a one-word response that made a million follow-up questions line up in her head, like soldiers in formation.

No

CHAPTER TEN

Grace pushed the café door open, sounding the bell overhead. Being late morning, the breakfast crowd had already left and the lunch crowd hadn't yet arrived, and for that she was grateful. As promised, Barb sat in a quiet booth clutching a mug of coffee. By the time Betts's car was out of sight yesterday afternoon, Grace had made a call to Barb, asking her to get the case files for August 12, 1955. The two had planned to meet at the café, away from the station, so curious fellow officers wouldn't catch on to what they were doing. Barb had taken an early lunch and Grace extended her morning meeting at the high school. She had to give one final safety lesson on social media to the graduating class, preparing them before they set off to college.

"Thanks for meeting me," Grace said, as she slid into the booth, making sure not to sit directly on the tear in the seat. The Bridgeton Café had been around for years and while it continued to thrive as a favorite for breakfast and lunch among the locals, the owners failed to upgrade the essential equipment—like furniture for the customers.

"You know me . . . always ready to sneak an old case file for you."

"You're the best."

Just as Grace was scanning the room for familiar faces, the waitress approached the table, presenting her with a steaming cup of coffee. "Good morning, Detective McKenna," the thirty-something waitress said. Grace stealthily scanned her eyes over the girl's nametag. "Good morning, Lexi . . . can I just get a side of rye toast with butter."

"Yes ma'am." Lexi looked over at Barb, tacitly requesting her order.

"I'll have the meat lovers if you're still serving breakfast?"

"All day every day." Lexi winked and turned on a heel.

"Princess, I always knew that you were a semi-celeb in this town but even the diner waitresses know who you are." Barb raised her eyebrows, mocking surprise.

"That's all Mark." Grace retorted. Ever since Mark had opened a successful gym in town her stardom as sole female detective seemed to skyrocket. She was like the first lady of the town fitness guru. "So . . . you got the file?"

"Would I disappoint you?" Barb pulled the file from her messenger bag.

Grace flipped open the worn manila envelope as surprise made an obvious expression on her face. "That's it?" The envelope contained only a few thin sheets of paper with notes.

"My thoughts exactly." Barb leaned forward on the table, her eyes set on Grace. "An accidental shooting at the home of one of the wealthiest families in town and this is all they have to show for it. Something's fishy." She brought her cup of coffee to her lips, a Logan Airport logo front and center. The café was known for having a selection of random cups for their customers, showcasing its quirky side. "I don't know how you do it, Princess, but you're always onto something with these cases . . . you got that hunch cops would pay millions for."

Again, Grace was on the fence about telling Barb about her gift. If she could tell anyone it'd be Barb, but she wasn't one hundred percent sure she could trust the woman to keep it a secret. Barb had a hidden heart of gold, but she liked to talk and pass gossip to the many people she talked to in town. Grace couldn't risk it.

The two of them were hovering over the sparse documents, trying to decipher the messy scrawl, when Lexi arrived with their plates. In a swift gesture Grace slammed the folder shut, shielding it from the girl with a flat hand. Lexi slid the respective dishes in front of them and topped off their coffees. "Enjoy your breakfast," the young waitress said, minding her own business and turning to greet another customer who had just arrived. Grace turned her head to see John Walsh gesturing to the waitress he was going directly to the bar.

"Shit!" Grace said, sliding the folder off the table and onto the seat by her side. Her nerves increased the grip she had on the tear in the seat, her four fingers anxiously feeling the exposed foam in the cushion.

Barb's gaze darted left to right, before landing on John. Since he was currently the only other patron in the restaurant, it wasn't hard for her to pick up on what Grace was trying to convey. "Is that?"

"That's John Walsh . . . Timmy's older brother . . . AKA the sibling who was at the scene of the crime." Grace hissed across the table, ducking her head as if she was hiding.

"Shit is right." Barb kept staring, looking over Grace whose back was to the bar.

"Stop looking . . . what's he doing? Did he see me?"

"Okay, *contradicting Cassidy* . . . he's ordering a coffee . . . looks like it's iced . . . and flavored. Maybe hazelnut?"

Grace realized how ridiculous the conversation sounded and sat upright, ridding her body of the sleuth-like posture. Her curiosity took control of her and she twisted her head toward the bar just as he was grabbing the iced coffee off the laminate and turning his body between two bar stools. Likely sensing that Grace was turned to look at him, his gaze landed directly on hers and there was no turning back for her. An awkward moment passed, like silence between two strangers in an elevator, before she waved a hand at him. Hoping that was all she needed to do to appear friendly and polite, while maintaining her introverted distance, she turned back around but the look on Barb's face told another story. Her eyes expanded, like rising muffins, as Grace heard the sound of his boots hitting the linoleum floor, getting louder with each step. She adjusted her position so she was sitting on the file, concealing it from view.

He passed the table and offered them a subtle nod, making eye contact with Grace long enough for her to see Timmy's ashen face with lips drained of color, and his vacant eyes releasing a trailing, glistening tear. And just like that he was gone, pushing his way out the side door that spilled out into an alleyway. Grace silently reprimanded herself for being so foolish, for forgetting about the side door and assuming he was walking over to her as if they were friends. She took in a deep breath, releasing all the worry that had washed over her when she thought he was going to approach their table and discover the file tucked securely under her bottom.

"He's creepy." Barb interrupted Grace's harsh internal critical comments.

"Isn't he?"

"Yeah, there is something off, and he looks so darn familiar . . . I can't seem to put my finger on it."

"Maybe you're thinking about his twin sister. Susan." Grace was certain Barb had met the woman at Sully's retirement party.

"Could be." She shook her head side to side, shaking out the nerves. "Close call." Armed with an elevated fork, Barb stabbed at the pile of potatoes filling a portion of her plate. Grace was relieved to see she wasn't the only one made anxious by the man's presence and that said a lot considering there wasn't much Barb admitted to being scared about.

Now that the butterflies in her belly had dimmed to a light flutter, she bit into the toast with her front teeth, the butter accentuating the rye flavor. She slipped the folder from underneath her and dropped it on the table. "So, where were we?" She used a napkin to cover her buttery fingertips as she flipped the folder open. Barb took one of the sheets and started scanning it as Grace went to work on another document, the two of them forming a perfect partnership without having to exchange a single word.

"Okay, now I know why Betts had worked hard to try and question her father about the scenario . . . looks like Joe Sullivan was the responding officer."

"That Sully's dad?"

"Yep." Grace remembered Sully mentioning he was named Joe Jr. after his father. "Betts must've assumed I knew that her dad was the responding officer."

"Small town like this . . . chances are pretty high that the incident would've occurred while he was on duty, especially if the responding team was at the scene for a while . . . and I imagine they would be for a case like this." Barb folded a pancake in half, soaked it in a pool of syrup, and took a hearty bite. The woman loved food and never lost her appetite. Grace vividly remembered Barb putting down a slice of pizza while she looked over a suicide case where half the victim's head had been blown off. Chunks of bloody skull fragments and brain matter, the same color of the pizza sauce, scattered over and dripping down the wall.

"True." Grace's eyes raced back and forth over the document, like a typewriter, scanning left to right. "So, it looks like the ambulance attendant declared it a DOA."

"Makes sense. Dead on arrival . . . but where was the bullet? That will be the most telling part of the puzzle."

Grace already knew the bullet was in the boy's chest but she had to fake like she was discovering it in the file. She sorted through the papers until she found a few photos affixed to the folder with a paperclip. In a square black-and-white photo was a picture of Timmy, facedown on the ground, the back left side of his shirt stained with blood. It only took Grace a few seconds of analyzing the photo to know something was wrong. In her vision, the boy is on his back, face up on the grass, which would be the natural way to fall if he was struck by a bullet while sitting upright on the swing. "The body was moved," Grace said, under her breath.

"What?"

"Nothing, sorry . . . just talking to myself."

"Whatcha got there?"

Grace turned the photo around so Barb could see it right side up.

"Damn, you weren't joking. He was so little."

"Exactly . . . so don't you think . . . that being so little, he would've been pummeled by the shot in the chest and landed on his back?"

"Depends if he died instantly, I suppose."

"According to Mrs. Walsh's statement, he did die instantly. See here . . ." Grace slid the first document she read over to Barb. In the handwriting matching the rest of Officer Sullivan's scrawl, the statement said Mrs. Walsh heard the gunshot and came outside to see Timmy lying on the ground. She immediately ran over to him and took his pulse."

"Which wasn't there."

"Allegedly," Grace said, as she continued scanning the rest of the documents.

"What about the brother?"

"Hmmm . . . let's see . . . he was only eight at the time according to Betts.

Grace's eyes captured the name John Walsh, again in messy scrawl, surrounded by limited notes. "It says . . . older brother, John Walsh, said he discovered his brother lying in the back yard after he heard a shot. He saw the gun in the boy's hand, then went to get his mother." In parentheses was a brief description of the pistol. *Walther PPK.* "A James Bond gun," Grace said, under her breath, knowing how big Bond was back in the day.

She thought about the sleek pistol used in all the movies, a fancy accessory for only the most elite. Only wealthy businessmen could afford this type of gun. Grace held the paper close to her face, trying to decipher the tiny print beside the lined paper. *Boy would only talk to mother. Refused to talk to police, mute.*

After Grace re-read Officer Sullivan's notes aloud, Barb reciprocated with an eye roll while releasing her pent up breath through vibrating lips, blowing the smell of breakfast meats in Grace's direction. "That's bullshit. If you were the boy's mother, wouldn't you force your kid to make a statement?"

"Maybe she was concerned that the boy was already scarred from finding his baby brother dead on the ground."

"You mean that whole mama bear protection thing neither one of us know anything about 'cause we don't got kids?" Whenever Barb got frustrated or annoyed, her grammar got shoddy. She went from being able to recite poetry with fluidity to sounding like she couldn't properly craft a coherent sentence. A red and silver strand of hair sprouted from her head as she spoke, bouncing up and down along with her frustration.

"Yeah, exactly."

"Why would Timmy still be holding the gun if he accidentally shot himself? Don't you think the gun would've fallen from his hand?" Barb asked.

Grace raised her eyebrows and nodded her head. "Yep, my thoughts exactly. Sounds more like the gun was staged. What else? Is there anything else that gives us major holes in this case?" Grace had already filled Barb in on what Betts said. The response time, the odd behavior of both the maid and John; although those could be completely due to the situation at hand. While Grace had never quite witnessed any type of shooting involving a five-year-old kid, she imagined it would be hard to take in.

Grace flipped through the haphazard documents and let out a frustrated response. "Why is there no write up about the angle of the shot? Isn't that a necessary part of a police report of this magnitude?"

"Yeah, but remember . . . they did shady things back then."

"Yeah, but this isn't the mob in New York City we're dealing with . . . this was a well-known, highly respected, wealthy family."

"Grace McKenna, I think you just said the magic words."

Grace looked up at Barb and everything clicked into place.

CHAPTER ELEVEN

"But why would they make up a story that Timmy shot himself?" Mark asked, as he folded one of Grace's T-shirts and placed it gently on the bed. Grace paused a moment to look at him in admiration. The man never stopped contributing; whether it was to his clients, their income, or to Grace herself. She sat on the bed, with the file open before her, surrounded by a sea of still-warm dried clothes on one side of her and piles of neatly folded garments on the other side. The smell of freshly laundered clothes making her feel more at home, already, in the new house.

"Maybe they were trying to hide something." While Grace had accomplished a lot since she got her hands on the files, there were still many pieces of the puzzle missing. The only thing she concluded was maybe John had snapped in a rage of jealousy. "Maybe John couldn't stand the fact that his younger brother was getting more attention from the mother? Think about it . . . he has a twin sister who is the only girl in the family. From what Betts said, Susan got whatever she wanted. And then there was Timmy who was the baby of the family . . . likely doted on by everyone. Maybe John was the outcast . . . the black sheep of the family."

"I'm the black sheep of my family and you don't see me shooting anyone." Mark was the product of his mom's first boyfriend, much older than his younger siblings and often used as a babysitter while his mother and stepfather worked and spent time socializing. While he didn't share stories of his past with Grace very often, he did mention that he never felt like he fit in with his family; with the exception of his younger sister Rain, whom he practically raised. His mother was a hippy and lived moment to moment, whereas Mark had always had to shoulder responsibility, making him a natural caretaker and someone who could be counted on whether it was in his career, or in their relationship. Grace thought of how Mark was a stickler for time management, never arriving anywhere a minute late and having his schedule planned out a month in advance. The man never missed an appointment and had once mentioned to Grace that he strived to be opposite of his upbringing.

"True."

"Here's a question for you." Mark shook out a pair of his tangled jeans with one breeze-inducing flick, the stiff denim snapping like a whip.

"What's that?" Grace blinked from the sudden rush of air.

"In your vision . . . isn't the boy on the swing set?"

"Yeah, he's on the tandem swing."

"Alright . . . so if he was seated on the swing and facing his shooter, then his body would've likely landed face up, due to the force of the bullet in his little body throwing him backward."

"That's very possible." Grace nodded following along.

"So, why is the body face down in the photos?"

"That's the question of the day." Grace's expression reflected *bingo*.

"My guess is that they . . . someone, tampered with the body . . . to make it look like he accidentally shot himself." Mark pulled a pair of Grace's underwear from the laundry basket, carefully folding it into a perfect square, something she never took the time to do. "But, any smart cop would pick up on what we just deciphered in two minutes, so why isn't there any mention of this in the file?"

"Because they were trying to cover something up . . . I just don't know what exactly they were trying to cover up yet."

"Well, we know that John pulled the trigger . . . maybe they were trying to protect him?"

"He was a minor, though. And wouldn't the mother be so furious that her one son shot her other son? . . . I don't know, if that were me . . . I'd probably tell the cops to take John away," Grace said, as she silently tried to picture herself in that situation. She imagined what it would be like to have two children pitted against one another to the point that one gets murdered by the other. "Although . . . maybe it was more about their reputation. Barb mentioned the whole high society reputation families of wealth had to uphold back in those days."

"Yeah, it was all about how things appeared on the outside back then . . . kinda like how people use Facebook in today's world. Everyone puts their glossy, picture perfect photos on their Facebook pages and hide all the real stuff that goes on behind closed doors." Mark moved around the bed, collecting a folded pile of clothes and making his way to one of the dressers they shared.

"That's a lot of work to always have to cover things up."

"It's kinda like keepin' up with the Joneses," Mark said, as he opened the top drawer and put away Grace's stack of freshly folded sports bras.

"Ugh, that sounds terrible. I'm glad we don't associate with our neighbors." Grace rolled her eyes.

"Um . . . yet." A wave of guilt washed over Mark's face. "I may have invited the Clarks over for drinks and apps tomorrow night."

Grace's chin jerked upward, shooting a glare in his direction. "No you didn't." She had strict rules about befriending the neighbors for two reasons. One was the fact she couldn't risk seeing into the eyes of a neighbor who was a criminal and the other was the result of her mother's neighbor friendship that had gone wrong. Ellen had become friends with a woman who lived next door to one of the many apartments they rented while Grace was growing up. The woman ended up being a leech, spending countless hours at their house and was even caught stealing from them. "You know how I feel about getting cozy with the neighbors and too quickly."

"The Clarks are harmless. And they are too wrapped up in their new baby to get too cozy with us."

"Baby? You invited a baby over?"

"Well, it kinda goes with the territory . . . I couldn't say, sorry but my wife doesn't like babies . . ." The two of them stopped. Grace looked up from her files again, locking eyes with Mark who was currently three shades of red. "I mean . . . girlfriend. Girlfriend, sorry."

Speechless, Grace stared at him. All it took was one word for her to be transformed into a world of possibilities. With the word wife, came a forever future with the man she loved madly. But, still, she was filled with an odd feeling, having never pictured herself as a wife of someone. "Freudian slip . . . that's okay." She looked back to her files, covering up the sheepish smile threatening to escape.

Mark turned toward Grace, walked toward the bed, and stood over her. He leaned down and pulled her head toward his lips, leaving a kiss on her forehead.

"So, when do the neighbors arrive with their baby?"

"Well, Peyton goes to sleep around six thirty so I said around four."

"Ohhh . . . I just remembered I'm working a double tomorrow night!" Grace faked upset. "I guess I'll have to miss it. Darn." She snapped her fingers for effect.

"Yeah, okay. You haven't worked a double since I met you."

"Not paid at least." Grace thought about the many times when she worked well into the night and made appearances at the station on weekends, her undying dedication to the job leaving a mark on her everyday life.

"I promise it will be painless."

"Babies go to bed that early? And you know the name of it?"

"It is a she . . . and yes, I even held her."

"When did all this happen?"

"On Saturday when you were hanging out with Barb in the library."

"You hold babies?"

"Are you forgetting that I had three younger siblings I practically raised single-handedly."

"That's right . . . exactly why you don't want kids of your own."

"I never said that."

"Oh . . . I must've assumed that." Grace directed her focus back on the files spread out before her, the papers yellowed along the edges, showing the age of the documents.

"And look at the bright side . . . I think the Clarks inherited the house from a relative."

"Why's that a bright side?" Grace only saw question marks dancing through her head, before a lightbulb went on. "Ohhh . . . they might have connections to the Walshes."

"They might. I think they inherited the house from an aunt or a grandparent."

* * *

Grace hugged a bottle of wine against her body as she pulled the front door open. It had been a long day at the station, dealing with routine visits to the schools to update masses of students on the bullying policy and caution them about the growing threat of social media predators. The last thing she wanted to do was socialize with the neighbors, but there may be a silver lining in tonight's visit. If Grace could get them to divulge any information on their relatives, the old owners of the house next door, then she may have another witness to draw answers from. She'd have to be sly about it, but she was used to putting on a performance by now, with her sidekick Mark by her side.

"I made it," Grace said, as she set the bottle on the countertop, after being intercepted by Brody who was demanding ear rubs. Mark was in full host mode, wearing an apron that said *The Grill Master, the man the myth, the legend.* The apron was a gift from Grace, which she later learned did not mesh with who he was. In an awkward Christmas gift exchange, after only dating two months, Grace found herself at a department store struggling to come up with a selection of gifts that didn't make her look like she was trying too hard. In the process she came up with a clichéd apron that was very much outside of Mark's personality. Not being a quintessential *grill guy*, the apron was even less fitting than the mug she got him that read *I may be wrong but it's highly unlikely.* Mark was far from cocky and he technically didn't even know how to start a grill. Grace knew this because months after Mark faked his love for the apron, he struggled with starting the grill during their first cookout. The poor gift choices were less about Grace not knowing Mark well and more about her desire to appear as if she wasn't a pushy girlfriend, with overly sentimental gifts. Both the mug and the apron were used frequently now as a private joke between the two of them.

Several cutting boards with a variety of sliced up vegetables were spread across the island. "I thought you said this was a little social hour not a three-course meal," Grace said, as she made her way to the closet at the backside of the kitchen, dumping her work bag on the floor beside a basket of shoes.

"It's just a few veggie appetizers." Mark spun around and tossed the top of a bell pepper into the sink, before he went to work transferring hummus from a store bought container into a small bowl Ellen had made them in one of her pottery classes. Even though she didn't remember her own daughter, Ellen McKenna would forever be present in their house, with the many crafts she left behind.

"Do you know for certain these people are even into vegetables?" Grace sat on a bar stool and plucked a sliced pepper from the tray. She tossed it in her mouth and let out a few loud crunches. "You know . . . some people actually prefer meat."

"For your information *these people* have names. Scott and Emily, thank you very much. And Mel and I had a conversation about how her life has changed dramatically since she became a vegetarian."

Grace rolled her eyes. "Great, another one."

"Yeah and you're gonna be outnumbered because Scott's on the vegetarian bandwagon too."

Just as Grace was about to engage in a meat versus vegetable battle, the door knocker sounded three times. Mark looked at Grace, jerking his chin in the direction of the door, suggesting that she answer it.

Reluctantly, Grace pushed herself up from the stool and ambled toward the front entrance. Through the glass paneling at the top of the door she could see two blonde heads. She pulled the door open and was greeted with near-matching megawatt smiles and two synchronized hellos and name introductions.

"Hi, I'm Grace . . . come on in." Grace pulled the door open farther, backing up slightly so the two could file in. A bundle protruded from Emily's chest. Grace could make out a tiny little body underneath the pale pink material wrapped around Emily like another layer of clothing.

"Oh sorry, almost forgot to introduce you to Peyton," Emily said, clearly catching Grace's curious scan of what appeared to be an extension of her body, an additional limb that needed introduction. A tuft of fine blonde hair peeked out the top of the wrap, and Grace could make out a slice of pink forehead.

"She's so tiny . . . how old is she?" Grace inquired. The bundle was so small, Grace questioned whether Emily had just walked out of the hospital.

"She just turned three months," Emily said, as a smile grew wide across her face. Grace knew nothing about babies but the amount of glee new moms expressed was never lost on her. While she had never really fantasized about being a mother, she had to admit she was curious about the perceptible happiness and adoration that new mothers passed onto their babies.

"Wow, this kitchen is gorgeous," Emily said, in a heightened whisper as she walked airily into the room.

"Hey, guys, thanks for coming." Mark wiped his hands on the front of his apron, stepped to the side of the counter, and reached out to shake Scott's hand, then Emily's. Grace watched as he tilted his head toward Emily, taking in the baby bundle attached to her, as he shook her hand.

"So far this little girl sleeps through everything, including Scott's snoring," Emily joked. "But enough about the baby, I want to hear more about this kitchen . . . it's absolutely stunning."

"Well, apparently the guy who lived here before us had it updated. Can't say that about the rest of the house though . . . so I'm guessing he was an aspiring chef maybe?" Mark's words fell together in the tone of a question.

"John Walsh . . . that's surprising." Emily responded.

"Really? Did you know him?" Grace jumped in, eager to get more from her new neighbor.

"Well, I didn't know him personally." Emily was swaying side to side as Grace's eyes rocked along with her. She paused. "Sorry, ever since we've had Peyton I've had the habit of rocking side to side . . . even when I'm not holding her." Emily smiled. "My grandparents lived next door from the time they were married . . . gosh I think they were only like twenty . . . you know how people got married young back then."

Grace nodded, silently urging her to continue.

"But anyway, from what they say, John was a quiet man and an odd duck. I don't think he exchanged more than two words with them the entire time he lived here. I'm assuming you guys know about his brother's accident."

"Timmy." The words came out of Grace's lips in an accidental whisper.

"Yeah, I think that was his name. Well, according to my grandparents, he was scarred for life after seeing his brother die in front of him. He never had any friends over, he went to work, came home, went inside."

"So, one of your parents grew up in the house next door then."

"Yep, my mother. She wasn't John Walsh's biggest fan. And anytime we came over to visit my grandmother when we were kids, it's like she would shield us from him. As she put it, 'he was creepy.'" Emily threw up a pair of air quotes. "But my mother is a bit paranoid about weird stuff, so who knows."

"She's not lying about that." Scott laughed, showcasing a smile that was a flash of white, void of any imperfections from what Grace could tell.

Mark used the bottle opener, on the side of the island, and popped off the top of a light beer, before handing it to Scott. "Thank you . . . much needed, my friend." He tilted his head back and took one giant gulp.

"Emily, can I get you anything?" Mark asked. "Wine, water, beer, Gatorade –"

"I'd love a glass of red wine if you have it." *A girl after my own heart* Grace thought to herself. "And yes, my mother can be a handful, but I don't think Scott will be complaining when she starts babysitting for us so we can go on dates again." Emily elbowed her husband.

"That's nice to have a babysitter so accessible," Mark said, as he poured two glasses of Cabernet into stemless glasses Grace plucked from the side of the island.

"It is . . . and it will give her something to do to take her mind off my dad. Kind of a win-win."

An awkward silence fell between the four of them, simmering in the air before Scott broke the ice. "Em's dad passed away a few months ago."

"I'm so sorry, gosh . . . that must be tough on everyone," Grace said, as she took a dainty sip of wine.

"Yeah, it's been tough, but Peyton has given us a ray of sunshine through all of this. Between getting pregnant unexpectedly and my dad passing, the last few months have been a whirlwind to say the least."

Grace looked at Emily, naturally wanting to hear more about her surprise pregnancy. Taking the cue, Emily continued. "Yeah, Peyton here wasn't planned, but sometimes the best things in life are surprises."

"If you asked us a year ago about kids, we would've scoffed at you . . . neither one of us wanted children, we were content with our careers and our weekend getaways," Scott interjected.

"And being forty, I really didn't think it was ever in the cards . . . but little Peyton here had other plans." She gently rubbed the pink fabric and Peyton's head shifted from right to left, her bum pushing outward as she made the movement.

"You're forty? I would've never guessed that," Grace said, genuinely shocked Emily was over thirty. Her skin failed to show any signs of age, free from the crow's feet starting to take up residence on her own face.

"Thank you. But since I had this baby, I feel like I'm approaching seventy. It's no joke when they say that you don't sleep." Emily took a sip of wine, swished it around in her mouth before swallowing. "This is good stuff."

Grace had always wondered how new parents survived on such interrupted sleep and the thought scared her away from ever fantasizing about a baby of her own.

"It must be kind of strange for your mom to babysit in the house she grew up in, huh?" Grace asked, as Mark and Scott were starting up a side conversation about fitness equipment, a topic that could keep Mark busy for hours. She saw them move into the living room out of the corner of her eye, next stop would surely be the basement to take a tour of Mark's vintage equipment.

"Yeah, she still avoids even making eye contact with your house, but don't worry I'll put in a good word for you." Emily winked. "She's going to have to get used to it sooner or later, she'll be here a lot once I go back to work."

"Oh, where do you work?"

"I practice law at Becker and Heaton . . . a firm in the city."

"I've heard of them . . . they have quite the solid reputation around here." Grace tried to hide her surprise learning Emily was a lawyer. *Beautiful and smart.*

"And Mark told me you're a detective." Emily scanned Grace from head to toe in a way that was less threatening and more of an applaud to a fellow female. "That's pretty darn impressive."

"Eh, it's a small town . . . I don't see a whole lot of action around here." Grace lied. She had more action than she could handle. Just standing in her own kitchen could cause her to drum up visions of little Timmy on the day that he died, memories of the eye contact she made with John Walsh searing into her.

"Well, evidently back in the fifties they had a lot more action around here, huh?"

"You can say that. Speaking of that, was your mom actually next door the day of the murder . . . I mean accident?"

"It's funny you just stumbled on those words because my mother was never quite convinced that it was an accident." Emily kissed the

125

top of Peyton's head, maintaining eye contact with Grace. "She was home that day, if that's what you're asking. In fact, she'll tell you exactly what she was doing when she heard the shot go off." Emily tilted her head and made a high-pitched sound with her voice. "I was playing marbles with your aunt Lizzy in the back yard and I thought it was firecrackers going off."

"So she was close enough to be a witness."

"Not necessarily, since she only saw the aftermath. I've heard the story a million times. After she and her sister argued over who got what marble, they heard commotion on the other side of the fence." Grace remembered seeing a modern white fence wrapped around the neighboring yard.

"They must've had a different fence back then."

"Oh yeah, it was some old fence . . . my grandmother had the new one put up a few years back when she fell deeper into her paranoia. She, along with my mother, was convinced John Walsh was watching her." Emily paused, letting out a gaping yawn. "Sorry . . . the whole lack of sleep thing. Anyway, I have no idea what a sixty- or seventy-something-year-old man would want with a ninety-four-year-old woman . . . I mean . . . if he was a so-called creeper, I think he'd choose to creep on younger chicks." She took another sip of wine then reached for a sliced pepper. She dipped it into the bowl of hummus and popped it in her mouth in a manner somehow graceful. Even in the middle of chewing, Emily's face was beautiful. Her full mouth contorting and moving in all directions, making her shapely pink lips stand out even more, her perfectly symmetrical face falling back into place as she swallowed. "Full disclosure, I peeked into your back yard from our upstairs window and I couldn't help but notice that old swing set was still there. Don't you think he would've gotten rid of it by now. I mean, look at what he did with this kitchen." Emily looked around awestruck once again by the magnificent lighting, every appliance and cosmetic update carefully selected. "I guess I just never pictured him dishing up a four-course meal so I'm surprised he'd have all the fixins." She smoothed a hand over the countertop and analyzed the vast six-burner cooktop. "And look at this pantry." She danced into the open door of the room pivoting her body every which way to show appreciation for the multiple levels of shelfing. Just as she turned to emerge from the pantry, Grace saw Peyton's wiggling body coming to life accompanied by a series of soft coos and gentle moans. "Looks like the little lady is awake . . . Scott honey, can you bring me the bottle?"

Within seconds Scott was back in the kitchen producing a baby bottle. "At your service." Emily efficiently unwrapped Peyton from the pink material, revealing her tiny little body dressed in a simple white onesie. As if suddenly invited into the room, Brody came from his spot by the door, curious about the new baby smells. Mark trailed behind, catching up to the big dog and grabbing his collar.

"Thank you, honey."

"I'll take her." Scott held his hands out as if he were about to receive a football. His arms had the muscular tone Mark's did, but the same golden glow Emily's skin tone retained. "Hey, my little princess." Scott's arms created a natural cradle for the baby and his voiced lowered to a soothing lullaby.

"She's beautiful," Mark said, still clutching Brody as he watched on, mesmerized by the tiny human. "I think Brody thinks she's beautiful too." Mark pulled Brody back as he tried to get closer to Scott, curiosity evident in his wagging tail.

"Well, what do you say, Brody, do you want to be the first doggie to meet Peyton?" Emily kneeled down to Brody so she was eye level with him. She held his head between her two hands and gave him a kiss on the snout, winning over both Brody and Grace. Anyone who loved her dog was a potential friend in her book. "Scott, why don't you sit on the couch and let Brody have a sniff. My uncle had this breed and I was surrounded by them growing up. In fact, a Newfoundland was at the top of my list when we were discussing dogs. Unfortunately, Scott here would prefer a Pomeranian, so I guess I'll have to meet in the middle with a Labrador or something, if we ever go down the dog road.

"Actually, Mark, do you want to do the honors?" Scott turned toward Mark, presenting the suckling baby to him.

"Sure, I'd love to." Mark received Peyton and made his way to the couch, gracefully sinking into the cushion. Grace took over Brody's collar and marched the dog over to where he was sitting. With his big beefy snout, Brody provided gentle kisses and left a dollop of drool on Peyton's blonde head.

"Oh my gosh, I'm so sorry." Grace panicked, not knowing what type of people Scott and Emily were.

"We are not neat freaks and, contrary to what my mom believes, we think that germs actually build up the immune system, so kiss away, Brody," Emily said, as she continued to sway side to side as if she were rocking her wine glass to sleep.

Grace found it difficult to take her eyes off the picture before her. Mark, completely content, holding a brand new baby, looking at it in awe as if it were his own. They had never talked about marriage, let alone children, but what if these two life junctures were the natural next step. As if he heard her thoughts he looked up, connecting eye contact with Grace, two thoughts mashing together and pushing their relationship along in a new direction. "Well, I hate to give up this sweet little bundle, but I better put the appetizer in the oven . . . Grace, do you want to hold her?" He asked, a test that only she picked up on. Mark was always the one pushing Grace to think outside the box, to shift her ways for the better. And right now he was presenting her with the opportunity to see what it felt like to hold a baby, to feel how precious life really was.

Grace's eyes darted in all directions, her gaze landing on Emily. "Oh no that's okay . . . I . . ." She was torn between her response. Frightened at the prospect of holding something fragile yet she didn't want to offend Scott and Emily. *Did parents get offended when you didn't hold their baby?*

"Fun fact guys . . . Grace has never held a baby, and she is afraid of breaking them," Mark said, as he rose from the couch, ready to pass the baby over to someone.

"It's true . . . I've literally never held a baby."

"Well, there's no time like the present, you want to give it a try?" Emily asked.

"Okay, but if she starts screaming—"

"She's not gonna scream," Emily said, already confident in the ways of her young baby.

Grace sat on the couch, and opened her arms, awkwardly extending them straight out in front of her. Mark leaned down, readying himself to pass Peyton along, while maintaining a handle on the bottle she was still fiercely suckling on. "Just make a cradle with your arms and I'll drop her right in," Mark said, as he settled Peyton in her arms. As if alerted to the fact that Grace was a first timer, Peyton's eyes shifted and locked onto hers. Her eyes, two pools of dark blue sea, moved around Grace's face, assessing her. And in that moment, Grace felt the fragility of life. She was holding a brand new baby, a fresh slate that would undoubtedly be tattooed by the world in some way or another. Grace had been used to looking into the eyes of criminals and being corrupted by the visions that passed from them to her, and now, here she was, holding a baby whose innocent eyes hadn't yet experienced hate, pain, suffering, or heartbreak. Peyton was a fresh slate, ready to be marked up, but until then, Grace couldn't help but feel solace in the clear, curious eyes.

CHAPTER TWELVE

June 1

After Grace found herself going through the motions of addressing a group of young students about summer safety, she sat in front of her computer waiting for it to wake up. As soon as the screen came to life, an alert popped up in the top right corner: *1:00 Susan Jacobi Talk at library.* The days had flown by and she had completely forgotten about the talk Susan was scheduled to host at the library. She knew Sully had finally been in touch with her, after she claimed she needed a few days to decompress and enjoy her grandchildren in Rhode Island, but Grace's guard was still up. Knowing how sensitive Sully could be on the inside, she didn't want anyone taking advantage of his heart. The man was like a father to her.

The thought of father figures reminded Grace she needed to schedule a time to meet her biological father at the assisted living home, to sign some paperwork for her mother's around-the-clock care. The two of them had come to a mutual agreement that Ellen was at the point of needing the additional care, and, as hard as it was to admit, Grace was glad she had someone else to help her navigate through such difficult decisions. If her mother was in her right mind, she would protest this high-cost care with all her power, but she had gone from bouts of anger and spurts of lucidity to practically catatonic, confined to a mind that was no longer attached to the life that she lived. With that came the need for assistance, for someone to make sure she ate, bathed, and moved from one piece of furniture to the next, depending on the time of day. It was beyond depressing for Grace. Like trudging through molasses, her emotions were stationary, a deep dark hole of nothingness.

Focusing on the Timmy Walsh case would help her escape the blackness of her mother's condition and offer a welcome distraction. As ironic as it sounded, solving mysteries was what brought Grace joy, even if that joy was the result of one person's tragic moment. While moving at a slower pace than normal, she had to celebrate the fact that she had made some movement on the case. So far, with the research she'd done, she discovered a few strong facts from promising sources.

According to Betts Sullivan and the police report there was an abnormally long length of time from when the gun was fired and the ambulance raced up the street. Betts also shared some information on the maid, Karina, and how she was over-the-top upset to the point that it seemed like she was putting on an act. Was she guilty of something in this bizarre family tragedy?

The police report also alluded to a mute John Walsh. And according to what Grace knew about gunshots, if Timmy Walsh was seated on the far side of a tandem swing, as he was in her vision, then why was his body face down? Surely the force of the weapon on such a small body would cause him to fall backward off the swing . . . unless the body was moved during the unnecessarily long period of time between the shot and the ambulance's arrival.

Her visions also brought a flash of green shattered glass, which was something she would have to examine during one of her case binge sessions. The wild card would be the father. While Mr. Walsh was seen in the family photos and society pages, he always appeared to be in the background, as if he were an understudy in the play of Mrs. Walsh's life. Maybe he just wanted to be behind the scenes and let his wife have the spotlight, or maybe he was there that day but made a run for it when the boy was shot. Seldom is there any mention of the man, but that very well could be because he was traveling the majority of the time. And then there was the most recent news she discovered about Emily's mother and grandmother always thinking John Walsh was odd. Grace questioned whether she would think the man was odd if she didn't have the visions of him shooting a weapon. She had to admit he was overly introverted, with darting eyes that rarely settled in place. And where was Susan Jacobi that day? In just a few minutes, Grace would hopefully learn a thing or two about the mystery woman.

* * *

By the time Grace got to the library, there was a gaggle of women encircling Susan, who appeared to be in her element. She would jump from one engaging gesture to the next, making sure to play the role of good listener. With arms crossed she looked intently into the eyes of one woman who was talking animatedly, and then she tipped her head back and laughed on cue, as all the other women joined in. From the outside, Susan Jacobi looked like any career-driven woman who was passionate about her craft. The inside may be an entirely different story.

Grace looked down at her watch. It was three minutes before the talk was scheduled to begin, not enough time to get information out of the woman, and at this point it looked like she would have to bulldoze her way through the circle surrounding Susan. Opting for the less obvious approach, Grace slipped into a chair in the last row. She spent the next three minutes gauging her surroundings and assessing the women who appeared to be Susan's followers. Like little minions, the women obediently sat down, filling all the seats except one, as soon as Susan stepped up to the podium. Even from the back of the room, Grace picked up on the tipped up gazes that landed on the speaker, the silent anticipation of the room, all poised and ready to absorb the information the woman had to offer.

As Susan talked about the family dynamic, Grace couldn't help but think of her own situation. Since Mark had been in her life, she lowered some of the defenses she had built around herself and felt like a better person. And then came the thoughts about her mother and biological father. It was inevitable Ellen wouldn't be around forever, but her father's shining health may give her a long future with him. Should she open up more and let him in her life? Grace pictured future holidays with Mark and her dad. What kind of guy was he? Did he prefer white meat or dark meat of a Thanksgiving turkey? Did he prefer cake over pie, like she did? These were all little facts children naturally knew about their parents, morsels of knowledge that made family members belong to one another. Grace's mind was drifting off in a direction far away from Susan's talk about marital relationships and bettering your presence with children. Before she knew it Susan was stepping away from the podium and heading to the table of coffee and refreshments. Grace popped up from her chair and raced across the room, in an attempt to beat Susan's fan club.

With a little more force than necessary, Grace cut in front of a woman who was standing behind Susan. Just as the woman readied her hand to tap Susan on the shoulder, likely inquiring about her own marriage, Grace inserted herself between the two bodies, not missing the incredibly loud forced sigh erupting from the annoyed woman's mouth.

"Hi, Susan." Grace leaned forward, craning her neck just enough so she could be seen.

"Oh, hi . . . Grace. You worked with Joe, right?" Susan turned, planting her gaze on Grace's and saturating her with a series of visions. An older woman gasping for air, her eyes wide with terror before they closed into two pools of wrinkles, the thin folds creating gentle ripples on her face. Tears trickled down her hollow cheeks and sagging skin, before landing on a white thermal blanket pulled flush to her chin.

"Yes . . . yes . . . sorry you caught me off guard when you said Joe." Grace stumbled, before catching herself from a mental fall. "I'm so used to calling him Sully."

"It's good to see you again, Grace." Susan started to turn away, putting her work face on for the next woman in line.

Grace's mind scrambled with ideas for how to divert Susan and keep her in conversation. "Hey, by the way . . . how was Rhode Island?" The question came out fast and more aggressive than she intended. Susan turned back again, a question evident in her crumpled eyebrows. "Sully mentioned you were visiting your son and grandkids in Rhode Island."

A wave of realization passed over Susan's face, causing her to catch up to speed on Grace's question. "Oh, yes . . . yes . . . I was visiting my son Timmy and the grandbabies." She paused, looking over Grace's shoulder for an escape. "You know how it is with little ones . . . busy, busy." Her eyes skittered around the room, avoiding eye contact with Grace.

"Yeah, it's funny you say that because I am learning about kids . . . we just met our neighbors and they have a brand new baby . . . I'm pretty sure they don't get a whole lot of sleep." Grace continued rambling, unaware of what she was saying. "My boyfriend and I recently bought a house and we've been talking about filling it up with a bunch of kids . . . we actually bought one of the oldest houses in town . . . you ever been on Court Street?" Like pushing coins into a vending machine, Grace wasn't stopping until she got what she wanted.

Susan dropped her head; apparently scanning the linoleum tiles on the floor. "I have . . . I actually grew up there. I grew up in the house you bought, Grace. Thirteen Court Street."

Grace nearly fell backward, in her dramatic overacting. "You did!?" she asked, excitement spreading her eyes wide, an exaggerated smile lighting up her face.

"Yep." Susan let the word out like a deflated balloon. "I'd love to chat with you, Grace, but it would be rude of me not to converse with those who came to hear me talk." Her words were less than friendly and borderline offensive, made from a mouth pursed together as she gave Grace one last bout of eye contact before turning on a heel and putting on a charming persona for her fans. One last vision brought Grace an image of the old woman, shaking her head left to right as if protesting vehemently. Her lips parted before her mouth fell slack and her head sunk deep into the white pillow behind her head.

* * *

As Grace pressed the gas pedal and made her way up Court Street's steep incline, she turned her head to the old staircase that connected with the neighboring street below; the staircase Betts fled to after she heard the gunshot that August day. If only she could transcend time and go back and sit beside Betts as she counted the minutes before the ambulance arrived. For the first time, Grace looked around her new street and took in all the beautiful houses with front doors and windows now open because it was June, when the weather made a turn for the better. The majority of front yards on Court Street confirmed that it was a neighborhood filled with children. Bikes carelessly dumped across lawns and driveways, strollers of various sizes, and plastic play structures and toys strewn about in front and side yards to Grace's left and right. Neon plastic driveway guards stood at attention, holding red flags that blew in the breeze, stationed at the end of properties, urging drivers to go slow because children were at play.

Once she reached the top of the street, she pulled into her driveway and exhaled a sigh of relief. It took a while for her to feel like this was home but she finally felt like she and Mark belonged here, even though the house had ghosts that she was hoping to put to rest. One day she hoped she'd be able to look at the swing set in the back yard and feel that Timmy Walsh had received justice. Twisting the keys out of the ignition, she was alerted to the sound of a drill, sending a bolt of discomfort across her temples. "Geez . . . could that be any louder?" she said to herself as she emerged from the Jeep, pulling her bag across the front seats and hoisting it on her shoulder. As she walked closer to the front door, the sound grew louder and she realized it was coming from the back yard. Diverting her route, she walked around the side of the house until she was standing in front of a somewhat comical scene. With Scott by his side guiding him, Mark's arms vibrated as his two hands gripped the handles of a gas-powered earth auger at his waist. His eyes intent on the motion of the red drill spiraling in and out of the dead lawn, transforming portions of their grass into piles of dirt.

"Just like that, hold it firm." Scott hunched over on bent knees as if he were coaching a kid on the rules of football. Both men were so caught up in the moment that they didn't see Grace standing there. She adjusted her stance and let out a cough but was overpowered by the drilling sound of the contraption. *What on earth are these two up to?* Scott was the first to notice her.

"Release the gas!" Scott shouted as he waved a hand in front of Mark, still hunched over, followed by a gesture to *cut it*, once he looked up. Mark pushed the rocker switch to the off position. He wiped his forehead with the back of a dirty hand as he looked around, completely removed from the trance of where he had been. "You're getting the hang of it." Scott gave him a pat on his sweaty back.

"This thing is fun," Mark said, as he released his grip after stabbing it into one of the holes to make it stand upright. Mark reached into his back pocket and retrieved a small bottle of water. He took a long swig as Grace stood clutching the strap of her bag with two hands, her eyebrows raised in question.

"Oh . . . hi, honey . . . how was work?" Mark asked, as he walked toward Grace in a pair of tan work boots she had never seen before.

"How is work?" Grace asked, lifting her eyebrows even further. "How about you tell me how our lawn is doing."

"Oh, this? Well, since our lawn is completely dead anyway, I figured I'd dig a few holes and add some perennials . . . you know . . . to jazz it up a bit."

"Do you even know what perennials are?" Grace asked, trying her best to maintain a serious look.

Mark pursed his lips together. "Nope, can't say that I do . . . but our trusty neighbor, Scott here, does."

"Talk about putting me on the spot, bro." Scott stood at attention like a soldier and scratched at his eyebrow with a couple fingers, a nervous reaction. "Okay, okay, you can blame this all on me. I provided the tools and made a few suggestions to Mark, but I promise you I won't let him get out of hand with the holes."

"Well, like you said . . . our yard is a disaster anyway. Between this ancient, creepy swing set and all this crabgrass, there isn't much that can make it look worse. So, have at it . . . perennial it up."

"Dang, bro . . . gotta say . . . that's not the reaction I was expecting." Scott bent down and picked something up off the ground.

"Grace is cool," Mark said, as if he were a teenager talking about his hip mom.

Grace's eyes swung over to Scott's hand. Whatever he picked up was now pinched between two fingers. Grace stepped closer to him as he mindlessly started rubbing the material between his fingers. "What is that?" She pointed to the green glass he was massaging.

"I don't know . . . an old piece of glass the drill must've pulled up from the earth."

Mark stood beside Grace, cued into her heightened alertness.

"Wait, this came up from the ground?"

"Yeah . . . along with like twenty other pieces over there." Mark pointed to one of the dirt piles, shaped like a giant ant colony, with pieces of green glass of all varying sizes and shapes.

"Oh my God!" Forgetting to hide her odd excitement over the discovery, Grace marched to the pile, letting her bag slide from her shoulder to the ground. She started gathering all the pieces she could find. Shards of varying sizes, some with jagged points and others with curved edges. One similar to the shape of Massachusetts and another was a perfect triangle. *The shattered green glass from my vision!*

Scott and Mark stood over her, swapping sideways glances as they questioned her next move. She gingerly gathered all the glass pieces she could find with one hand and placed them delicately in the palm of the other. Without looking at the two men and leaving her bag on the grass, she headed to the sunroom door. When they first looked at this house, Grace imagined this room would be the one she'd spend the most time in, but it served only as the occasional route to access the back yard and back inside. The floor talked backed to her in cracks and squeaks as she stepped on its uneven boards. She barreled through the door leading to the living room and made a beeline for the cigar box. For some reason she kept putting it back where they found it, afraid if she kept it out a million ghosts would emerge from the photos and haunt her long after she solved the case.

"Thanks, I'll get this back to you as soon as I finish up . . . yeah, that sounds great . . . thanks, Scott." Mark's muffled voice came from the front of the house, where Grace could hear from the second story turret window, followed by a gentle click of the door closing behind him. "Grace?" His voice rang out, accompanied by footfalls as he ascended the stairs in search of her. He found her kneeling beside the bench seat. "What's going on? Why the excitement over the glass?"

Revved up with the latest clue, Grace asked, "Remember when I told you about the vision of the green glass raining down and the flash of something round and red?"

"Vaguely? Was that the first time you met John?"

"No, I think it was when I went to his house to return his mail . . . I'm not sure. All the visions are starting to blend together. Anyway, this has to be that green glass!" Grace held up a piece of glass, as Mark crouched closer, to present him with her clever detective work.

"But, does glass—"

"Last this long? Yes, it does and I only know because I had to research it for a case a while back. Glass is, in fact, one of the strongest materials . . . it can take one million years to decompose in the environment. In Egypt they are still finding glass artifacts dating back to the thirteenth century BC." Grace passed the glass pieces from one hand to the next gently, as if handling valuable gems. "There have been several studies showing that even if glass bottles break into smaller pieces, the glass will retain its chemical composition for thousands of years."

"And what are you hoping to learn from the glass?" Mark asked, his eyes revealing he was intrigued, yet minorly confused about its significance.

"Well, the glass obviously plays some type of role in Timmy's life . . . maybe it was just a minor cast member in the play of his death, but it could be a simple clue that leads to something else."

"Wow, since when did you get so . . . so . . . metaphorical?"

With eyes wide, making her appear maniacal, Grace moved to sit on the bench and patted the peach seat cushion beside her. As Mark sat down, she opened the cigar box and pulled the entire stack of photos out, setting the glass pieces in the bottom for safekeeping.

"What can I do to help?"

Grace separated the photos into two piles, handing half to Mark like she was dealing a deck of cards. "Look through these and tell me if you see any signs of something with glass . . . anything with glass."

"Got it."

Grace started looking through the now-familiar photos and realized how different things looked when you were searching for something specific. In the past she had always been looking at the people in the photos, analyzing the relationships between subjects and gaining a sense of family dynamic. Now, she was searching for objects, something she barely paid attention to before. As she went through the photos one by one, the scenes played out in her memory. She held the black-and-white photos up close to her face, taking in the furniture, food, and décor. A photo of John, Susan, Timmy, and Margaret all cuddled closely in front of a well-decorated Christmas tree. Stockings sat on the children's laps and Susan looked up at her mother with adoration. It was a postcard photo. The only thing missing was Charles, but Grace assumed he was the one capturing the moment. She guessed that one day they had looked at this photo and it made them grieve Timmy even more, remembering such a happy memory. The next photo was similar to several of the others, with a group of women and men all smiles at some celebratory event. From the look of this one Grace could tell it had to be a New Year's Eve party. Margaret and three other women were clinking martini glasses together and animatedly blowing into horns. Balloons decorated the background of the photo, marking the occasion. "Martini glasses!"

"Is there such a thing as green martini glasses, though?" Mark kept his eyes on his pile of photos.

"Doubtful, but I'll set it aside for further analysis."

Mark didn't miss Grace's scientific tone and took the opportunity to make fun of her. "Okay, Dr. McKenna."

"Shut it," Grace said, elbowing him in the side.

"Wait a minute, I think I got something." Grace looked to the photo Mark was squinting at. "That's a bottle of liquor right there . . . hold on . . ." Mark leaned sideways to retrieve the phone from his back pocket. He typed something into Google and in seconds had the answer they were both searching for. He held the phone out in front of them with images of Tanqueray gin filling the screen, bottles all with the same antique green glass.

"How did you know it was Tanqueray gin?"

"Easy . . . you see that red wax seal on the bottle?" Mark pointed to it located near the top of the bottle shaped like a 1920s cocktail shaker. "That could be the flash of red you saw in your vision."

"What made you think of it?"

"My mom liked her gin martinis . . . I also know Frank Sinatra had a love–hate relationship with gin, and his daughter once said 'Dad loved Tanqueray gin but it didn't love him.' I used to have a man crush on that guy." Mark gazed off into space for a moment.

"The things you learn." Grace leaned closer to the photo Mark was still holding. "So, does that explain the martini glasses that seem to be in every picture?"

"I would say yes . . . someone liked their gin martinis." Mark held the phone closer to Grace. "Based on your visions, would you say this is an accurate depiction of what you saw?"

"I'd say so . . . but this seems to take the confusion up a notch. Why would a liquor bottle be involved at the scene of Timmy's shooting? If John wanted to kill him . . . he was successful in doing so with the gun. Where does the liquor bottle come into play?"

Just as Grace was about to start digging further into the photos, she heard her phone ringing downstairs. "Did you bring my bag in for me?"

"I sure did. Left it by the front door." Mark beamed with pride, as Grace pushed off from the bench and headed for the stairs.

"You're a saint. I was so caught up in the glass pieces, I left it in the piles of dirt," she shouted, as she ran down the stairs with a barking Brody following, nearly tripping her at the landing and catching herself before she face planted. "This dog is gonna kill me one day." She reached her phone just in time to see Betts's name displayed on the screen. "It's Betts!" She yelled the words at Mark, overstimulated from the Tanqueray discovery.

"Answer it!" Mark came back at her as he descended the stairs at a normal pace, his excited tone mocking hers.

"Hello." A winded Grace hoped she hadn't already hung up.

Betts's voice came through equally winded, creating a crackle as she spoke. "Grace . . . sorry . . . I'm in the middle of exercising right now . . . but I figured. . . I'd call you to let you know . . . I have your family photos . . . and they look amazing." Betts kept talking out of breath as Grace wondered how she exercised with her bum leg. "Anyway . . . I want to apologize for the delay . . . I got caught up . . . taking all these prom photos for friends' kids . . . you know . . . favors I owed friends in town. Anyway . . . any chance you guys are free . . . say tonight . . . to look over the photos? I always like to be present . . . when the client sees the photos for the first time . . . so I can capture their reaction, ya know."

"Yeah, we can be free tonight." She looked down at her watch. It was already six o'clock. "In fact we are free now if you want to come over when you're done exercising." She could feel Mark's questioning gaze. Grace had completely forgotten about the photo shoot and really wasn't interested in reviewing the pictures, but she had a sliver of hope that Betts would be able to shine some light on the Tanqueray bottle.

"What are we doing tonight?" Mark was still looking at the photos as he asked the question.

"Photo viewing with Betts."

"Oh good, I've been wondering how those bad boys turned out." Brody lifted his head as if he was remembering the photo shoot that he starred in.

* * *

Eager to get out of her work clothes and change into something more comfortable before Betts arrived, Grace stood over her open drawer and stared out the window abutting the piece of furniture. A dark cloud dragged across the sky, contrasting with white clouds that were transforming to a pale shade of grey. Mark, usually obsessed with keeping tabs on the hourly weather update, had been distracted as of late and was unaware a storm was moving in. Grace loved storms since she was a child. It was a time when she and Ellen would gather all the blankets and pillows in the house and make a nest on the couch, snuggling in close as the rain pelted the windows and the roaring thunder pushed them closer together, all that was visible was their two heads peeking out from the fort of comfort.

Now, as Grace looked out the window, she was haunted by the realization she would never be able to cuddle with her mother, at least not in a way that was comforting for them both. Instead, Ellen would likely be afraid of who the stranger was sitting beside her if Grace dared make them a storm fort. The words *never again* attached themselves to all of the memories she had of her mother. Never again would they enjoy a holiday meal together, never again would Ellen give Grace a hard time for being so rigid and career-obsessed, never again would Grace receive a reciprocated hug from her mother. Adding to that was all the things she would never experience with her mother for the first time. As her relationship with Mark continued to grow, Grace couldn't help but think about what the future held. If they took the natural next step, would Ellen not be mentally and physically present at a wedding if they ever decided to make that commitment. It was already hard for her to accept that Ellen would likely never see their new home, offering her stamp of approval. Grace could hear her mother's voice now. While she would likely joke about her daughter's choice of a big home that needed updates, Grace would inevitably be gifted with one of her mother's brief talks of pride: "I'm so proud of you Grace . . . you are my gift in this world."

The crack of thunder sounded, along with a simultaneous flash, interrupting her thoughts. The sky opened up in an angry torrent, releasing buckets of water. After Grace slipped on a pair of comfortable leggings, she walked closer to the window, watching through the downpour as a blurry turquoise silhouette hobbled up her walkway. *Betts.* From what she knew of the woman so far, she was a lot like her mother. A hippie heart and a straight-talkin' mouth, with a quirky style that was all her own. Every time Grace was in the woman's presence, she felt relaxed. It took Grace a long time to trust, and her faith in a person would often oscillate like the old tandem swing that rocked ever so gently even in the steadiest weather.

As Grace made her way down the stairs, she heard greetings and laughter passed between Mark and Betts. Brody had risen from his spot by the door and was circling their visitor, working diligently to get pets.

"Hi, Betts . . . thanks for coming . . . especially on such short notice and in this unexpected weather." Grace peered through the top window of the door to see if it was letting up any.

"Well, I would've been here a long time ago but I got so caught up getting those prom photos done." Betts leaned in as she held a hand to her mouth forming a mock whisper. "I have a tendency to promise everyone everything and prom photos aren't top on my list of photography I'm passionate about. Remind me not to agree to do those incredibly annoying photo shoots next spring will ya?" She laughed as she slipped off her turquoise raincoat. Water cascaded to the floor in a series of splattering droplets. "Oh, geez . . . now I just made a massive puddle on your floor." She looked at Mark and Grace with apologetic eyes.

"Are you kidding me, Betts . . . you just did Brody a favor. He'll gulp that up in no time," Mark said, as he pulled mugs out of the cabinet. "Tea? Coffee?" He raised his eyebrows in Betts's direction as his hand hovered over a cigar box filled with teas. Same brand as the one holding the photos, Mark recovered it from one of the kitchen cabinets. He cleaned it out and filled it with rows of his beloved teas.

"Do you happen to have peppermint tea?" Betts asked, as she set her cane alongside the island and skillfully hoisted herself up onto a bar stool.

"Ask and you shall receive." Mark tore open the package, removed the teabag, and dropped it into a cup, letting the string drape over the side. He twisted the knob on the stovetop, with a *click click click* of the gas followed by a *woosh* of the blue flame, to heat up the kettle of water. Knowing Grace was more of a coffee drinker he went through the motions of pouring her a cup of coffee. Even though it was evening, Grace could drink coffee without the stimulating aftereffects that kept some up all night.

"For whatever reason, peppermint tea is my go-to when my leg is acting up . . . and this rain is making it ache something fierce." Betts pulled a laptop out of the bag she set on the countertop and started punching in some keys. Grace thought about how tech savvy the woman was at her older age. Ellen didn't even know how to check her email, even after Grace had taught her multiple times and, before her Alzheimer's set in, she struggled to press the right buttons on the remote to get the shows she wanted.

Having been curious about the cane since the moment she met Betts at Sully's retirement party, Grace jumped at the chance to ask her about it. "What happened to your leg anyway?"

"Actually, it's kind of a funny story and it happened on your street."

"Really?" Tiny questions prickled at Grace. *Why wouldn't Betts have brought this up before, when she visited last time?*

"You see, as the only girl in a family of boys, I was always trying to prove myself and on one particular day . . . my ego got a little out of hand and led to an injury that would follow me throughout life."

"What happened?" Mark spun around with the cup of peppermint tea and presented it to Betts.

"Well, it was the one time our family and the Walsh family got together. And if you remember me telling you before . . . Mrs. Walsh had asked me to stop coming by to take photos . . . and suddenly our entire family was over there, having a barbecue with them. I'll never forget it because it was only weeks after the accident . . . when Timmy passed." Betts tucked her chin into her chest and cleared her throat. "It was sometime in September after school had started for the year. Anyway, we were barbecuing in the front yard because Mrs. Walsh still couldn't bring herself to go in the back yard . . . since the accident. So, it was my parents, Mr. and Mrs. Walsh, and us kids. One of the boys brought out a skateboard and someone brought up a dare. Who would go down the hill on the skateboard? It was a somber day and quite honestly, I had no idea why we were there . . . I mean, it had only been weeks since Timmy's accident. Maybe the family just needed a distraction and they invited us over." Betts dropped a hand to her lap and rubbed circles in her leg as she squinted her eyes, the pain evident on her wincing face. So, once again trying to prove myself to my brothers, I stepped in and declared I'd take the dare. The deal was that if I did it I'd be able to take any photos of the other kids that I wanted, posing them any which way." Betts laughed. "I know, it doesn't sound like much of a prize, but to me it was the world. To be able to use them as my subjects and practice my craft . . . well, to ten-year-old me . . . that was a dream. So, I kneeled down on the skateboard, locked my eyes on the road, and set sail down the steepest street in town."

"That's crazy . . . weren't you scared?" Grace asked, as she tucked a strand of hair behind her ear.

"Scared out of my little girl panties. But there was no stopping me from trying to prove myself to my brothers. I've lost quite a bit of my stubborn pride over the years 'cause, now, I know I'm the black sheep of the family and I simply don't give a damn." She lifted her hand onto the countertop, smoothing her palm over the surface in a self-soothing motion. "Well, this is where it gets dicey. I think I would've made it down that hill intact . . . if my attention hadn't been diverted." She raised her eyebrows for added drama.

"What do you mean?" Mark leaned forward on the island, hugging his mug of tea with both hands.

"Well, you guys know how I was suspicious of the accident because of the whole ambulance response time and stuff?"

"Yeah." Mark and Grace shared the word, their stares glued on Betts as if they were watching an intense baseball game.

"Well, as I was speeding down the hill, something caught my eye. On the side of the house I saw Mr. Walsh and my dad talking privately. But they weren't just talking . . . they looked like they were in the middle of an argument . . . arms were flailing and I caught a glimpse of Mr. Walsh's heated expression. It was in that moment that I lost my balance and tipped to the left, barreling down the hill."

Grace felt her mouth drop open, and Mark's expression mirrored exactly how she felt. "Oh my God!"

"Yeah, but at the time it was more like a 'thank God.' Thank God a car wasn't pulling out of a driveway or turning onto the street at the bottom of the hill. Because this leg injury here . . . would be the least of my worries." Betts patted her leg as a grateful expression peeled across her face. "Anyway, I landed on my leg in a position that I was never able to recover from. Back then, medicine wasn't as advanced as it is today."

"Geezus," Grace said, selfishly thinking she wanted to get back to what Mr. Walsh and Mr. Sullivan were arguing about.

"Dumb question, but did the kids let you take photos of them?" Mark asked.

"Darn straight they did. They all felt so bad that I spent the next few weeks taking photos of all of my brothers, anytime I wanted. Only lasted about a month before it got old for them too, but I gotta say . . . I got some of my best photos then. That's how I learned to hobble around with a camera in my hand. First it was crutches and then it was a cane, and I've never been able to get rid of it. It's kind of like an extra limb." She let out a gentle laugh.

Grace jumped in. "Did you ever find out what your dad and Mr. Walsh were arguing about?"

"No." She paused, looked around the room as if searching for a hidden camera. "I have my opinions though."

Grace raised an eyebrow, urging Betts to go on.

"Between the three of us . . ." She looked down at Brody. "I mean four of us?"

"Between us." Grace responded.

"I think the day of the accident . . . something else happened. Something more intentional. Maybe it wasn't an accident at all. Maybe it was . . . I don't know . . . an act of jealousy? Or maybe someone else was supposed to be shot and poor little Timmy got caught in the crossfire. I really don't know, but it has haunted me all my life."

"I bet you'd love to have been a fly on the wall that day," Mark said.

"Or a fly on the swing set." She rolled her eye around until it landed in a wink.

Grace slapped her hands on the countertop before sliding off the barstool. "Hold that thought." She raced into the living room where Mark left the cigar box of photos and glass. In the thirty seconds it took her to make it back to the kitchen, Betts and Mark had exchanged a few words. Grace placed the box on the counter, where she stood across from Betts, and lifted the lid. "So, when Mark here was digging up our back yard on his attempt to beautify it with some perennials . . ." Grace smirked in his direction.

"Oh, if you need any advice on gardening, I'm your gal," Betts said, clearly unaware that Grace was going in a completely different direction with this.

"See, now you can get some professional advice, honey," Grace joked, lifting the lid of the box. "Anyway, as he was pulling up our lawn, we came across some broken green glass." Betts furrowed a brow, showcasing an obvious question mark on her face. Answering her implied question,

Grace carried on. "So, I was wondering if this glass, buried fairly deep, was from when the Walsh family lived here."

"You mean the family and not just John Walsh himself?"

"Correct."

"That looks like glass from a liquor bottle."

Grace looked over at Mark, a smile coming to life on her lips. "Exactly." Mark remained quiet as Grace watched Betts's expression, as the cogs turned before clicking into place. "John Walsh didn't drink alcohol."

"He didn't?"

"Nope, and I know this because he was a recovering alcoholic. And I *know* that because my father was and I accompanied him to a meeting once when he was receiving one of his milestone coins."

"Isn't it supposed to be anonymous?"

"Oh, geez . . . I'm sorry . . . I wasn't supposed to say anything about seeing John there." Betts slapped her forehead with a palm. "Can we promise to keep this a secret between the four of us?" She angled a smile down at Brody once again.

"He's not saying anything . . . and neither are we," Mark said, holding up a pair of crossed fingers like a kid making a pact.

"I know it was a long time ago but do you remember the Walshes drinking out of any green liquor bottles."

Betts eyes scanned the wall behind Grace, searching for the memory in her head. "Yes, the one with the red wax seal . . . Tanqueray. They used to drink Tanqueray. I'll never forget it because when I got hurt on the skateboard that day my dad came running down the hill, he was the first one to get there, followed by everyone else who was at the gathering that day. I'll never forget him reaching into his pocket to get me his hanky for my tears and seeing a red medallion that looked like a flat, round chip, fall out and onto the ground." Betts paused, took a deep breath and released it. "You know how some memories just come in flashes? Well, I remember my dad hovered over me as I was screaming in pain, and I remember him pulling that hanky out like he always did when I cried or when my brothers and I had a runny nose."

"What did he do with the wax seal?" Mark asked.

"It all happened so fast . . . it was like in one fast motion he picked it up and pocketed it before anyone else made it to the bottom of the hill."

CHAPTER THIRTEEN

John

I'm doing everyone a favor by going away. It will save Susan the pain when she bumps into me in town, which will inevitably happen. I knew that she would find out the truth someday, so when she came to me asking why I sold the family home, I figured there was no time like the present. But, looking back, maybe I should've sheltered her from all of it, from what she didn't know…from what happened that day. I was just glad that she wasn't there to witness it. She was always so sensitive, if she had seen it unfold, she wouldn't have been the success that she is today because it would've eaten at her and haunted her for years, like it has me. But Susan didn't have the same angst that I had. I was the one who received all of our mother's abuse, a punching bag that she took her own bottled up pain out on. And then there was Timmy. He was next in line when Mom couldn't get to me and I knew that it would just get worse the older he got. Poor Timmy was old enough to witness our mother's abuse but not old enough to fight back and save his own life. Being the youngest, Timmy was born fighting for attention, trying to compete against his older twin siblings who had already established themselves in their parents' graces. That fighting for attention was his Achilles' heel with our drunk mother and over time, as she sunk deeper into alcoholism, she would shift her abuse from me to him. I had received my fair share of slaps, slices, and belittling. I had been victim to her tying me up and keeping me locked in her bedroom walk-in closet for days when Dad was on business trips. Other times, she made a jail cell out of the shed in the backyard, locking me in the dark well into the evening hours. I could still remember the feel of the metal floor, the little slits in the material that would cause tiny cuts on my rear end and legs. My only safe place was the attic, where I would stare out the windows and long to be somewhere else. She never found me up there. As if her beatings were out of convenience, the kitchen was the place where I took the most abuse. There were times late at night when the rest of the family was sleeping, when she would rip me out of bed and sit me at the kitchen table, forcing me to eat the things I hated. Broccoli. Liver and onions. Brussels sprouts. It was as if she couldn't rest her eyes until she saw me suffer. When I renovated the kitchen, I took an axe to the old space, picturing her face with every crack of wood. Every busted cabinet, I heard her drunken slur. Every broken tile, I saw her nasty lips badgering me and telling me I'd never amount to anything.

While my mother was a mean, sloppy drunk, she was somehow a genius at hiding secrets from Susan, telling her that I was sleeping over a friend's house or at a sleepaway baseball camp. I'll never forget all those years later when the movie Mommy Dearest came out and my sister laughed about it, questioning how a mother could treat their child in such a way. All of my scars were caused by sports and boyish accidents and all were hidden well. Nine stitches along the right side of my forehead when she pushed me into a dresser and my head and the sharp corner collided. That was the result of me tripping and falling as far as my father and sister were concerned. Boys are so clumsy she'd tell them. She was an award-winning actress for all who were watching her life movie. My father coddled her knowing that she was alone with us three kids for lengthy bouts of time while he traveled. The local doctor who made house calls and patched up her dirty work, actually felt sorry for her…having to bear the brunt of seeing her child hurt on more than one occasion. While she was messy with her pushes, slaps, and shoves she was precise when it came to the burns. The woman loved her Lucky Strike cigarettes and she loved making artwork with them on my skin. Burn dots in the shape of a heart on my chest because she said she loved me so much and she believed in the motto that pain is temporary and pride is forever. According to my mother, if we never endured pain, then we'd have no pride to show for, and in turn we would amount to nothing. I was always grateful for the tattoo artist I hired years later. He never questioned the burn dots and simply covered it up. It made me believe that I could become someone else, someone who was worthy of love and it gave me hope that I could forget the past. But I couldn't. And I still can't. I can't forget seeing Timmy's tiny body tossed down the stairs, his pleading eyes shooting questions at the woman who had hugged him and kissed him just moments before. That little boy became more like a son to me than a brother, and to think I was only eight years old at the time of his death. Most eight-year-olds were just learning how to read and do simple math, and there I was protecting my baby brother from the horrible mother that gave birth to us. For years I questioned why we had to be born to a mother like her…why couldn't we have someone else? My protection of my baby brother ended up being my undoing, a slap in the face in what was a freak accident, a collision of angers that resulted in the death of an innocent boy. A boy who, at only five years old, knew he wanted to be a baseball star.

I had stopped at the general store on my way home from day camp and, wanting to cheer Timmy up after our mother's rage from the night prior, I bought him a Red Sox cap. I had stopped at the general store on my way home from day camp and wanted to cheer him up after our mother's rage from the night prior. Susan was at a Girl Scout meeting when my mother let loose on us two boys. When I got home, he was already in the back yard. He had been playing in a pile of dirt that my dad had accumulated for him, a makeshift sandbox. As soon as I pushed the front door open, I could hear the ice being scooped and dropped into her shaker. I had looked at the watch on my wrist…the one my father had given me for my birthday. It was nearing 4:00, and my mother was likely already well on her way to being inebriated. I could hear the sound of Frank Sinatra's voice permeating the air. She always played Sinatra when she was drunk and he'd become the background noise to our beatings. As I entered the house I was pushed into a cloud of cigarette smoke. When I passed our maid, Karina in the hallway, she gave me the look that she always gave me when my mother was in a mood…a sly warning to stay hidden, unseen. She was always looking out for us. In some sense she was the mother that Timmy and I never had.

I regretted opening the front door and quietly pulled it closed, praying that my mother wouldn't hear. Out of sight out of mind usually kept me out of danger. I immediately made my way to the back door, assuming that Timmy was in the back yard. Sure enough, he was knee-deep in dirt, wearing his school clothes. That is something that I never understood…why he was wearing his school clothes on an August day. My mother would later tell the cops that he wanted to play dress-up, and pretend he was at school. I never bought that because Timmy hated being in his school uniform, so much so that he couldn't stop fidgeting in the discomfort of the high socks and the button-down shirt that chafed his skin. My guess is that my mother made him wear it for that very reason…because he hated it. It was one of the many cruel ways that she messed with our minds, twisted our trust.

Like always, Timmy was excited to see me, his big hazel eyes opened wide when I approached him, where he was standing proudly as king of the mountain on his dirt pile. "I'm king of the mountain," he said, as he raised a fist in the air. Most kids in this situation, would engage in play, but I had to jump into action. "Timmy, you're dirty… Mom is going to be so mad…let's get you cleaned up, buddy." I started to usher him toward the hose so I could spray off his dirt-encrusted legs. I spit on my hand and started swatting at the mess on his face. I looked up and saw Karina knocking on the window, giving me the warning. Our mother was coming. And then the back door slammed open, crashing into the house's wood panels. I gripped Timmy's hand, and I could feel the sweat in his palm, his heightened sense of fear building right alongside my own.

"Timothy John Walsh!" The demand came out in slurs, the words smashed together and barely comprehensible, but to us it was familiar. It was our drunk mother, getting ready to beat on us. Behind my mother, I could see Karina watching from the window, ready to break up yet another fight. Since she was hired shortly after Susan and I were born, my mother had gotten drastically worse. A sliver of my memory holds onto few moments where my mother treated us with care, but they were always in the presence of my father or friends that she had to impress. Straight from Poland, Karina had no family in the area and with limited options she had to hold on tight to her job as our maid.

As my mother closed in on us, I grabbed Timmy's hand and started to pull him toward me, but my mother, driven by anger, caught his other hand. "Come on, baby...mommy just wants to snuggle you." For a moment, even I had bought my mother's affectionate words and soothing tone. Timmy bent down to retrieve his flannel security blanket that was crumpled on the lawn, it's colorful polka dots standing out against the green grass backdrop. He stepped toward her, eager to win his mother over, a game he had been striving to win since he was born. Once he was in her arms, she shook him side to side. "Maybe I can shake the dirt off of you, you dirty boy," she said, disgust tinting her made up face, the same face that just hours before, was smiling at her friends over a late morning tea. The same eyes that maintained contact with her friends, who were fellow mothers, completely blinded by her false persona. She tore the blanket from his clutch and tossed it as far as she could, an evil laugh erupting from her lips when it landed behind the tandem swing. I stood there and watched as she started to spiral into a fit of rage, all aimed at Timmy. I begged her to shake me instead, begged her to leave him alone, all the while I was moving my eyes from Karina to Timmy, back and forth, not knowing what to do. And then, when she hoisted Timmy up in one arm and stumbled toward the swing set, something spoke to me. The numbers 10 16 46. I had remembered seeing my father put his pistol away. As his oldest son, he had a moment of man to man talk with me before he wrapped the gun up in a silk material and punched in a few keys. Whether he assumed I didn't see or he simply didn't care because he never guessed that I would try to get in that gun safe, I retained the combination. 10 16 46. My parents' wedding anniversary. I took direction from the voice in my head and I raced into the house, past Karina, and up the stairs to my father's closet, where the small dresser was pushed against the wall. In seconds I was standing there, the silky texture of the material smooth between my fingers, at a crossroads. I walked slowly to my room at the back of the house, with the gun pressed to my side like I'd seen the police do on television so many times before. I looked out the bedroom window and I saw my mother setting Timmy on the swing with urgency, taking his little hands and forcefully pressing them around the bar as he screamed. His face, beet red and lined with dirt, said all I needed to know. I couldn't take it anymore. I barreled down the stairs and went out the door on the other side of the house. With the gun held to my side awkwardly, I pressed my back to the house like I was a police officer in the cops and robbers shows that I had watched with my dad on the rare occasion that he was home. The louder Timmy's screams got, the wider my steps got, until I was at that corner of the house that greeted the back yard. Replaying what my father had showed me when he unlocked the gun, I aimed at my mother, ready to pull the trigger on her. Even at the young age of eight, I knew the difference between right and wrong and I knew that what she was doing was beyond wrong and if I let her get away with it, Timmy would end up scarred for life, or even worse…dead. I pulled the trigger, and in that moment, I heard a sound from the door that led directly to the back yard. "Stop!" The Polish accent was strong, barely decipherable, but what happened seconds before is what changed my life forever. Karina, on a mission to stop my mother from hurting Timmy anymore, had hurled a Tanqueray gin bottle at my mother's head. With the ambition of a professional baseball pitcher combined with the anger that was fueling her, Karina's aim was spot on, hitting my mother in the back of the head and knocking her onto the ground. Simultaneously, Timmy flew backward off the swing, from the force of the bullet that was intended for my mother. As if in slow motion, the next few moments sat heavy in the air. Karina looked at me, her jaw dropped and in an instant, she was racing toward Timmy and surpassing my mother's limp body. I followed her lead. In a few steps we had Timmy bookended between the two of us. We yelled his name as if that would drive some energy into his lifeless body. As Karina's determination subsided, her facial features shifted from severe angles to a softened sadness. She pressed her index and middle fingers gently to his neck, detecting the answer that we didn't want. I fell onto my backside and hugged my knees in close as my shock transferred to reality…I killed my brother. As my head and knees dropped to the side on the prickly grass, my gaze locked with Timmy's blanket, now splattered in fresh droplets of blood, another image I would have stamped on my memory forever. The words replayed themselves in my head like a broken record, taunting me. Those same words still taunt me today, and the memory of those few moments surge through my veins with the pressure of a punch in the gut every single moment of my life. I've never been able to let go and accept what happened that day. Yes, it was a freak accident. If Karina hadn't thrown the bottle, Timmy would be alive and my mother would be dead. But instead, she lived and continued on with her life. While she never laid a hand on me again, she could also never make eye contact with me after that day. Even in her drunken state, she knew that my intention was to kill her, she knew that her bad choices resulted in my brother's death, but she would never admit fault. At the same time she'd never allow the police to know that it was me that killed my brother, because after all that would tattoo our perfect high society family with disfunction. Instead, my little brother had to take the fault for his own death. It was an accident, a little boy whose curiosity got the best of him. This was during a time when accidental gun shootings among young children were fairly common. Timmy's alleged curiosity painted a picture of a family that was dealing with a tragic accident, instead of a mother who abused and mistreated her children, hiding behind a schedule that was committed to town committees, social gatherings and volunteer work. To this day, people still offer my mother their condolences, layering on the sympathy that she gladly breathes in.

Lying in a heap on the grass, beside the mound of dirt, my mother's body started to gradually move. As if she was the star of a Hollywood movie, she fell right back into her role as soon as she saw the blood on Timmy's shirt. It was like someone had pressed play on the movie after it was paused for a brief time. "Timmy! My Timmy... what did you do to my darling boy!" The hit on her head must've caused her to sober up because the slur had diminished and she charged for my brother, lifting his body up in her arms and cradling him, rocking him back and forth the way new mothers do. Black tears streaked down her face, leaving behind an angry watercolor painting. "What did you do to my baby boy!" Her silky white dressing gown was now smudged with blood, chunks of her dark hair stuck to her cheeks where the tears continued to furiously carve misguided paths in her skin.

Karina stood up, her tall Polish build hovering over my mother. "How dare you act as if you were anything more than a reckless, coldhearted roommate of that boy. You are the reason he is dead."

As if someone had hoisted a rock at her, my mother fell backward, her dramatic emotions flaring up, transforming her into the role of victim, a character she had always played well. Timmy's lifeless body landed face down in the dirt. "I love my children... how dare you accuse me of anything else...since the day they were born, I've given everything to them, sacrificing myself."

"You don't know the first thing about sacrifice." Karina started walking toward the house. "I'm calling the police."

I'll never forget how I felt hearing those words. At the time I had thought that Karina was calling the police on me. I hadn't yet thought about the legal aspect of me shooting my brother, I was still so shocked that it was me who took his life.

"Wait no! We can't let them know. I can't lose another baby."

"Are you more afraid of John getting hurt or are you more afraid that the police will find out why your eight-year-old son tried to shoot you in the first place?"

"John honey…did you really try to shoot me?" Her eyes shrunk into two slits as her brow crinkled together. She made it sound like being the target of anger was so unexpected, like she didn't deserve it after all the years she spent abusing her sons.

Suddenly filled with a surge of energy, my mother pushed herself up off the ground and followed Karina into the house. Moments later, Officer Joe Sullivan was in our back yard assessing the scene while simultaneously tending to my grieving mother. And then, the sound of sirens crept up our street.

CHAPTER FOURTEEN

Grace pulled a loose-fitting tank top over her head. June weather could vary greatly in Massachusetts, extending from the low sixties to the mid-nineties. It was nearing mid-June and the heat index was already skyrocketing, which is why she opted for something that wouldn't reveal the sweat stains that would inevitably make themselves known. It was Saturday and while she was off duty, the station was taking part in the I Love Bridgeton festival. While it wasn't necessary that she attended, she figured it wouldn't hurt her to put her face out there a little more. It was also an opportunity for her to mingle with townies who might have a grasp on the Walsh family. Surely there were classmates of John who still lived in town and who were diehard fans of Bridgeton.

"You ready?" Mark called up the stairs. Grace could hear some type of equipment being rolled across the living room floor. There was no way Mark would be late for the fest. It was an opportunity for him to share his fitness expertise with potential clients while he mingled with his current fan club. This type of event was a dream for him.

"Yep. Coming!" Grace said, as she paused by a hutch beside their bedroom door. On top of it was one of the photos they selected from Betts's collection. While it wasn't a picture perfect family photo, it summed up their life and it was Grace's favorite of the selection. Brody, sitting upright in between the two of them, had a big smile on his face, as Mark and Grace were caught mid-laugh with wide open grins as they looked at each other instead of the camera. It would likely be their Christmas photo, if they decided to step it up a notch and send out cards this year. Grace retrieved the photos from their home in the window seat before heading downstairs. She seldom left the house without the Walsh family photos these days, always scanning them for more clues. Every opportunity she had, she would pull the photos out and look, as if she could conjure up some answers or get the family to speak to her. Sometimes she even talked to them as if they were characters in her own life.

Grace's sleep had been light, as it always was when in the middle of a case, and her body felt heavy as she trotted down the stairs, one step at a time. Mark was already out the door and pulling a bin filled with fitness equipment across the front lawn and to the Jeep. With her bag over one shoulder and her other arm squeezing the box of photos against her side, she stepped over Brody and pushed her way through the front door. "Bye, buddy. We'll be back."

Just as she slipped into the passenger seat, she could feel her phone vibrating in her bag. She slipped it out of the front pocket and saw it was her father. "Crap."

Mark looked over as he buckled his seat belt. "What . . . who is it?"

"It's my dad . . . he wants to meet up to discuss my mother's care."

"And? Shouldn't you answer?"

"Of course I should, but I don't want to," Grace said, as she stared down at her phone, contemplating whether she should press red or green.

"Honey, you're gonna have to talk to him eventually. And I know this isn't the topic you want to be discussing with him, but your mother needs the care . . . so the sooner you talk to him, the better it will be for her. Maybe it will help to think of it like that." He rested a hand on her thigh as he turned out of their driveway and down the street.

"Hello?" Grace answered on the last ring before she could change her mind.

"Hi, Grace, sorry to bug you . . . I know you're really busy." Grace was still surprised by how well-spoken her father was. After having a not-so-nice picture of him painted in her head all these years, it felt odd to discover that he was a well-rounded, highly educated, successful businessman with a heart that led him to donating to multiple charities.

"No worries. Sorry I haven't been the best communicator lately." Grace looked at Mark, her face softening. Maybe it was time to just let the guy in her life.

"I understand. Really, I do, Grace."

"Thanks."

"Any chance you have time to meet over the next few days?"

"How's tomorrow?" Grace asked, surprising herself at the quick response. She could feel Mark's eyes on her and she turned and motioned for him to pay attention to the road.

"Tomorrow? Tomorrow is great . . . that works. How about ten o'clock at the The Willows? Your mother is usually her best around that time, according to the staff."

"Sounds good." Grace felt a rush of emotions surge through her. She so badly wanted to not like this man, but he was keeping tabs on her mother the way she had done for so many years. It was like the roles had shifted when he came into her life. Part of her was sad to let go of the reigns, to hand over the relationship that had molded her and made her who she was today. Letting him in wouldn't be easy, but it would be even harder to let her mother go.

By the time Grace hung up the phone they were pulling into the parking lot across from the town center. "Feels weird driving such a short distance, doesn't it?" Mark asked, as he removed the keys from the ignition. He leaned toward Grace, planting a kiss on her cheek.

"Yeah, considering we live literally one minute from here." She turned her face toward Mark, sneaking a kiss on his lips. "Thanks."

"For what?"

"Just being so understanding and supportive and talking me down from the ledge when necessary."

"Hey, this hasn't been an easy time for you. Between the new case and your mom . . . not to mention this new relationship with your dad." Mark tucked a strand of hair behind her ear. "It's a lot. Go easy on yourself."

Changing the subject before it got too serious, Grace pressed on. "So, do I really have to help you demonstrate your fitness equipment?" She pushed the door open and stepped out.

"Do you really think I didn't have a backup plan for this? I've got it covered. Kayla and Jason will be more than happy to demonstrate."

"Of course they will." Grace laughed. The gym couple was the epitome of health and fitness with their picture perfect bodies, glowing skin, and bright white contagious smiles.

The sound of tables being set up and directions being tossed about grew louder the closer they got to the town center. The streets that made up the center were all lined with equipment, vendors pumped up to tout their supplies and services. From across the way Grace could see Barb's red head bobbing up and down as she pulled bike helmets from a box and lined them up on a table in front of the station. "I'm going to head over to the station table but I'll come by as soon as I can, okay?" She turned to Mark and planted another grateful kiss on his lips.

The sun was already gearing up for the predicted ninety-two degrees, and it penetrated her shoulders as she made her way across the patch of grass containing the small town garden. Inside the black steel fence, a few kids played and a mom sat on the wooden bench rocking a stroller to-and-fro in an effort to get her fussy baby to sleep. A couple of rookie officers were taking instructions from Barb at the station table, their eyes shifting to each other every few seconds, likely questioning something odd she had said.·

"Good morning."

Without looking up from fanning out safety pamphlets on the table, Barb said, "Hey, Princess, I got you an iced coffee . . . it's gonna be a scorcher today." On the table next to a row of helmets, Grace saw a large iced coffee with The Bridgeton Coffee Depot logo on it. The rookies only held bottles of water. Classic Barb move to let the rookies earn their keep before she bought them a coffee or even had a solid conversation with them.

"Thanks, Barb. I'm gonna need this." Grace lifted the coffee to her lips, sipping out of the fat straw. She hoped the caffeine would put some pep in her step. Everything that had been piled on her plate recently, had caused her to feel incessantly exhausted.

Barb turned and stepped closer to Grace, officially invading her personal space. "Hey, any movement on the Walsh family saga?"

Grace looked around, making sure the rookies weren't paying attention. "Yeah, I got a little intel from our new neighbors. Turns out they inherited the house from a grandparent who lived there at the time of the incident."

"So, you got anything good from them?"

"Just that they were always weirded out by John Walsh. Said he was odd but that's nothing that we didn't already know." Grace paused, looking around again to make sure no one was eavesdropping. "I also did a little recon on Susan."

"Yeah, how did that go?"

"Well, I gotta say . . . after she disappeared for a few days, to allegedly go see her son in Rhode Island, she was acting kind of strange. I'm hoping Sully has something to say about that. Any idea if he will be coming to this shindig today?"

"It's Sully and it's a town event . . . I have no doubt in my mind that he'll be here today. The guy can't get away from us even if he tried." Barb laughed.

"True. So, what can I help you with?"

"I would love for you to be the face of the station . . . you know . . . just stand here and look pretty, Princess . . . mama will do the rest."

"You know that's not gonna happen, right?"

Barb looked up, her attention directed past Grace's shoulder. "Well, speak of the devil." Grace turned around to see Sully strolling up with a coffee in hand and a colossal grin on his face.

"You look awfully happy to be here." Grace greeted him with a hug.

"It's always good to be back with my people."

"In other words . . . you're bored out of your mind."

"I happen to be incredibly busy these days actually . . . with bowling, history book club, the dog park committee—"

"Your new girlfriend," Barb injected her wisecrack into the conversation.

"Yes, that too." Sully's face became speckled in pink blotches, as if he were a schoolboy caught staring at his crush.

"How is Susan anyway?" Grace asked, hoping he'd unknowingly share some intel on the woman. "Did you ever get a hold of her?"

"Oh, yeah . . . she was just caught up helping her son out with the grandkids. Stayed a little longer than she had planned."

"So, when are you going to meet the stepchildren, Sully?" Barb asked, with a wink.

"Funny," Sully said, just as he was distracted by the ringing of his phone. He reached into his back pocket and pulled it out. "Speaking of . . ." he lifted the phone to his ear. Out of what Grace assumed was habit, he answered with a simple, "Sully."

The visible grin on his face, since he showed up, suddenly disintegrated, transforming into an expression of concern. "Where? Okay. I'm on my way." He looked down at his phone in confusion before he looked up at Grace. "McKenna, what are you doing right now? I think I may need your help."

* * *

After Grace raced over to Mark's booth to get the keys to the Jeep, she led Sully to the vehicle, offering to drive since he was caught in a frazzled moment. Susan, in a state of panic, called Sully saying her brother John was on the verge of committing suicide. She was at his apartment trying to talk him out of pulling the trigger on a gun held to his temple.

"Why . . . why would John want to commit suicide?" Grace asked.

"I'm not sure . . . she said it had something to do with the past."

Ideas circled through Grace's head as she made her way to his apartment.

"How do you know where he lives?" Sully inquired.

"Oh, I uh . . . had to deliver some mail sent to us after we bought the house from him."

Five minutes later they were standing at the intercom outside of John's apartment. After Sully announced his arrival, the door clicked open and Grace followed him inside. Sully failed to share that Grace was accompanying him and instead promised Grace it would be best if Susan didn't know. Susan had the door open by the time they stepped in the corridor leading to John's apartment. "Sully! Come quick, I don't know what to do." Tears were streaming down Susan's crumpled face, her hands reaching for Sully before she even noticed Grace standing behind him. "What's—?"

"Susan, Grace is here to help . . . don't worry. She knows how to handle these situations," Sully said, knowing Grace had dealt with a few suicide attempts in the time they worked together. Women tending to be better at talking people down from pulling the trigger. Susan didn't have a choice but to let her in, to submit to Grace's expertise.

She stepped in front of Sully, and though she didn't have her weapon since she had been off duty, her hand automatically went toward her hip, reaching for her invisible gun. Several photo albums were lying on the floor, some splayed open and others facedown. Grace stepped over the albums, making her way to a brown leather recliner facing an open window.

She passed a tipped over bottle of Tanqueray gin on a glass coffee table as she made her way to the sounds of heavy breathing. Outside the window birds perched on a tree branch emitting gentle, peaceful chirps and going about their lives as a much different scene unfolded inside; a collision of two separate moments.

"John?" Grace looked back toward the door she entered, seeing Susan crouched and crying in the corner as Sully rested a hand on her shoulder, maintaining one eye on Grace's movement and one on Susan. As she got closer, Grace saw the chair swivel to one side slightly, revealing a red and green flannel shirt. She thought about how it was such an odd clothing choice given the heightened temperature. "John?" Grace tried again. "There is no need to do anything rash, we can sort out anything . . . it's not worth taking your life. Think about your sister."

"It's too late." Grace heard the click of a gun disarming followed by a shriek coming from Susan.

"No . . . John don't do it!" She gasped and Grace could feel Susan's voice getting closer, approaching from behind. "John . . . there is something you need to know . . . something that will make you want to live. Please . . . just listen to me . . . I'm begging you. Please."

Grace took one step forward, ready to use force if she had to. She turned toward Susan, who was fast approaching, and, as she locked eyes with her, she saw a frail hand fall onto a white sheet, its knobby knuckles raised like tiny mountain peaks. Grace stepped toward the window, taking in John's profile, the gun in hand dropping heavy from his temple to his lap. Grace knew that the next few minutes would determine the outcome of the situation. Would John snap and shoot Susan? Would he just shoot himself, or would he take all of them down with him? Only time would tell. A bead of sweat cascaded down his face, spilling onto the collar of his shirt. Susan passed Grace and sat in front of him on an ottoman that matched the recliner. "There's something you should know," she said, reaching for his free hand.

CHAPTER FIFTEEN

Grace woke to the smell of maple syrup and fresh coffee, the sound of cups clinking as they hit the countertop. Sitting up in bed, she was pummeled with memories of yesterday's events. Susan had successfully talked John out of harming himself and by the time Grace had left, they seemed to have a stronger sibling bond than they ever had. She told John how important he was to her and no matter what happened in the past it was time for them to move forward together as a family. At first Grace and Sully stepped out to give the twins time alone, but between Sully's concern for Susan's safety and Grace's need to learn more about the family, and ensure John wasn't going to harm himself, they both went back inside to find two sobbing siblings. Evidently, John told Susan the truth about how he accidentally killed Timmy while trying to stop their mother, out of protection. He told her how Karina, the maid they loved so much, attempted to protect Timmy that day too, and how she threw the Tanqueray bottle at their mother's head, which ultimately led to Timmy's untimely death.

"Is that why Karina stopped coming to our house after that?" Susan had asked, her eyes wide as if a lightbulb had gone off in her head.

"That's what I always assumed. How could she go on dealing with the dysfunction of our family, of constantly being on edge trying to protect us." John shook his head. "I don't blame her for leaving."

"But, if Mom treated you so horribly then why didn't she just say that you accidentally shot your brother?"

"One main reason. She didn't want anyone to know that I was aiming for her, then all of her little skeletons would be out of the closet. People would question why on earth I would want to kill my mother, and with that I would have to confess to her horrible abuse. Her perfect high society image would be tarnished forever. And even you can admit that all Mom wanted was to live a life of luxury, to spend Dad's money and be viewed as a socialite."

"Are you saying that Dad never knew the truth?"

Matter-of-factly, John said, "Dad never knew the truth. Like you, and everyone else, Dad believed Mom . . . that Timmy somehow got his hands on Dad's gun and accidentally pulled the trigger. Imagine how terrible Dad felt about that?"

Grace stepped into the conversation, after locking eyes with Sully. "Wait a minute . . . what about the police that showed up on the scene that day . . . didn't they conclude that it was near impossible for Timmy to shoot himself in the chest. If that was an accidental shooting, don't you think the bullet would've been somewhere else . . . an arm, the head, a leg. How often have you seen someone accidentally shoot themselves right in the chest?" Grace had looked over at Sully, searching for answers from the retired cop.

Sully's eyes had darted left to right, before settling into place. "My dad was the responding officer that day."

"Yeah, I know. He tried to get me to make a statement but I was so shaken up that I could hardly speak."

"You were only eight years old. Oh, John . . . I'm so sorry you went through that." Susan leaned over, pulling both of his hands onto her lap. I'm so sorry I never knew."

"It's not your fault."

"But I was your twin, I should've known."

"I didn't want you to know, Sue, I wanted to protect you."

Grace knew this was her opportunity to get more out of John about the day that seemed to be slowly unraveling itself before them. But she had to be cautious about what she said around Sully. "John, how long did Mr. Sullivan . . . Sully's dad . . . try to get you to make a statement . . . do you remember?"

"I remember that day like it was yesterday. It has haunted me for nearly sixty-five years. It didn't take Mr. Sullivan long to give up . . . he had other things to worry about, like my mother who was frantically running around the yard, trying to cling to Timmy's body as the ambulance rolled him away. It's like Mr. Sullivan was there for damage control . . . he was there trying to calm down Karina and manage my mother."

"And where was your dad through all of this?" Grace asked.

"He was scheduled to come home the next day, but Mr. Sullivan had contacted him about the emergency and he arrived home that evening." John looked down and wiped at his eyes. "To a family that was changed forever."

"How was he when he returned?" She pried.

"As you could expect . . . not good." John started. "But my father wasn't the best at showing his emotions. He was a wonderful father but sometimes it was hard to tell if he was happy or sad. I remember seeing him with a stoic look on his face. Like he couldn't quite process how he was feeling."

"Did he ever find out about what your mother was doing?"

John took in a deep breath before releasing it in one long drawn-out exhale. "My father died a year later of a sudden heart attack." John rubbed his chin, setting his eyes on his sister.

"I always assumed he died of a broken heart," Susan said, "I remember how close he was with Timmy even at such a young age. They had this special bond, you know. My mom had me, my dad had Timmy, and . . . I'm sorry John, I'm so sorry."

"What did your mom do after your dad died?"

"What any widow in the limelight would do . . . she put on her Jackie Kennedy sunglasses and black dress and mourned him in front of all the funeral attendees."

"Oh, geez." Susan dropped her head in her hands. "Why didn't I ever think about this before . . . but I remember how fast she seemed to bounce back into her social life . . . like here is this woman who lost her son and husband over a one year period and she seemed fine a year later."

"That's because our mother was never capable of real love, Sue. I never wanted you to know that but she was a monster."

He shared the abuse that he endured all those years when Susan was at a friend's house or in bed at night, even going into detail about how his mother's abuse often took place in the kitchen. It was for that reason he renovated the kitchen making it look and feel as if it was a different house when he was in that room. In the evenings, after Margaret Walsh had reached her mean drunken state and Susan had gone to sleep to the sound of classical music, she would pull John out of bed. Sometimes she would torture him verbally, belittling who he was, and other times she would physically harm him, going so far as to trap him in the dumbwaiter. These occurrences never happened when their father was home and, on the rare occasion Charles Walsh had a long streak home, Margaret would shower John with love, showing a side of herself that greatly contradicted her manic abuse.

At eight years old, John always hoped his father would get a job that kept him home, so he could be safe. The kindness his mother showed him is what he clung to when he was trying to act normal around Susan all those years. At some point, John unbuttoned his shirt revealing the Celtic tattoo he had done to conceal the cigarette burns on his body. Susan gasped with a hand clasped over her mouth. Grace could sense the shame and sadness the woman felt. She reiterated how she had been stuck in her own world that she missed everything going on in her own house. Grace could see the emotions boiling inside of her, showcasing a display of anger and sadness on her face.

"That explains why you never took your shirt off in the summer months."

John nodded simply; no more explanation was needed.

Unknowingly, John mentioned the reason for the gin bottle in his apartment. Prior to pulling out the same gun that had shot his brother Timmy, he decided to have several glasses of gin on the rocks, his mother's choice of poison.

"That was always my father's go-to drink too, on the rare occasion that he had a cocktail. He was more committed to his La Palina cigars." Sully had said, which struck a chord in Grace. She thought back to what Betts had told her about the red Tanqueray seal her dad slyly picked up off the ground and slipped into his pocket. She also remembered the image on the cigar boxes she and Mark found in their house, and jumped to the next question. "Those were popular cigars back then . . . did your dad smoke them too?" She directed the question at John and Susan.

"No, I never remember my dad smoking anything," Susan said, as her eyes darted to the photo albums strewn about the floor. She picked one up and flipped through the pages, as more tears cascaded down her face. "These are the albums I brought over last time?" She asked the statement. "From the outside looking in, our upbringing looked perfect didn't it?" She asked anyone in the room. "And I guess it was for me technically, because I knew nothing about what was going on behind the scenes." She raised a shoulder and wiped at her tears with the cotton short-sleeved shirt. This was the most underdressed Grace had ever seen the woman. "Looking through these photos is drumming up some memories that I likely forced myself to forget." She paused, pulling the book closer to her face. "I remember this Christmas. It was the Christmas before Timmy died. I remember I got this game that I had asked for and I was so happy when I opened the package. But there was something else. I remember as the night went on, Mom started saying mean things . . . to me, to you . . . to Timmy. Even to Dad. I had never seen her that way before. And then, when all of us kids were supposed to be in bed, I got up and went downstairs to get some water. That's when I saw it. Mrs. Sullivan was sitting at our kitchen table with Dad, having a really intense conversation. When I heard the voice that wasn't Mom's, I tiptoed and slowed down my steps and peeked around the corner of the wall at the bottom of the stairs. Mom was nowhere to be seen, so I went back upstairs and cracked her door open but the bed was still made, so I went to your room and when I looked at your bed I saw two lumps under the covers and Mom's hair sticking out."

John had looked up at Susan and locked eyes. "That was one of many nights Mom was in her drunken state, where she promised to stop hurting me. It usually happened when Dad was home. She'd cuddle me and pass drunken promises about how she would never hurt me again, but by the time Dad was off on his next trip, she'd have forgotten and been back to her same self. A socialite saint by day who presented herself as a caring mother, a committed community member, a doting wife, and a friend of many. Nobody really knew who she was . . . who she is . . . the only photos I had, I left at the old house. I couldn't bear to look at them any longer."

"Oh, John . . . I'm so sorry." Susan sprung up from the chair and fell into her brother's arms. The two embraced one another as if reuniting after a long time apart, a rekindled relationship that now had a clear past and a bright future.

* * *

As Grace rolled out of bed she thought about Sully's words. His father, the responding officer, had a love for Tanqueray and La Palina cigars. Then she thought about Betts's words about her father's quick work of picking up the liquor bottle's red seal on the Walsh's property just a few weeks after Timmy died. The odd exchange that he and Charles Walsh had on the side of the house during a barbecue invite that spurred from nowhere. And she needed to find out where Susan was when she was supposed to be visiting her son in Rhode Island. Grace had a hunch she hadn't been taking care of the grandkids at all. It seemed like there was a bit more to discover about the Walsh and Sullivan family dynamics. After Grace sorted out her own family dynamics. In less than two hours she was scheduled to meet her father to discuss her mother's quality of life.

She would need coffee before anything else and the smells that were rising from downstairs nearly made her float down the steps in a haze. Without saying a word, Grace hoisted herself onto a barstool as she watched the back of Mark as he effortlessly lifted pancakes on a spatula before flipping them onto a plate. He turned to place a stack on the island but stopped midmotion. "Geez! You scared the crap out of me! What are you . . . a ghost . . . sneaking up on people like that?"

"Hey . . . I was just following my senses . . . and they brought me right down here, to watch you in action. What's the occasion?"

Mark turned again, grabbed the coffee pot and started filling the cups on the island. "Well, this is kind of a big day for you . . . seeing your dad again and all . . . so I figured I'd try to ease the stress a tad by making your favorite pancakes."

Grace looked around the countertop with raised eyebrows. "I mean, not that I don't appreciate this and all but . . . did you forget something?"

"I most certainly did not," Mark said, as he reached into the fridge, retrieving a small pottery bowl her mother made years ago. "I just decided to make your whipped cream from scratch this time." He set the bowl in front of her and her eyes grew as she dipped a finger into the white pool of thick, wavy cream.

"Damn that's good!" Just as Grace was about to fill her mouth with a forkful of fluffy pancakes, the doorbell rang. She looked down at her watch, surprised by such an early visitor. Mark paused in the middle of taking a long swig of green smoothie, mirroring the same expression Grace felt on her face. "I'll get it." Grace slipped off the stool and padded to the front door. Out the top windowpane, she could see a blonde head rocking side to side. *Emily*. She was greeted with an apologetic smile when she opened the door.

"I am so sorry for bugging you guys so early but . . . do you happen to have any creamer?"

"Of course . . . come on in." Grace led her new neighbor into the kitchen. While she was not one for early morning visits, she had to admit she really enjoyed Emily's company.

"Hey, neighbor!" Mark said, as Emily entered the room.

"I'm so sorry to bug you guys . . . but I had a late night with Peyton . . . and I'm not gonna make it if I don't have my coffee. Personally, I'd prefer to inject it in my veins but mixing it with a good creamer is my second favorite way of having it."

"Say no more." Mark went to work pouring her a fresh cup of coffee as Grace retrieved the french vanilla creamer from the refrigerator. Also a fan of creamer, Grace added a generous amount to her cup and slid the bottle over to Emily.

"Take a seat . . . is Scott home with Peyton now?" Grace asked as she spooned a dollop of whipped cream onto her pancake.

"Yes, he's actually there with my mom . . . she just arrived. We are going to go into the city today and have a little adults-only lunch. I figured I'd have her come over a little early so I can take a proper shower in peace for once. Thank God for grandparents."

Grace couldn't help but be saddened by the comment. If she ever went down the parenthood route, her child would never have a grandmother who was present and she would never have the convenience of a relative caretaker.

"Well, you might as well go all out and have a pancake or two while you're here . . . I won't tell Scott." Mark winked as he used a spatula to transfer a pancake from the top of the pile onto a fresh plate, before setting it in front of her.

"Oh my . . . this looks delightful. But are you guys sure I'm not crashing your private romantic breakfast?"

"Nothing romantic about this breakfast . . . and you need to add this if you really want to live the life of luxury." Grace pushed the bowl of whipped cream toward her and watched as her eyes expanded.

"Gosh, I gotta say . . . I miss having simple quiet breakfasts with Scott." She continued to talk as she shoveled bites of pancake into her mouth. "Don't get me wrong, I wouldn't trade Peyton for the world, but there is something to be said about a quiet cup of coffee in the morning." She wiped a glob of cream left behind on the outer edge of her lip. "Everything is interrupted by a cry or a diaper change or a feeding now . . . but like I said, I love being a mom . . . it just takes some getting used to." With a now empty plate in front of her, she picked up the cup of coffee and cradled it between her hands, taking a slow slip and reveling in the moment.

"Well, you are welcome to sneak over here any time you want," Grace said, "and maybe next time we can incorporate wine into the mix."

"A girl after my own heart," Emily said, as she threw her head back and took one final sip. "Well, I better get home before my mom changes her mind." She winked and turned on a heel toward the door.

"Emily?" Mark held up the bottle of creamer as she turned around. "I think you came here for this . . . if you went home empty-handed, they might catch onto your little escape." He laughed.

"I'm losing my mind." She laughed and took the creamer.

* * *

Grace's nerves were churning inside her as she pulled into The Willows Assisted Living facility. She wasn't sure if it was because she was going to see the father she had just recently met for the first time or if it was because she was likely to be presented with a long list of questions she needed to answer. She hadn't seen her mother in a couple of weeks, ever since the nurse had urged her to keep her distance, as her presence had a tendency to cause upset. Grace remembered when her mother would glow with happiness every time she walked into a room to join her, and now all she did was drum up bad memories and formulate stories about her. Between the excess coffee, the sugary whipped cream, and the nerves she was feeling about this visit, her stomach was in shambles and she was swaying in between waves of nausea and bouts of lightheadedness. She was surprised to see her father standing at the front steps of the building. For someone who carried a lot of pain from the past, his posture was immaculate, free of the sloping and sagging of someone holding onto bad memories and regrets. Until Grace approached the steps, he had been looking off into the distance, his black sunglasses perched on the upper half of his face, contrasting with salt and pepper hair that fully covered his head.

"Good morning," he said, as he lowered his glasses and allowed them to settle on the bridge of his nose as he offered her his wide-set green eyes that matched her own. Normally Grace would think the gesture was cocky but everything about her father breathed a nonchalant apprehension. The man was a millionaire and it may show from his attire but it was discreet in his disposition.

"Good morning." Grace reacted opposite, pushing her sunglasses up and over her head. Instead of giving him too much eye contact she looked ahead at the glass doors, ready to get the meeting over with.

As they walked in together, he asked her how work had been and how Mark was doing. Before she could stop herself, she told him about their new house, about the odds and ends they'd had to tend to with such an old home. When she regretted her overshare, she realized how hard it was becoming to keep him at a distance. It would be so much easier to let the man in her life and not have to monitor every single word that came out of her mouth. But she was on a mission to make him prove himself.

"You know . . . if you ever need help with fixing things up around the house, you can call me . . . I'd be happy to help."

Grace was well aware of her father's construction expertise. The man owned a prestigious development company that had received major accolades in the city of Boston and beyond. "Thanks." Her word came out simple but the eye contact she gifted him with, as they sat in the lobby, proved she was starting to open to the idea of letting him into her life.

In a matter of seconds Frances Dupont was sitting down beside them, holding a beefy file folder to her chest. She set it down on her lap and got right to business, which Grace was grateful for. "So, as you both know, Ellen has been rapidly approaching a more aggressive stage of dementia and she is at the point where around-the-clock care is, in my expert opinion, a necessity." She paused, gauging their states of mind and allowing for any comments.

"I'll pay for whatever we need to get her the best care possible," Bruce said. He rested his forehead on steepled fingers.

"I appreciate your generosity in this matter but, Grace here, has the ultimate say, as Ellen's next of kin." Frances tilted her head toward Grace. Her cheeks were puffy pillows beneath her eyes and patches of rosacea marked her sagging cheeks. She was likely nearing the end of her career, ready to retire from a job that Grace imagined was beyond draining. She applauded the woman for maintaining professionalism and staying in a field that Grace could never imagine doing. Being surrounded by people who were perfectly capable of using their physical bodies, yet completely unable to recall their most momentous memories. It had to be depressing, but, then again, Grace thought about how depressing her job could be, how sad her gift could be. She was attempting to solve a case about a five-year-old boy who was accidently shot by his older brother, leaving behind a lifetime of sadness and anger. What was worse . . . not being able to control your thoughts and memories or being trapped by them? Her mother was walking around unknowingly in a world of her own, while John Walsh spent his life being haunted by his memories, likely remembering them far more clearly than he would like.

Ready to move on for her mother's sake and for her own, Grace said, "Okay, let's do it . . . my father . . . I mean Bruce, gets my consent to place my mother in around-the-clock care." Saying the words out loud generated a tear in the corner of her eye as a lump expanded in her throat. There was nothing left she could do for her mother and in some sense it felt as if she was giving up on her, accepting the fact that all her promises to take care of her mother were no longer relevant. She was not in control. A mutual understanding passed between Grace and her father, and she accepted his hand when he reached for her in an act of comfort. If it weren't for this man who entered her life at the most fateful time, there is no telling where Ellen would be right now. Grace wouldn't have the money to provide this type of quality care for her and she would've had to spend every penny she made, resulting in a life that was lived paycheck to paycheck. She wouldn't have been able to buy a house with Mark, the love of her life, and in turn, she wouldn't be solving a sixty-five-year-old case that may free up some angst and pain for a family. Life had a way of intersecting in bizarre ways.

Sometimes, regardless of the chosen path you take, your destination plans a scheme all its own.

* * *

After signing an extensive amount of documents, some of which were tear-stained, Grace and Bruce emerged from The Willows. As if they were saying goodbye on an awkward first date, they hesitated at the bottom of the steps, looking at one another. Grace was grateful she no longer saw the horrific visions in her father's eyes.

"So, like I said . . . if you ever need help with home projects, I'd be happy to help."

"Thanks, I appreciate that. I'm sure Mark would too . . . he's not the handiest guy around." Grace let out a slight giggle.

"Ahhh . . . I wasn't always handy either . . . it just takes some trial and error. You tell Mark I'll be happy to teach him a thing or two . . . in exchange for one of his personal training sessions of course." Bruce held his sunglasses in his hands and shared his full expression, gifting her with his kind eyes and perfectly aligned bright white teeth. Grace didn't know all that much about dental work, but most men his age didn't have such glowing smiles so she naturally assumed he had some assistance with achieving perfection. "I hear he's a pretty top-notch trainer."

"Oh yeah?" Grace wondered if Bruce had been Googling her boyfriend. Mark had already attained quite an online following for his workout videos that had been shared thousands of times.

"I have a friend . . . Cynthia . . . she's a big fan of Mark's. She's been seeing him a couple of times a week for one-on-one sessions."

"Should I be concerned?" Surprised at her ease, Grace shared a joke.

Bruce let out a hearty laugh. "I don't think so . . . considering she's my age, I'm pretty sure you have nothing to worry about."

"Good to know." Grace smiled as she hugged her bag close like it was a teddy bear comforting her. "Well, thank you again . . . you know . . . for this." She waved her hand in front of the building, afraid that if she said the exact words, they would feel that much more true. That her mother no longer belonged to her. Instead, she belonged to her dismantled mind.

"Of course . . . keep in touch, Grace." He extended a hand, as if sealing a deal on a business agreement. Grace knew that was because of all the hugs she had denied him in the past.

"I will." She started to extend her hand, but a swell of emotions pushed her forward and before she knew it, she was embracing him, holding onto him tight. He held her in his arms for as long as she allowed, and when she released, he stepped back and swatted the tears ambushing his eyes. Blinking rapidly, he replaced his sunglasses, covering the unannounced tears.

"Thank you," he said, as he rubbed his chin in a nervous gesture.

"You're welcome," Grace said, the odd exchange playing tricks on her.

CHAPTER SIXTEEN

Susan

When I learned that my brother sold our childhood home, I was filled with sadness. It was in that home that I grew up and had all of my first experiences, filling my heart with memories year after year until I went to college. Before Timmy's accident I had been the happiest child alive, blessed with two wonderful parents who brought me into a life of high society. Timmy's death upset me as you would imagine it would upset an eight-year-old, but it did something different to my brother John. It broke him. There is no doubt that John had always had his guard up, never going out of his way to share too much of himself to the rest of the family, but after the accident, he walked around as if his heart was on the outside of his body…if he got too close to anyone he could damage it, if he moved too fast or talked too much he would exhaust it. Over time, we got used to it as a family.….John was the black sheep. Maybe that is because he was there that day when Timmy supposedly shot himself. It was for this reason that I was so concerned when John decided to sell our childhood home.

The day after I made the discovery, I called him and he agreed to meet me at my house, on the other side of town in the Bayview neighborhood. At first, I blasted him with insults. How dare he sell the home without consulting me? How could he give away a piece of our past so easily, a piece of our parents. My father had died not long after Timmy's death. A sudden heart attack had taken another one from us, a rippling effect of grief. But my mother was still mentally adept inside her frail, withering body in a nursing home just one town away. She couldn't get around well but she was still very much mentally alive, and I know this because I visited her every week. My brother John kept his distance. Another thing that I insulted him for. I always harassed him for not going to see my mother. He always said he was too busy but he never even had a girlfriend, or a family. After I pummeled insult after insult at him, he finally lost it. For the first time in my life I had heard him yell. With force that seemed to make the furniture in his apartment rock. He told me to sit down because it was his time to talk. And in a few moments, everything I knew about my childhood would change from recollections that were laced in color to shades of grey. A storm had moved into my memories, and my mother was now painted as the corrupt one, the hurricane that swept through our family unbeknownst to me. How had I never seen it? She kept me protected because I was the girl, but to my brothers she was evil. Maybe I secretly knew but I didn't want to admit it to myself. John's words started to connect multiple dots, forming a complete picture. The bruises on both of my brothers' bodies. I had assumed that they were too rough during play. And the way Karina, our loving maid, always had her sight on my mother, as if she was a hidden camera, trying to catch her in the act. It now makes sense that Karina left the job not long after the incident. How could she stay with a family that had such dysfunction, how could she spend her life witnessing abuse and rage every single day and not be able to do anything about it. Much in the same way that Karina had reached her boiling point on that day with the gin bottle, my brother John had reached the day he told me the truth. And that is why he was leaving…selling the family home because he couldn't bear to live with the memories from all those years ago. If what he said was the truth, then I honestly don't know how he lived within the confines of those walls where his worst memories came back to life every time he entered a different room. I just don't know how he managed to hold it in all these years, how he suffered knowing the truth about my mother while I continued to put her on a pedestal.

I had to find out for myself whether my mother committed the abuse so I took my anger and I brought it to her, presenting her with my questions during my weekly visit to the nursing home. Did she really abuse my brothers like John had said? Much to my surprise she confessed. To everything. She confessed to the most major instances of abuse. It was almost as if she had been waiting all these years for me to ask her what she did. Maybe she had expected John to tell me that it was her fault that he accidentally shot our baby brother. And just like that, without an ounce of regret in her shaky voice, she told me how she herself was abused by her own father and it was her way of removing her own pain and anger. Right then and there she transformed into a monster that my brother always knew. And that's when I knew that justice must be served and she didn't deserve to breathe anymore. Without a second thought, I pulled the pillow out from beneath her head and I held it over her face until her brittle hands went slack and all the fight in her relented. I put the monster to bed.

The day John was threatening to commit suicide, I needed to convince him that things would be different. When Detective McKenna and Sully stepped out, to give us a moment, I informed my brother of what I did to our mother. He was clearly affected with mixed emotions, but he got nervous that the timing of our mother's demise could lead back to my being out of town, and so, as we heard the two returning, John instructed me to follow his lead and play along that I was learning of the real nature of our monster mother, for the first time, and so we began our ruse. A lot of it was organic and new territory we hadn't discussed previously, and as much as I hated to deceive Sully like that...he and Detective McKenna seemed to gobble it up and even engaged in the conversation. I believe any chance at suspicion falling upon me has been thwarted.

CHAPTER SEVENTEEN

Court Street was more alive than Grace had ever seen it. As she pressed the gas harder to make it up the steep road, she took in the activity around her, with wide open windows. Two little girls played hopscotch in front of a dark blue house with freshly painted white trim. In front of another house Grace saw two brothers tossing a baseball back and forth on their front lawn. The older brother, who looked to be about the age John was when he accidentally shot Timmy, dove for the ball with an extended glove as it barreled by his right side. He fell, landing right on his arm and rolled over on his back emitting a loud "Owww." The little brother, who looked to be about Timmy's age at the time of his death, raced over to the other boy, and offering him a chubby arm, hoisted his older brother up and off the ground. Grace couldn't help but relate the two sets of brothers to one another. This little boy in present day was helping his big brother up off the ground and consoling him, much in the same way that John was finally feeling freed from sharing the burden of his secrets.

As she pulled into her driveway, she saw another sight that brought on an unannounced emotion. In Emily and Scott's front yard, Peyton was lying face up on a blanket and wiggling around. A woman, who Grace assumed was Emily's mother, held a book out in front of her and made animated gestures as she read. Grace could hear Peyton's coos carrying through the air. She watched as the woman matched her facial expressions to the character she was reading. As soon as she shut the Jeep door, Peyton twisted her head in Grace's direction, forcing her to emit a friendly response. "Hi, Peyton!" Grace said, as she hefted her bag out of the car. She walked across the driveway until she was a few feet away from them. "You must be Emily's mom."

"I sure am." She stood and Grace could see that Emily had been blessed with her mother's good looks and flattering figure. Even at retirement age, Grace could tell the woman took good care of herself. Her skin, the same tone as Emily's, had a glow that could only be the result of proper eating and high quality skincare products. "And you must be the lovely neighbors that my daughter has been boasting about. I'm Jane."

"Grace. Nice to finally meet you."

"Likewise. I'm sure Em told you about how I was raised in this house."

"She did."

She bent down and lifted Peyton in her arms, dropping a kiss on the top of her head. "So, many memories on this street. It's crazy to think that my grandbaby will grow up in the same house that I did."

"It's a great neighborhood and we're lucky to have Scott and Emily as neighbors," Grace said, as her eyes locked with Jane's.

"It is . . . it was a lot like this when I grew up here. Kids everywhere. We were always outside playing games and chasing one another." She wiped the slight sweat starting to collect on her forehead with one hand, as she continued to balance Peyton in an expert hold in the other. Her hair, pale blonde and shaped into fat curls that touched her chin, had a few wiry flyaways protruding from the top. She tucked a strand of hair behind her ear and shifted her position. "I was quite surprised when I found out that the Walsh house was sold. I guess I never imagined John living anywhere else. This was like his sanctuary . . . he never left except to go to work."

"He seemed a bit odd when I met him at the closing." Wasting no time, Grace jumped right into it.

"You could say that." She looked down at Peyton, whose eyes were fluttering as she fought sleep.

"Besides being somewhat of a recluse, what was odd about him?"

"Honestly, I think that I'm biased. Ever since Timmy's accident I've had trouble viewing that family the same. I'm not sure if I feel bad for John or if I'm scared of him. I know that my mother was kind of scared of him, but she was also a bit paranoid in her later years. I always thought the family was a bit off . . . it wasn't just John. And then of course there was Margaret. She was nothing like my mother. That woman was all about being in the spotlight and my own mother didn't even like her photo taken. I think my mother had some anger toward her . . . for good reason. Margaret ditched her the second she settled into the elite group. You see . . . when the Walshes moved into town, they didn't know anyone. So, my mother took Margaret in with open arms, befriended her, and showed her around. From what I hear they were together nearly every day for a while . . ."

"And then what happened? Why did they stop being friends?"

"Margaret found her group . . . the high society women who spent all their time getting primped and hosting parties. One day she and my mother were having coffee . . . and the next day Margaret was throwing a party at her house and can you believe it? She didn't even invite my mother. She dropped her like a box of rocks. I think that's why—"

"Why what?" Grace wanted to pull the words out of her mouth.

"Well, my mother had witnessed Margaret and Officer Sullivan having an affair . . . it's not like the woman did a good job at hiding it. I'm pretty sure I witnessed them sneaking around even as a young kid. Their . . . *your* side kitchen window looks right into our back yard. Before the fence was there . . . well, let's just say I could see things as a young child that I probably shouldn't have been seeing. The problem is my mother was best friends with Officer Sullivan's wife. Had Margaret stuck around long enough to discover that, then maybe she wouldn't have been cheating on her husband and breaking up another family.

Grace couldn't help but wonder if Sully and Betts knew that their father was having an affair all those years ago, and whatever came of it.

"What do you know about Mr. Walsh? Did he ever find out?"

"He did, but by then it was too late."

Grace thought about what Betts said about the two men arguing on the side of the house. Were they arguing about the affair or something about the shooting?

* * *

August 19, 1955

Charles Walsh looked out his bedroom window into the back yard. The midday sun was casting a glow on the metal swing set, the light breeze causing the tandem swing to rock back and forth. He watched as John sat up against the shed with knees pulled to his chest, his head buried, covering his eyes as if playing hide-and-seek and he the seeker. In previous months the boy was likely in that scenario, ready to launch into a yard game with the competitive nature of an eight-year-old boy. But today, the day after his baby brother was buried, Charles didn't know if his son would ever be the same. Having witnessed his brother take a bullet, in what was an accidental shooting, was too much for a boy to take; but he vowed to do what he had to, to keep his family together. He looked over at the bed, taking in the outline of Margaret's curled up body, the tangled nest of hair erupting from underneath the bedspread. Since he had rushed home from the airport the night of Timmy's accident, Margaret had maintained a steady distance from him, seldom making eye contact. Aside from the initial monumental moment, when he came home, they embraced in a collision of tears while crumbling to the floor in their joint sorrow, she refused to look at him. And all he could do was blame himself. It was his gun, which was unsafely tucked away inside its case beneath his undergarments in the top drawer inside the closet. He thought he locked it in its safe and twisted the combination out of the order of its code. 10 16 46. But, evidently, he did not and Timmy did what most little boys would do. He unknowingly took a loaded gun and reenacted what he had likely seen his television heroes doing. Holding a gun in a cops and robbers stance, twirling it around in his tiny grip, not knowing that the fun little game would lead to his death.

Charles's father had always taught him to do what he had to do to protect his family, to provide for them, to keep them safe and happy. And here he was a day after burying his youngest son, because he failed to keep him safe. Charles's father had also taught him to move on in life, to overcome and prevail. And that's what he would do. He'd overcome and prevail for his family. As he pushed through his bedroom door, and headed down the stairs, he knew he would soon be a different man. Karina stood before him at the bottom of the stairs in the foyer, her packed bags by her feet.

"Are you ready?"

Without a word Karina nodded obediently. Charles had always liked her and considered her family, but the woman had witnessed too much in their home, too much that could taint their reputation. Officer Sullivan had warned him that if Karina stuck around then she was bound to accuse them of neglecting their children, and because he had an unlocked gun in the same home as minors, Charles could be held responsible. As his father always said, "Do what you have to do to keep your family together." He picked up two of her bags as she held the other close to her side and followed him out the door. He couldn't help but think of how little this woman could survive on while his wife wouldn't be able to fit a day's worth of belongings in these two bags. He opened the door for her and gently placed her bags in the back seat of the car. As he made his way to the airport he attempted to make things better.

"I'm really sorry that we have to let you go like this, but I think our family needs some alone time to adapt. We are so grateful to have had you with us. Karina, never forget you are like family to us." He twisted his head toward the passenger seat, hoping to gain a response. While she had seldom spoken with him during the time she lived at the house, she could often be seen unveiling a smile or offering a greeting. Today she was silent, her face empty of emotion. She would be going back to her family in Poland, which was not a desirable destination for someone with her background who had scored a solid income working for a wealthy family. And Charles felt her pain. He was ripping all she had worked for out from underneath her, sending her back to poverty. She had nowhere to go in the States, the Walsh family was all she knew and the only job she'd ever had in the country. He pulled into the departure section of Logan Airport, in front of the sign that read LOT Polish Airlines. When a police officer approached to hurry him along, he flashed the badge he used to access the airport on the rare occasion he wasn't on the road and had to do business here. It was typically to meet with the higher-ups who made the decisions regarding the part he sold worldwide. The officer passed a mock salute in his direction, certifying that he was all set. Karina emerged from the passenger side as he slid her bags out of the back seat and motioned for an attendant. He leaned in to give her a hug but she backed off, searing him with unwavering eye contact. "She prays but has the devil under the skin." She started to walk away, and then turned to meet his confused expression. "Your wife." She turned on a heel and walked toward the airport entrance, the escort following closely behind. Charles stood there in a cloud of confusion, watching her broad body marching away.

CHAPTER EIGHTEEN

"Hello?" Grace called out as she pushed the front door open. It was only one o'clock and she felt like her emotions had run a marathon, leaving her exhausted. Between the meeting with her father and the new intel she received from Emily's mom, her mind was reeling with speculation. Unfortunately, Peyton's need for an early morning nap cut their conversation short, leaving off at the point where Charles found out about the affair. Following Officer Sullivan's advice, he sent Karina back to Poland so she wouldn't reveal any of the family's secrets to the police. As a well-respected officer in town, Sullivan's word meant something to Charles and he listened, upending Karina's safe and secure life in the United States. Grace still had to figure out what Jane meant when she said Charles had found out about the affair between Margaret and Officer Sullivan too late.

"How do we manage to have so much laundry?" Mark asked rhetorically, as he walked toward her, his arms cradling a laundry basket. "How did it go?" He asked the question after he planted a kiss on her forehead and continued to the couch.

"Which part?" Following Mark, Grace dropped her bag and sunk into the cushion.

"There's more than one part?"

"The saga continues," Grace said, throwing her head back as she closed her eyes in exasperation. "So, it turns out that Officer Sullivan, Sully's dad, was having an affair with Margaret Walsh."

"So do you think that has anything to do with what happened that day?"

Grace pulled a T-shirt out of the basket and started folding it. "Maybe not that day, necessarily, but I think it may have to do with why the case was closed so quickly."

"Why would Sullivan want to protect Margaret if she was such a wreck?"

"He didn't know she was such a wreck. From what I gather, everything she did was behind closed doors."

"True."

Grace recapped everything for Mark she learned from John and Susan. Margaret abused John and Timmy when no one was looking while she was in her drunken states. Then, on the day of the accident, Karina couldn't take it any longer and threw a bottle at Margaret to prevent her from hurting Timmy anymore. Then, in what was a twist of fateful timing, John shot the gun at his mother from behind the house . . . the gun he took out of his father's case in the drawer. The bullet hits Timmy after Margaret falls to the ground. Timmy falls backward off the swing from the power of the bullet firing into his small body. When Margaret comes to, she puts on all the drama; but when Karina threatens to call the cops and the ambulance, Margaret panics. After all, she doesn't want anyone to know the bullet was intended for her because she was such a horrible mother. She doesn't want to taint her reputation, and she most certainly doesn't want her husband to find out she was, technically, the cause of Timmy's death. Because then he might take away her posh lifestyle. A life that she never had growing up poor.

Grace told Mark how a week later, after the burial, the Walshes oddly have the Sullivan family over. A family they never really interacted with. When Betts sees Mr. Walsh and Mr. Sullivan arguing, on the side of the house, it's because Mr. Sullivan is urging his friend to get rid of Karina. Having her around is threatening to them; at any moment she can accuse them of being neglectful parents because of the unlocked gun. But at this point Mr. Walsh still doesn't know Timmy was accidentally shot by John because that would, of course, lead him to learn his wife had been mistreating the boys. On the day when Betts got injured, skateboarding down the hill, she witnessed her father picking up the Tanqueray seal and tucking it in his pocket—no one could know the bottle Karina threw was intended for Margaret.

Mark continued to ask questions throughout Grace's recap. "But why would Mr. Sullivan be so set on covering things up for this family?"

"Because he was in love with Margaret."

"Even though she was a drunk socialite who abused her kids?"

"Evidently love does not discriminate." Grace laughed, setting aside another piece of folded laundry.

"Is Margaret still alive?"

"Well . . . that's another thing I haven't had a chance to brief you on yet. Remember how Susan was away for a few days, allegedly visiting her son?"

"Yeah."

"Well, I decided to do a little intel on her. So, I went to hear her talk at the library."

Mark raised his eyebrows, silently questioning what happened next.

"When I looked in her eyes I saw images of an old lady . . . taking her final breath, right before her head sunk into a white pillow."

"Did Susan kill her mother?" Mark's eyes were wide as he followed the story.

"I'm guessing when Susan found out the truth about her mother hurting both of her brothers all those years and the role she played in Timmy's death . . . she was compelled to kill the woman. And I don't believe, for a moment, she only learned the truth that day of John's attempted suicide . . . because I saw the visions of the dead woman before that . . . but she of course couldn't have known that. I believe she took the opportunity, when Sully and I stepped out, to allay her brother's anxieties and do a little confessing of her own. I played along, as if I was duped, and ended up gleaning further information in the process."

"So now what?" Mark stacked the folded clothes in the basket, pressing them down with a flat palm so they all fit.

"Well, I have one major question remaining . . . what ever happened to Karina? The kids remember Karina leaving shortly after Timmy's burial and they never saw her again."

CHAPTER NINETEEN

Susan

Susan looked over at John one last time before they opened the door to the nursing home. She had been anticipating this moment since John first told her that he had been in touch with Karina all these years. The last time she saw the woman she was only eight years old and was grieving the loss of her little brother.

"Do you think she'll even remember me?" she asked, as John checked them in at the front desk.

"She will most certainly remember you. The woman may be ninety-five but her mind is still as sharp as a knife. Must be something in her Polish genes."

"She must've been well taken care of by her new family," Susan said, her tone shaky from the nerves playing a game of ping-pong in her body. After John told Susan everything about his mother's secrets and the abuse he endured, he told her about how their father sent Karina back to Poland. Having always considered Karina to be his real mother, the one who tried to protect him from Margaret, John tracked her down years later. While working at the airport he met a salesman who was out of town often and in need of a maid for his wife and three children. Knowing the family didn't have the same dysfunction his own did John found Karina and brought her back to the states, to a home where she could work and make a living. He told Susan how he felt he owed it to her. Karina ended up staying with the family until she could no longer care for anyone except herself. She tended to the children of the family, then their children, and so on; watching the family blossom and thriving right along with them. She had expressed her appreciation to John repeatedly, declaring she would've never survived during Poland's severe economic strife in the early sixties.

While she had tried to save him and his brother, Timmy, all those years ago, it turned out John was the one who saved her.

"Are you ready?" John looked over at Susan as they stood outside the door marked eight. They could hear the television playing on the other side.

"Ready as I'll ever be." Susan thought about all the years she spent as an expert counseling families on how to communicate with one another and here she was afraid she wouldn't be able to form a sentence.

John took the lead, walking ahead of Susan as they entered the room. A chair perched in front of the television rocked slightly, a white head of hair bobbed up and down. "Hey, Frannie, you ready to watch our program?" The voice penetrated Susan's ears. It was not as heavily coated in the Polish accent it was all those years ago but it was the same voice she remembered. The voice of home.

"It's not Frannie . . . it's John." Susan followed John as he walked toward the front of the chair but stopped when John held up a hand.

"John . . . my dear. How are you? Did you bring me my chocolates?" The woman cut right to the chase like she always had. John told Susan he had been bringing her favorite chocolates every week like clockwork. He reached into the small grocery bag he carried in and pulled out a bag of Dove milk chocolates. He opened it and handed it to her.

"Of course I did . . . have I ever disappointed you?"

"That you have not, my dear."

Susan felt a tear break through her right eye. The sound of the woman's voice filled her with feelings of nostalgia. She thought about how stern yet loving Karina was when she lived with them, how she was always a safe place to go to when her mother wasn't available. Until recently she didn't know her mother wasn't available because she was too consumed with being the monster she was. Traumatizing one brother and basically killing another before he ever had a chance to live and explore the beauty of childhood. Yet this woman, who had so little, had been a lighthouse in her childhood; strong and centered among the crashing waves of her family. And while her time with the Walsh family had ended too soon, it had left a permanent print on her heart.

"I brought someone with me today, K," John said. Susan picked up on the nickname, the bond that had formed between the two of them after years of staying in touch. For a moment she felt like a third wheel but she knew John had just been protecting her. Maybe she went into the field of family communication because she subconsciously knew her own family was a mess.

Karina started to turn herself in the chair before John stepped forward and spun her around slowly, until she was facing Susan. Without a word Karina leaned forward, her faded blue eyes peeking out from behind wavy wrinkles. Her chin, still robust, now framed with lines that were engraved from, what Susan hoped was, years of smiling. Her nose sat heavy in the middle of her round face, centered between two pink splotches on her chubby cheeks. She may have been ninety-five years old, but Susan could tell she still ate well and had lived a full life. Karina pushed herself up from the chair slowly, but with an independent strength not typically found in women her age. She took two steps forward until she was close enough to cup Susan's face with her hands, pulling her even closer.

"Oh my goodness, it's really you." Karina's eyes scanned Susan's face, as if she was assessing every feature, comparing it with her memories.

The intensity of Susan's joy at seeing the woman after so many years ignited tears in her eyes and before she knew it she was pressing Karina's hand to her face with her own, as tears streamed down.

"I can't stop looking at you. You beautiful grown girl. You look just like your father . . . both of you." Karina stepped back and assessed Susan from head to toe, taking in her well-dressed figure.

"Well, I can't say I'm a girl anymore . . . I'm a grandmother." Susan laughed, swiping at her tears and pulling a tissue from her purse to catch the moisture running from her nose and eyes. After she cleaned her face up, she stepped forward and pulled Karina into a hug, her entire body shaking as they embraced one another. She always felt like the woman towered over her when she was a child and now she was the taller of the two. Susan looked up and saw John wiping away his own tears. For a moment she felt like they were kids again, telling Karina about their day at school, sharing the things they couldn't tell their mother.

"Sit, sit . . . both of you." Karina, still with the ability to take charge, was demanding they get comfortable in the chairs beside her own.

Susan looked around the room, her eyes landing on a large windowsill that held a menagerie of picture frames, all of various sizes and from different points throughout her life. In the front row was a four-by-six black-and-white photo of John, Susan, and Timmy gathered around Karina in front of their home. Susan leaned forward and picked up the frame, taking in the happy moment. Timmy with his short blonde hair parted to the side, his mischievous grin looking up at Karina like he was about to bolt from the photo. John stood to the left of her and Susan to the right, the way they always set themselves up for photos. It had been an unintentional habit the twins had since they were toddlers and Susan couldn't help but wonder if maybe that was how they were positioned in their mother's womb. John on the left and Susan on the right; a formation made to support and defend one another from the time they were conceived.

"I remember this day," Susan said, tracing a finger over the glass frame, outlining their figures like she was drawing a piece of her past. "Betts took this photo." Susan remembered that their mother had been upstairs taking a nap and Karina had taken a few minutes away from her chores to play in the yard with them.

"That was the day Betts was walking by with her camera and you asked her to take a photo of us . . . she had stopped coming around for a while but she had been walking on our street and you called her over to take our photo. You were so determined to have that photo." John recalled, looking at Karina.

"I wanted to have a photo of myself with you three. I loved you like my own and I didn't have any of just the three of us . . . and I know your mother told Betts to stay away . . . so I took the opportunity knowing your mother was sleeping. Glad I did because it's one of the items I cherish to this day."

"Wait . . . did you say Mother told Betts to stop coming around?" Susan set the frame back on the windowsill and turned to face Karina, confusion lacing her eyes. "Why would she do that? Betts was my friend."

"Well for a number of reasons . . . your mother was so concerned about her appearance; she didn't want Betts capturing any of her hostility on camera. And then of course she didn't want Betts knowing she was having an affair with the little girl's father."

Both John and Susan angled inward, locking eyes with one another. Karina nodded, observing their questions. "You may not have known this because you were just kids but . . . your mother was having an affair

187

with Officer Sullivan. And it went on for a long time." Karina paused and plucked a chocolate from the bag sitting on her lap.

"When Dad was away," Susan said, matter-of-factly. So many things she never knew were being presented to her, suddenly making her question every aspect of her life.

Karina offered them each a chocolate before she unwrapped another one and nibbled the square. She set the bag down in her lap and grabbed each of their hands, gripping them tightly and pulling them in close, just as she had when they were children. "There is something you both need to know."

Susan didn't know if she could take any more shocking news. It was like these tidbits of information were punching her in the gut, causing her to question every move. Again she locked eyes with John as Karina continued.

"Officer Sullivan was Timmy's father."

CHAPTER TWENTY

Grace looked up from her phone when she heard the door of The Depot swish open, letting in the sounds of summer. Sully ambled down the ramp, leading to the dining area, in his classic slow-moving way. Puffy bags evident beneath his eyes, no doubt from lack of sleep since learning about the Walsh family saga that now included him. Grace lifted the coffee cup that sat across from her. She had ordered him his go-to hazelnut coffee with a drop of milk and an herbal tea for herself to calm the nerves in her stomach. The last few days had brought on a rush of intense emotion. She let him slide into his seat and take a sip of the coffee before she spoke.

"How are you?"

He cupped his beverage in both hands on the table and looked around with skeptical eyes. Grace understood. If she learned what he had, she would question everything around her too. She compared it to the moment when she discovered her father was a stand-up citizen, completely different than what she had been told about him her entire life.

"Well, I've been better . . . as you can imagine."

"I'm so sorry, Sully . . . that you had to go through this . . . that you had to learn all of this now."

"Better now than never, right? I'd hate to have gone to my grave never knowing that Timmy was my little brother."

Grace thought about her own situation. She could easily find out she had siblings she had never known about. But to learn they were killed when they were only five years old would bring an entirely different level of sadness. "Did you talk to Betts?"

"Yeah, she's pretty broken up about it . . . but she seems less surprised than I am." He circled his index finger around the lip of the mug. "But she spent a lot more time at the Walsh house than I did when we were kids . . . so maybe she picked up on things."

Grace pictured the question marks in Betts's eyes when they spoke about the past. She had always suspected something was out of the ordinary with the Walsh family, and the exchange between the two fathers, but she probably never expected that her father had a child with Mrs. Walsh.

"I just feel so bad for my mother . . . and to think she knew all along. She knew about the affair. I still don't know if she knew Timmy was the product of her husband but she knew about the affair and she kept it together for us kids. The last thing she ever wanted to do was break up the family and she carried on knowing her husband was going behind her back with the town socialite."

"It was pretty common for women to turn a blind eye to their husband's philandering back then," Grace said, as she thought about how different a person Mr. Walsh had been than Officer Sullivan was. Sully had learned from Susan that Mr. Walsh gave Karina a good sum of money to live off of when he sent her back to Poland. And the only reason why he sent Karina back to Poland was because Officer Sullivan urged him to do so, saying that his family would be ripped apart if the woman decided to bring up the fact *his* gun was the reason for the accidental shooting. He later found out from Mrs. Sullivan about the affair but neither one of them ever knew Timmy wasn't his. Charles Walsh went to his grave thinking he was responsible for the death of his son, carrying the blame for the next year of his life before he died far too young. He never knew Timmy wasn't *his* son and that the boy was ultimately shot because of Margaret.

"Yeah, so I hear. It's just hard to take in. Grace, my father was always my hero. For me and my brothers. I wanted to grow up to be just like him from as far back as I can remember. And in some sense, I did all that. I followed in his career footsteps."

"But you aren't him . . . you didn't do what he did and you shouldn't compare yourself to his poor choices."

"He essentially covered up a crime scene to protect his mistress."

"Do you think he knew about Margaret abusing the boys?"

"To be honest I don't know. He had to know to some extent right? He had to question why John would aim a gun at his mother. Unless he just chalked it up to John being off." Sully took a sip of his coffee and set the cup down gently, as if he was afraid to draw any attention to the two of them. "I should've listened to Betts all those years ago when she brought up her speculations that something shady was going on at the Walsh house. But I put the trust in my father . . . assuming that being a police officer he was a truth teller and out for the best interest of the greater good."

"Sully, first of all there is no way you would've known. You were a little boy. Listen, if you want to compare sordid pasts . . . I can tell you all about my own father."

"I thought you and your dad were working on your newly formed relationship." Grace had vented to Sully about her dad not long after she received the first call from him. "We are but my past, just like yours and everybody else's, is a tangle of lies, deceit, and disloyalty." Grace rubbed the tea bag label with two fingers, a calming gesture in the midst of a cloud of chaos. "I guess that is what makes us who we are and helps us appreciate the good people in our lives."

"Like Mark," Sully said the words matter-of-factly.

"Like Mark." A genuine smile splayed across Grace's lips. "But even Mark isn't free from a tough past. He didn't always have it easy, but . . . he learned to take the good with the bad and move on from the things that you can't change." Grace shook her head left to right. "You can't change what your dad did. But you can grow from it and surround yourself with solid people." She paused, hesitating before she dove into the next question. "Speaking of . . . where does all of this leave you and Susan?"

Sully scrunched up his nose and raised his eyebrows. "That's the question of the day. I mean we just found out my father had a child with her mother . . . but technically we aren't related by blood. So . . . you tell me, Detective McKenna, where does that leave me and Susan?"

"Do you like her?"

"A lot."

Grace could see the flush of red creeping up Sully's cheeks. It was unlike him to be so open about a love interest, so she imagined it meant a lot to him.

"Well, then you gotta do what you gotta do to keep the girl."

CHAPTER TWENTY-ONE

August 12, 2020

Grace looped her arms around Mark's and shuffled her feet through the uneven grass leading to Timmy Walsh's grave. Already standing by the headstone was Sully and Susan hand in hand. Next to them was Betts leaning on her cane, her camera bag on the ground touching her foot as if it was an extension of her body. Beside Betts, John stood behind a wheelchair that held Karina. Grace had met the woman a few weeks before when she bumped into John and Susan sitting outdoors having lunch with her at Renzo's. Since John had brought Susan in to see her, the three of them got together every week to talk about the good memories of the past but more importantly the good memories that the future held. For John that was accepting his past was not his fault and moving on from there, while always remembering to honor Timmy. For Susan that was building the relationship with her twin brother and making up for lost time. While they hadn't been estranged, by any means, they had been more distant over the years than she preferred. Now she would be able to hold onto some of the burden John had been carrying for so many years and he would have a sounding board when he needed to vent.

While the moment was a somber one, Grace and Mark received smiles from everyone present, a gesture showing appreciation for their being there. Without any of them knowing, Grace had been present through the entire process, from the moment she first met John, when she thought he was a cold-blooded murderer. With the help of Barb and Mark she was able to untangle a family's darkest secrets. Beside Timmy's grave was a fresh mound of dirt that covered the plot where Margaret had just been buried. While the staff at the nursing home said she died suddenly in her sleep, Grace, John, and Susan knew the truth. After Susan visited her grandchildren, she made a trip to visit her mother—to kill the monster. Knowing what she knew about the woman Grace didn't feel the need to press the crime and, instead, she'd let it sort itself out. Margaret Walsh was a monster that hid behind a life of luxury. The center of her circle of socialite friends, the charity work that bolstered her do-gooder appearance even further, and the show she put on for the family photos.

Susan reached into a bag she held close to her side and pulled out several small candles. She passed them out as John followed behind lighting the wicks one by one, until they formed a glowing circle meant to keep Timmy's memory alive. Every year on the anniversary they had committed to gathering here, to remember the boy who got caught in a crossfire and left the earth too soon. Grace watched as tears rolled down Karina's cheeks and slid onto the candle, softening the flame until it was gone completely. The woman had seen poverty, abuse, and death and was somehow guided back to a place of love and a place of belonging.

As the flames slowly faded, Grace thought about her own life. Her mother's last days were likely upon her and her father was a new place of guidance and love. She had spent the last two months contemplating whether she would let him in and had swayed side to side on many occasions, afraid to get too close yet afraid to miss out on the only family bond she had the opportunity to grow.

"You ready?" Mark said, cutting into her thoughts.

Grace turned to Sully, hugging him tightly, her strong grip a silent message telling him not to take blame for his father's actions.

As they were about to turn away and walk toward the path, that greeted the cemetery entrance, Grace paused and watched as John knelt down by the grave with Susan beside him. He folded a small polka dot blanket up neatly and set it in front of the tombstone. Catching Grace's eye on him, he said, "It was his favorite blanket. He always had it with him. And all these years later I haven't been able to let it go. Now, hopefully he will be at peace having it with him once again."

Grace noticed the uneven splatters of blood, now blurring with the faded polka dots on the small cotton blanket and answered her own question. Timmy had been holding onto the blanket, likely for protection, during the moments before he died, when his mother was berating and abusing him.

"Wait a minute." Grace pulled Mark's elbow back toward the grave where John was kneeling. She pulled the apron out of her purse. It was still folded in a neat square, pressed from years of being in the same position.

"I think this belongs to you." Grace held the apron out so it was in between Karina and John. The tiny red flowers faded like an old family photo, blending into the blue and white gingham. She never told them how she knew the apron belonged to Karina, and they never asked.

CHAPTER TWENTY-TWO

Grace stood in the bathroom staring at the Apple watch on her wrist, as the white numbers of the timer counted down. She wasn't sure if she wanted the three minutes to go by fast or slow. With one minute remaining, she was about to find out whether or not she was pregnant, a surprise conception that may have been the result of a few missed birth control pills. "There are no accidents in life." She could hear her mother's words echoing in her head, blending with a collage of fears that were slowly creeping up in her mind.

Closing her eyes she took three slow and steady breaths, holding onto what may be her last moment of freedom. When the timer vibrated, it sent a roller coaster of nerves through her body and she had to force her eyes open. On the sink, she looked down at three pregnancy tests. She couldn't rely on just one and took three for good measure. She swallowed and allowed the six lines to register. The realization took another thirty seconds to settle in and soon she was sliding down the bathroom door, onto the tiled floor. She held her knees to her chest, against breasts that were already aching. And she cried. Her tears were laced in fear, each droplet conveying a different reason for why she was incapable of being a mother. Motherhood was never on her list of things to accomplish in life, for many reasons. What she imagined as an innate skill, being a mother simply wasn't in her DNA. She had never felt compelled to have a baby, to raise a human being. She was always the one who ran in the opposite direction of a new baby being passed around at a gathering, afraid she wouldn't know what to do if it cried. She could dissect a murder scene, face traumatizing visions from unsuspecting tragedies, and she could work around the clock on limited sleep. But caring for a helpless baby was something she wasn't confident she could do.

She heard a knock on the downstairs door and looked at her watch, this time it wasn't at the timer. It was ten o'clock. Her father had arrived right on time. Next she heard the sound of Mark's feet padding down the hallway and soon he was standing outside the bathroom door, completely unaware of what was going on, on the other side. "Grace . . . your dad's here. What are you doing? Surely, you're not getting primped for him, are you?" He laughed, again oblivious to what she now knew.

Having always been an ugly crier, with obvious bloodshot eyes and blotchy red patches on her skin, Grace knew she had to say something about why she was crying. Before she could change her mind, she stood up, tucked her hair behind her ears, and pulled the door open. She stood with her hand by her side, embracing the red patches that were undoubtedly speckling her face. She allowed Mark to see it all, including the fresh set of tears racing down her cheeks, spurred on by the sight of him.

"Grace . . . what's the matter? What happened? Do you want me to tell him to leave?"

Without saying a word Grace shook her head left to right and then fell into Mark's embrace. He held her in his arms and stroked her hair, and then suddenly he released the hug and transferred his hands to her arms, squeezing them as his eyes burned into hers. It was at that moment Grace knew he had seen the tests over her shoulder, lined up like dead soldiers on the bathroom sink. His eyes grew wide and the biggest smile peeled across his lips. "Oh my God! Are those—"

"Yes," Grace said flatly, still unsure of how she felt. She watched him take one step closer to the tests, lifting one in his hand and holding it up to the light as if he was trying to look inside an envelope. "Two lines mean . . ."

"Two lines mean I'm pregnant." Grace sniffled. She used the back of her hand to wipe away the tears on her right cheek.

"Oh my God."

"You said that already."

"But, Grace . . . this is amazing. I'm gonna be a dad." He looked over at her and she could see his eyes growing misty. As if something even bigger just dawned on him, he continued. "And you're gonna be a mom."

The sound of the word *mom* felt heavy in her heart. She thought about her own mother and how she wouldn't be there, at least mentally, to guide her through being a parent. That paired with the hormones racing through her body, made for an emotionally charged moment. Mark, still gripping the pregnancy test, stepped forward and pulled her into another hug. Picking up on the fear she felt, he whispered in her ear, "It's all gonna be okay. You're gonna be the best mother ever."

* * *

Mark had jumped into action, greeting Bruce at the door while Grace took a moment to pull herself together, wiping away the mascara smudges from her tears and doing her best to cover up her blotchy skin with a light foundation. She smoothed her hand over the front of her T-shirt, pausing to rest her palm on her abdomen. Her body was no longer hers alone, she'd be sharing it with a roommate for the next nine months. Now, as she walked down the stairs, she was especially careful, knowing that one falter could hurt her growing baby. She stepped off the bottom step and followed Mark and Bruce's voices into the kitchen, where Mark was already dressing a cup of coffee for her father. Bruce turned when he heard her approach the room and greeted her with a warm, genuine smile. And with a thousand different emotions colliding into one another, Grace darted across the room and landed in her father's arms, allowing herself to be truly held by him for the first time.

The End

ACKNOWLEDGMENTS

To some, a book is a one-time escape, and once that final page is read, it's closed for good, the plot and characters a long lost memory. For many authors, books are never fully closed, and instead they are endless, alive in our hearts long after we put them on the bookshelf. As one who never likes to say goodbye, I'm grateful that I get to spend so much of my time creating boundless worlds, and characters that I would personally love to befriend in real life. None of this would be possible without my team of artists, editors and dedicated readers who offer their time to polish my books through what can sometimes be a very long publishing process. Avree Clark, from here on out you have found a spot on this page. I truly believe that editing and writing is something that you were born to do, and I hope to always have you in my corner. Your attention to deal and love of the written word are exceptional, and the fact that our work relationship has seamlessly spilled over into a natural friendship is more than I could ever wish for. Thank you Helen "Vrouts" Giavroutas for linking us, you'll always be the heartbeat of our friendship. Maria Aiello, since day one you've not only been producing beautiful covers and graphics, but you've been cheering me on like a dedicated fan. Thank you.

As always, thank you to my husband who puts up with my constant state of daydreaming. I'm glad I have someone grounded and realistic to live in this fictional world with. Emily June and Charlotte Rae, thank you for "holding on" all those times when mommy is in mid-thought, crafting a scene, a setting, or a plot twist. And thank you for naming my characters and giving me your honest opinions about *everything*.

To Timothy, who this book is dedicated to-thank you for surviving all those near-death experiences so you can continue to be my marketing manager. I'm pretty sure there are still some people on the east coast who haven't heard your "my daughter is an author" speech, so you have a lot more work to do. I love you more. Thank you, Baron, for working alongside Rex to share my books with the world.

Thank you, mom, for always cheering me on, participating in my contests and spreading the word. Your support will forever be remembered.

A crime fiction novel wouldn't get very far without the expertise of a few police officers. Thank you, Brian Allaire, and Dawne Armitstead for teaching me how dead bodies fall and what type of gun would be used for an era-appropriate murder. Heather Hildebrant and Janet Fox, thank you for your knowledge of the Polish language. A special thanks to Peter Heald for teaching me about the funeral industry and those little tidbits surrounding the deceased.

Thank you, Jen Salsich, for helping me navigate my way through the ever-changing world of social media marketing. Terry Shepherd, I am so grateful I met a guy wearing a ThrillerFest hat during a panel discussion at Bouchercon in October 2019. Since then you've become my brainstorming buddy and the first person I call with an author question. I'm looking forward to our future projects. Thank you, Kelley Demers, Courtney Demers, Michaela Archambault, Kristina Caverly, Christie Conlee, Leslie Kreb, Kasey Andruski, Gillian Teixeira, and Khrissy Wyman, for taking the time to be the first set of readers and typo-catchers. I think I speak on behalf of many of today's authors when I say thank you to the Bookstagram community. You give our books a face and a home on readers' bookshelves everywhere.

Made in the USA
Monee, IL
16 February 2023